KINDRED SPIRITS

ALAN BRENNERT

TOR

A TOM DOHERTY ASSOCIATES BOOK
NEW YORK

This is a work of fiction. All the characters and events portrayed in this book are fictitious, and any resemblance to real people or events is purely coincidental.

KINDRED SPIRITS

Cover art by Steve Brennen

A Tor Book
Published by Tom Doherty Associates, Inc.
175 Fifth Avenue
New York, N.Y. 10010

Tor ® is a registered trademark of Tom Doherty Associates, Inc.

ISBN: 0-812-52414-4

First Tor edition: December 1984

Printed in the United States of America

0 9 8 7 6 5 4 3 2

They fell into a snowdrift, holding one another; Michael kissed her, and Ginny eagerly returned it, filled with wonder and astonishment, unable to believe that someone would really want to kiss her like this. Michael stroked her back as they embraced, astounded by her nearness, by the fact that she was not drawing away, like so many others had drawn away. They lay there in wondrous silence for a moment, then Michael raised a hand, stroked her face tenderly, and smiled. "I love you," he said, and tears came to his eyes.

Ginny bit her lip, didn't know whether she would smile or cry. "I didn't think anyone would ever say that to me," she said, softly.

Michael touched her face again. "I didn't think anyone would ever let me."

Ginny could hardly believe the words were coming from her mouth. "I love you, too, Michael."

KINDRED SPIRITS

Tor Books by Alan Brennert

Her Pilgrim Soul and Other Stories
Kindred Spirits
Time and Chance

ACKNOWLEDGMENTS

The author gratefully acknowledges permission to quote from the following: "Saturday Night at the World," words and music by Mason Williams, copyright © 1967 Irving Music, Inc. & SFO Music, Inc. "J.B." by Archibald MacLeish, copyright © 1956, 1957, 1958 by Archibald MacLeish. Reprinted by permission of Houghton Mifflin Company. "The Love Song of J. Alfred Prufrock" in *Collected Poems 1909–1962* by T.S. Eliot, copyright 1936 by Harcourt Brace Jovanovich, Inc.; copyright © 1963, 1964 by T.S. Eliot. Reprinted by permission of the publisher. "my father moved through dooms of love," copyright 1940 by e.e. cummings, renewed 1968 by Marion Morehouse Cummings. Reprinted from *Complete Poems 1913–1962* by e.e. cummings, by permission of Harcourt Brace Jovanovich, Inc. and Faber & Faber Ltd. "Revelation" from *The Poetry of Robert Frost* edited by Edward Connery Lathem, copyright 1934, © 1969 by Holt, Rinehart and Winston. Copyright © 1962 by Robert Frost. Reprinted by permission of Holt, Rinehart and Winston, Publishers.

KINDRED SPIRITS

I

I have seen them riding seaward on the waves
Combing the white hair of the waves blown back
When the wind blows the water white and black.

—T.S. Eliot

1

Sometimes, on slow summer nights when he had nothing better to do, which was most of the time, Michael Barrett would catch a bus to Kennedy or LaGuardia, find a comfortable seat in the passenger lounge near one of the gates, and watch the flow of travelers passing through, en route to somewhere else. There was a special feel to the airport at night, the air thick and warm and moist, relaxing and tranquil—the meteorological equivalent, he supposed, of Darvon. The people seemed to move through the terminal as if in a dream, slowly, unhurriedly; as though, just returned from some exotic retreat, they had brought back a piece of Hawaii or Tahiti or

Jamaica with them. Michael could almost see it, an aura, a glow, a memory of a time and a place surrounding them like a bubble, their pace relaxed and leisurely. And he saw that glow dim and diminish the farther they walked, as the clamor of traffic outside grew louder and New York began its jackhammer assault on their nerves. By the time they reached the street, they were rushing for cabs, cursing at the sky, tense and anxious and combative—their auras gone, reduced to a dim memory to be summoned up at times of particular stress, then forgotten. New York, Chicago, Los Angeles, by whatever name, the city had won again.

A rattle of hail against the windows shattered Michael's romantic vision, reminding him that tonight was no moist summer evening, but rather a chill November night, bone-cold with occasional flurries of hail and rain. The terminal was shut tight as a drum but still felt cold; he started to turn up the collar of his jacket, then balked, not wishing to look like something out of a Graham Greene novel.

He sat holding a newspaper, only occasionally reading it, more often simply looking around the terminal with a carefully designed expression of boredom, as though impatient to pick up a friend. He scanned the TWA display monitor by Gate 29, double-checking the arrival time of a flight from Mexico, then, with a studied sigh, returned his attention to the Sunday *Times*.

Once, he had felt self-conscious doing this, as indeed he did about nearly everything, especially his appearance; he was a twenty-nine-year-old man with a plain, somewhat horsey face, diffident eyes, and a slightly sloping forehead which he tried to conceal by combing his unruly brown hair down to his eyebrows. Women, he felt, looked right through him, and on balance he supposed he could hardly blame them.

His self-consciousness at being here, however, had faded more and more with each visit, as he had come to realize that compared to some of the other night-side denizens of the airport—the bag ladies, the proselytizers, the derelicts who seemed to have some sort of lease-option deal on the stalls in the men's room—compared to them, Michael was positively respectable.

"Flight 58 from Mazatlan, Mexico, now arriving at Gate 29 . . ."

Michael got up at the announcement, joining a dozen or so other people clustered around the entrance to the gate; as the passengers began trickling out, he craned his neck and looked expectantly about, as though awaiting his first glimpse of a girlfriend, or a wife, or a parent.

Tanned and happy travelers cried out and embraced waiting loved ones, suitcases swinging as they hugged and kissed and chattered. Michael stood, continuing to scan the incoming passengers, but his expectant smile was getting harder to maintain. Once, all this had filled a hunger within him; he had gotten pleasure from these reunions, had enjoyed basking in the special glow of people returned from places he himself would probably never see.

But that pleasure had given way over the months to a quiet, wistful envy, then a stubborn melancholy, then finally, perhaps inevitably, a bitterness. Watching the reunions now made the hole inside him grow larger, not smaller, and after a few more moments Michael dropped his pretense and began sidling away, the game no longer fun.

A pretty female reservations clerk noticed him as he walked glumly past the check-in counter, and, after a moment's hesitation, called out to him. "Sir? Were you . . . waiting for someone? Can I help you find anyone?"

Michael, a bit startled, recovered himself quickly. "Oh no. That's quite all right," he said, smiling. He quickly made the smile smaller, conscious as always of his slight overbite and the way his gums showed when he smiled too broadly.

"Oh," the woman said, seeming confused. "You just seemed to be waiting so . . . eagerly . . ." Michael felt suddenly guilty at his pretense; to mask his anxiety he started talking, spouting the first things that came into his head. "No, no, it's all right," he assured the woman. "You see, my . . . my ex-girlfriend was supposed to be on this flight. She was visiting Mexico. Little town called, uh, Styx. About ten miles south of Chichen-Itza. Very hot tourist spot. The ferry ride is supposed to be something else. Anyway," he went on, starting to get into this now, "I guess she heard I'd be waiting and decided to take another flight. Her name's Charon. Had a thing about dogs; we could never quite work it out. Thanks for your concern, though. G'night."

Michael smiled politely, turned, and headed for the escalators, leaving the young woman blinking uncertainly behind him as she tried to sort out exactly what had just happened here.

Once safely on the escalator, Michael wondered

why in hell he *did* things like that, berating himself
as he was wont to do after saying anything more
complicated than *hello*. God damn it, he told himself,
that was an attractive woman back there; why did he
always get so flustered, launching into comedy
routines instead of saying something like

—Excuse me?

—I said, were you looking for someone, sir? You
seemed so . . . expectant . . .

—Yes. Yes, I was waiting for someone. I was
waiting for you.

—Sir?

—In a manner of speaking, I've been waiting for
you all my life. My name is Michael; Michael Barrett.
Listen, I know this is unusual, but . . . would you
like to have a cup of coffee with—

Oh come *on*, Michael objected as he stepped onto
the moving sidewalk which would take him to the
main lobby of the TWA terminal. Sounds like an
Italian movie, for Christ's sake. Maybe more like

—Excuse me? Sir? Were you . . . waiting for
someone?

—Me? Oh, no, I . . . it was nothing . . .

—Are you sure? You looked so . . . expectant.
And then when no one showed up, you seemed so
. . . so sad.

A moment of nervous trepidation, then:

—I know this may seem unusual, sir, . . . I don't
even know your name, but . . . would you like to
have a cup of coffee with—

No, no, *no*! What the hell did he want—pity? He
liked to think he had some pride left. He marched
through the lobby and onto the street, ignoring the

continuous stream of daydreams which ran like an undercurrent beneath his conscious life, and waited for the bus that would take him to the East Side Terminal and, from there, to the Port Authority. He noted with a certain sadness that the same people he had just seen emerging happy and languorous from Gate 29 were now wrestling with baggage or scrambling for cabs, anxious and tense. Michael looked away and stepped onto the bus, which, amid a cloud of exhaust, began the long drive back to Manhattan.

From the Port Authority Terminal he took the 42nd Street IRT south toward Houston Street, doing his best to ignore the human detritus sitting all around him in the half-empty subway car. A wino slept soundly despite the rattle and squeal of the train as it stopped and started every few minutes; a sad-looking transvestite in a faded print dress stared into space, eyes fixed on something just beyond his reach; and a pair of teenage girls, obviously loadies, giggled and laughed between themselves, their baby-fat cheeks flushed, their pupils dilated from here to Poughkeepsie. Something about them all filled Michael with a vague unease, an inexplicable anger and irritation—more with himself, even, than with them. Suddenly restless, uncomfortable, he got off the subway two stops too early, walking the eight blocks to Houston Street and his apartment, trying to push the unease to the back of his mind.

The phone rang at six-thirty the next morning, a full half-hour before Michael had to get up to go to work. Startled awake, limbs splayed at unnatural angles like a sand crab roused from deep slumber by a sharp stick, he groggily snatched the phone from its cradle, his "Hello?" only vaguely recognizable as English.

"Mike? George. Listen, I've been thinking."

Michael sighed, forcing himself awake. This was not a good sign. His boss, George Kaplan, had the unfortunate habit of thinking out loud—of gnawing at a particular worry or problem like a dog chewing on a bone, going over and over and over all the options available to him until everyone around him wanted to grab him by the collar, spin him around, and hurl him into the path of the nearest oncoming truck. As yet, nobody had, but Michael suspected it was only a matter of time.

"Thinking about what, George?"

"What else?" came the voice on the other end of the line. "The Christmas party this afternoon."

Michael gazed wistfully at his alarm clock. "I picked up everything on the list. Everything's taken care of."

"Yeah, but did you get paper plates or plastic?"

Michael pinched the bridge of his nose. "Call me madcap, George, but I didn't even look at the package before I bought it. I honestly don't know."

"Jesus, Mike, we've got some important people coming to this thing! Executives from MCA, from Columbia . . . I don't want them sitting there with their three-bean salad falling off some drooping paper plate into their *laps*."

"George, what do you want me to do? Go to Tiffany's and pick out a silver pattern?"

George sighed. "All right, all right. I guess it's

too late to do anything about it. You got all the booze, right?"

"Two cases of beer. Three cases of wine. A drum of eggnog the size of Puget Sound. I think we're okay."

"I just thought. These are *record* people coming, y'know. You think we should've laid in some cocaine? You know, sort of like party favors?"

"Sure," Michael said, deadpan. "And how 'bout a *piñata* filled with amphetamines, while we're at it?"

"Okay, forget the cocaine. I know I'm missing something, but I'll catch you when you come in to the office. See you."

He hung up. Michael lay there, the receiver bleating a dial tone at him, now fully and irrevocably awake at the absurd hour of six-thirty-two in the morning. He looked around his bedroom . . . looked at the familiar beige walls, at the pleasant but nondescript rented furniture . . . and felt momentarily disoriented, as though he awakened in a stranger's house; even after five years, the apartment did not feel quite like home. But then, neither did anyplace else. Prying himself out of bed, he readied himself for work.

It had snowed during the night; by morning the city was covered with a dirty blanket of snow. Plows rattled and shook their way uptown and down, scattering salt on glassy streets, pushing and molding the icy drifts into new shapes: embankments, bulwarks, frosty battlements from some forgotten war. It was easy to envision the city as some Medieval fortress, assaulted by a raging winter, its knights buried, its king ensconced in a lonely turret.

As he made his way down Canal Street—bundled up in ski jacket and gloves, leaning into the wet, chill wind—Michael wondered, not for the first time, just why he remained in New York. But of course he knew the answer to that: this was where his friends were. It had taken him five years to build a nest here, and perhaps it was not as large a nest as some, but it was more than he had ever imagined he would have back in those lonely, desolate days of high school, and he treasured that small group of friends he did have. The thought of starting all over again somewhere else, even in a warmer climate, terrified him more than the thought of winters like these.

Besides, he told himself, he could never have made it in California; he didn't have enough chest hair.

Within minutes he had arrived at work. Multigraphics, Inc, was located in a fifth-storey loft overlooking Canal—a print shop specializing in advertisements, album covers, and related promotional materials for record companies. It was as drafty as commercial lofts usually were, though today Michael noticed upon entering that someone had cajoled the landlord into turning up the furnace, precluding the usual necessity of stuffing paper towels around the edges of the windows. Michael was hanging up his coat and scarf when George—a thin, neurasthenic sort with long hair and a drooping mustache—cornered him.

"Mike, what do you think? Is it warm enough in here?"

"Hell, yes. Warmer than it's been all year. How much did you bribe the super, anyway?"

"Maybe I should've had him turn it up a few more degrees . . ."

"George, it's fine, honest."

"Maybe I'll go down and talk to him again . . . see if he can jack it up a little more. . . ."

Michael started looking around for a truck. *"George, the temperature is fine.* I mean, we're not talking about the Donner Party here, you know? They're not gonna start turning on each other if the thermostat drops below seventy."

George looked unconvinced. "Yeah. Yeah. Hey, Mike, thanks a lot for taking over these party preparations. Frankly," he added in a low voice, taking Michael aside, "you're the only one of these bozos working here who I'd trust to walk across the street unaided, know what I mean? You give most of them a thousand bucks and a list of party refreshments, they'd come back with nine hundred dollars worth of Trail Mix and a case of Coors."

"C'mon, George. You're being a little hard on them, don't you think?"

George half-smiled, shook his head. "Come on, Mike. All you need in this job is the ability to line up blocks of copy and artwork along straight lines laid out by other people, wax 'em in place, and send them off to the camera room. I mean, we're not talking applied physics here. You see the kind of drifters this business attracts. Hell, not that I'm looking a good thing in the mouth, but I've kind of wondered what someone like you is doing here as long as you've been."

"I came for the waters."

"Seriously, Mike."

"Seriously," Michael said, moving off, "I've got to get down to work. After lunch I'll start getting the refreshments set up." He turned and headed for his desk, where he began his daily ritual of pulling out pen, X-acto knife, and straightedge. Although he'd quickly changed the subject, part of him was basking in the admittedly faint but still warming praise his employer had given him. As he surveyed the other graphics workers in the design room, Michael had to agree with George: most of them were professional drifters, going from one minor graphics job to another, people with talent but no great ambition, skill but little drive. Emotional vagabonds. What *was* he doing here, anyway?

Then, just as he started feeling good about himself, he opened the largest drawer of his desk and the first thing he saw was the battered, slightly tarnished brass of his horn. A French horn, bruised by time and disuse, it lay half-wrapped in brown butcher paper, nestled on a bed of cardboard shavings and other debris of previous weeks' work. Michael had forgotten he had it here, in the office; he'd brought it in weeks ago, thinking that finally, all these years later, he'd pawn the damned thing for something useful . . . but had not yet been able to bring himself to do so. It lay there, a brassy reminder of a failed career and discarded dreams, and it mocked him. But still he could not quite bring it to the pawnshop. Still.

His face hardened; he slammed shut the drawer. Today. After work. Today he'd get rid of the god-damned thing, and no further procrastination. *This* was his career, now: layout, paste-up. This was the closest he would ever come to music again, and he'd damned well better get used to it.

Turning back to his work, he was pleased to discover that he had an album cover to paste-up today, a task always more interesting than promo items. Unwrapping the package from RCA, he found the art, photos, and pre-set jacket copy for the new Dolly Parton album, including a five-inch cutout of Dolly in a low-cut, spangled gown that still only hinted at the awesome body beneath. Michael stared, finding it difficult to believe that this was a photograph of a real person and not a Vargas cartoon from *Playboy*: not just the fabled breasts and pneumatic thighs, but the warm, laughing face framed by an incongruous cascade of platinum hair. She seemed somehow accessible, the kind of person you wouldn't be afraid to talk to, or joke with, if you ever . . .

—Mike? Ah good, you're working on it now. Mike, this is Eric Denten of RCA, and I'm sure you recognize Miss Parton. They dropped by to check on the production of Dolly's new album. Eric . . . Dolly . . . this is Michael Barrett.

Michael shakes Denten's hand, then nervously extends a hand to Dolly. He feels faint as she warmly returns his grip. She seems smaller in person; all Michael can see is her wide, open smile and the twinkle in her eyes. —Pleased to meet ya, Mr. Barrett. I'm happy to see my album's in the hands of someone so . . . capable.

My God, is she flirting with him? That quick, enigmatic glance she gave him . . . . —It's my pleasure, Miss Parton.

—Dolly.

—Uh, yes. Dolly.

She turns to Denten. —Why don't you two go on to the . . . what do you call it . . . the camera room? I'd like to give Mr. Barrett some o' my . . . input on the cover layout.

Denten and George exit, leaving Michael suddenly alone, beyond all imaginings, with her. Dolly motions him to sit, and as he does she moves closer, standing right behind him; she is wearing a bright red sweater that clings to every staggering contour, and as she leans over to look at the album cover on his desk, he feels her arm press against his side, and Michael has an immediate hard-on, perhaps the greatest, most monumental hard-on he has ever had.

—Now, how do you usually go about laying out one of these things, Mr. Barrett?

Her breath on his neck makes his nape hairs stand on end; he never imagined before that nape hairs could be an erogenous zone. She smells of lilacs. He begins to think that his cock is going to explode. —Well, I, uh . . . I line up the art . . . the photographs . . . on these blue lines, you see, and . . . uh . . .

She leans over, her scented platinum hair brushing his cheek, and Michael stops in mid-sentence. He turns, ever so slightly, and looks at her. She looks at him, smiles mischievously. —Y'know, Mr. Barrett (she drawls teasingly) what I'd really like to see is your typesetting room. You think you can arrange a little . . . private tour?

Within minutes, Michael has given Pat, the typesetter, twenty bucks to go take an early lunch, and soon he and Dolly are alone in the small typesetting room, its machines silent for the moment. Dolly makes sure to close the door behind them; Michael leads her on a mock-tour, gathering from somewhere the courage to put his arm lightly to her waist as they walk. God, it feels so soft, so small, so . . . —Now this is the main equipment, here . . . this is where they . . .

She stops, turns toward him, smiles; her eyes shine expectantly. Oh God, this is it; this is the moment. With only a second's hesitation, Michael takes her in his arms and kisses her. She embraces him and Michael feels the lushness of her lips, the wonderful softness of her body. He feels her breasts push against his chest and somehow he gets even harder. They fall back against one of the stacks of cardboard Pat uses to pack between frames of type; quickly Michael strews some onto the floor, and they drop down onto them, her hands under his shirt, caressing his sides. Michael, always too damned ticklish for his own good, restrains a giggle. Please, God, not now. All his life he has broken out into ticklish laughter at all the wrong moments, but not *now*. Dolly starts to unbutton her blouse. Michael stares in open-mouthed wonder, watching her long red fingernails undo the first button, then the second, the lush crescent of her cleavage peeking out, the promise of something even grander starting to appear; her fingers undo the third and last button, and as she does

"Hey, Mike, got a minute?"

Michael jumped. Unaccountably, tears sprang to his eyes. George stood behind him, looking puzzledly at him.

"Uh, something wrong, Mike?"

Michael quickly composed himself. "No. No. Nothing at all. What's up?" The phrasing reminded him of a potential embarrassment, which he quickly crossed his legs to avoid.

"I want to take a look at the paper plate situation. Where'd you put them?"

"They're in the—" Michael's eyes misted over as he realized. "In the typesetting room," he said, with infinite sadness. George nodded, moved off. Michael sighed and returned to work. Briefly, he attempted to continue the fantasy, but somehow, it just wasn't the same. . . .

An hour into the Christmas party Michael found, to his surprise, that he was enjoying himself. Actually, calling it a "Christmas" party seemed unconscionably premature; it was only the last week in November. But since Multigraphics, like many graphics firms, shut down entirely for December, it would be the only opportunity this year.

Michael wandered through the crowd, a mixed bag of staid-looking advertising people, coked-out record company execs, and some of the most astonishingly beautiful women Michael had ever seen—most of whom seemed welded to the arms of the coked-out record company execs. Getting his third cup of eggnog, Michael noticed that the room was starting to sway somewhat, and realized that he was well on his way to getting hammered. Well, why not. Christmas, after all, albeit prematurely. He was having an enjoyable talk with a couple of advertising writers when, through the pleasantly inebriate fog, he heard a young woman's voice, saying, "Hey, whose horn is this?"

He turned to find an attractive young blonde standing in front of his desk, an unlit cigarette in one hand and Michael's French horn in the other. He sobered quickly, went toward her. "Uh, that's . . . mine," he said awkwardly.

The blonde laughed. "I'm sorry, I don't usually ransack people's desks, I was just looking for a light. Do you play?"

There was something warm, something friendly about her face; Michael forgot to react defensively. "Not much these days, I'm afraid."

"Can you play something now?" she asked, suddenly taken with her own inspiration. "How about a Christmas carol?"

"Oh no—I couldn't—"

Her eyes twinkled. "Oh, come on. Just one carol; I'm dying to hear one. Do you know 'It Came Upon a Midnight Clear'?"

Michael took the horn. He felt good, and whether it was due to the eggnog or to the blonde's merry eyes, he didn't know. What the hell. "I don't know that one, but . . . how about this?"

Without stopping to think, Michael put the horn to his lips—and played.

The familiar strains of "Hark, the Herald Angels Sing" filled the room. The notes were sharp and clear; the melody flowed effortlessly from Michael, his breath strong, his fingers moving surely over the valve buttons; slowly, conversation in the room stopped as people began to listen. At auditions, years ago, Michael had never had this feeling; he would freeze, fear gripping him in a cold hand. Fear that he would play badly. Fear that halfway across town, Zubin

Mehta would hear him, storm into the audition, and announce, "Young man, this is a crime against art. You must forsake the horn immediately, or submit to euthanasia. The choice is yours." And so, of course, he *would* play badly.

But not today. Not now. The triumphant melody carried him higher than he had gone in years—filled him with the kind of joy he had felt when he had first taken up music, the joy of being a cherished vessel for something older and grander and more beautiful than he could dream of, but more than a vessel, too, for without him that music could not live; without him it was mere notations on paper, chords and quavers and breath marks and accidentals, waiting to be brought to life. He was, compared to the music, unimportant; and yet he was all-important, as well. He served the music, and the music, in turn, served him, each making the other truly alive.

It wasn't until he finished that he noticed the rapt attention of the other guests—and then, (to his surprise), came their apparently sincere applause. Suddenly embarrassed, Michael smiled gratefully, nodded, and put the horn back in the drawer.

The blonde was smiling appreciatively. "You're very good," she said.

"It's kind of you to say that," Michael said, not believing her.

"Have you thought of playing professionally?"

The defensiveness was creeping back in. "Not for a . . . long time. I was never able to break in. I just keep the horn around for old time's sake."

"Well, you're very good." A brief silence, then, as they looked at one another, the blonde perhaps waiting for Michael to make the next move, and Michael as usual wishing to high hell he knew what the next move *was*. Awkwardly they stood there, until, finally, the blonde cleared her throat. "Well. Thanks for the performance. It was nice meeting you." Michael's heart raced; he searched for something, anything, to say to her, to engage her in conversation to keep her there, but his mind was a blank, nothing came to him, and in moments the woman had edged past him and melted into the crowd once more, forever lost.

From the heights he had just scaled, Michael plummeted to earth. Once again he had let opportunity pass by; once again he stood watching life, real life, recede away like a tide gone out for the last time. He felt suddenly ashamed—ashamed of being so goddamned shy; ashamed that, with his thirtieth birthday drawing ever nearer, he still felt so much like a child.

Suddenly, he had to get out of this party. He started for the door, then, as he was getting his coat, stopped—turned—and, obeying some silent impulse, went back to his desk, opened a drawer, and took out his horn. He held it for long moments, turning it over and over in his hands, remembering how the music had filled him just minutes before, remembering again how much that music had meant to him, once . . . and, slowly, he came to realize that he would never, could never, bring himself to pawn it. Tucking the instrument under his arm, he made for the exit, and as he descended the five flights of steps to the ground— shame consuming him, making him move faster,

faster down the stairs—the sounds of the party dimmed behind him, the laughter and the music mocking him all the way down to the street.

The depression passed, as it usually did, but this time it took longer than the last, even as the last had taken longer than the time before that. And he suspected that he might not have pulled out of it at all were it not for the fact that he was having dinner Thursday night with some of his closest friends— Bob, Susan, Morrie, Val—and, especially, Shelley.

Shelley Loventhal was probably his closest friend; although they'd known each other for only a few years, they had become immediate soulmates. After a period of initial infatuation with her, Michael had come to realize that she was far more valuable to him, and he to her, as a friend and a confidante than as a would-be lover. When Shelley was depressed, Michael was able to make her laugh; when Michael despaired of his life, Shelley always found something to pique his interest—a new restaurant, a new book, a Broadway show—and suddenly they were off on an adventure. When Shelley had broken up with the man she had been dating for two years, plunging into a despondence deeper than anything Michael had yet seen in her, he had spent an entire night with her, talking till four in the morning; then, later, they had lain together in bed, not making love, just holding one another against the terrors of the dark.

Lately, they had not seen as much of each other as either would have liked; Shelley was dating a med student named Josh, and it looked as though things were, as they say, Getting Serious, and Michael . . .

Michael found himself drawing back, not wishing to intrude on her happiness, and preparing himself, perhaps, for the inevitable moment when she, like so many of his friends, would take the plunge into marriage.

Still, he was not prepared for it happening quite so soon. . . .

Dinner at La Crêpe in the Village was fun, as always. At one point Michael found himself looking around at his friends and marveling at his good fortune—to be blessed with people such as these in his life. Some, like Bob and Susan, he had known in college and continued to stay in touch with over the years; some, like Shelley and Will and Val, he had met in classes at NYU and City College, in that familiar ritual of night classes known so well to singles—the most socially accepted way of Looking to Meet People without actually seeming as though you're Looking. He looked around at the faces surrounding him, and he knew they loved him, as he loved them. But . . .

As the evening went on, Val and Morrie produced snapshots of their youngest daughter, Alexandria, just three months old and currently under the eye of a babysitter; Bob and Susan talked about the home they had just purchased in Westchester, throwing about terms like equity, points, straight notes, and all-inclusive trust deeds; Shelley and Josh exchanged playful kisses every once in a while; and Michael, not for the first time, sat staring at his salad plate, feeling a little out of it. These people were his contemporaries, of the same generation as he, and yet he felt so much *younger* than they, somehow, so much more . . . backward. Nor was the feeling ameliorated any by what happened next.

Shelley stood up, wineglass in hand, poised as though for an announcement. She was an attractive woman with curly black hair and dark olive eyes, but tonight, it seemed to Michael, she looked even prettier than usual. "Settle down, you animals," she declared, tapping her spoon on a glass. "Josh and I have an announcement." A suitable pause for effect, then: "We're finally going to *do it*."

Morrie, with typical mordant humor, widened his eyes in astonishment. "You mean you haven't *done it* already? My God, Josh, don't they teach you *anything* in med school these days?"

"No no no," she reprimanded, "marriage, you fool, marriage. We're getting married next month."

An immediate babble of delighted voices followed, offering congratulations, but the smile on Michael's face belied the sudden fear he felt welling up within him; fear and a certain sad resignation, a sound of doors closing and pages turning, as another life moved ahead while he stood still. . . .

Later, outside the restaurant, Michael found a moment alone with Shelley; bundled up in a fox jacket, Shelley looked very soft, very vulnerable, as she took Michael's hand and squeezed it affectionately. "Is this really happening?" she said, laughing. "Am I really getting"—a look of mock-horror passed across her face—"*married?*"

"Sure are," Michael said, smiling, genuinely happy for her. "I told you it would happen, didn't I?"

"Yeah. And I never believed you. I felt like I was, I don't know, destined to go from one disastrous relationship to another, till the end of the time. You've heard of the Wandering Jew? I thought I was going to be the Wandering JAP."

Michael laughed. They continued to hold hands, looking into one another's eyes in a way only old friends can, seeing things only old friends can see . . . and, very softly, Shelley said, "It'll happen, Michael. It may seem impossible now, but it will. I have it on very good authority."

Michael smiled, a bit sadly. "And who might that be?"

Shelley squeezed his hand again. "Fella named Barrett," she said. "*He* told *me* it would happen— and it did."

Touched, Michael didn't know what to say. So instead he hugged her, the two of them holding each other for several moments before Josh appeared, feigning jealousy. "Okay, you two, break it up," he announced good-naturedly. "God, every chance you get, huh?"

"You bet," Shelley said. "Sorry, Josh, I've changed my mind. Michael's going to take me to Maui instead."

Michael blinked. "Maui? Your, uh, honeymoon?"

Josh nodded. "Surf . . . sand . . . seventy-degree weather . . ."

"Yeah, well, if you like that sort of thing," Shelley said with studied indifference. "I mean, there's still time to make reservations at the Buffalo Marriott."

Michael laughed, but he felt something sink within him: Hawaii. Of course. What else. He refused to allow his envy to show, however; he gave Shelley a kiss on the cheek, shook Josh's hand. "Congratulations again, you two. Looking forward to the wedding."

They waved goodbye to one another, and Michael turned, headed for the nearest subway station. After a minute, he glanced back; Shelley and Josh were small figures in the distance, walking arm-in-arm away from him. Michael watched their receding figures, and for an instant he smiled, recalling what they must be feeling: the excitement, the anticipation, the sheer wonder of having someone you cared for so much, someone who cared as much for you. Michael had known that feeling perhaps once or twice in his life, and never for very long, but while it lasted it had been wonderful. To have someone to *think* about, to lie awake in bed and dream about . . .

Their figures rounded a corner and were gone. Michael turned and headed for the Chambers Street station. True, he'd known the anticipation, the excitement, but he had never really known the joy, the culmination . . . and knew now that he probably never would. He had overcome his shyness far too late, not losing his virginity until he was twenty-five, for Christ's sake; he had never learned how the game worked, what you said, how you acted . . . he assumed that there was some instruction manual you got when you were twelve years old, and he had missed it. Probably the day he'd cut gym class. He couldn't understand it; some men didn't think twice about asking a woman to go to bed with them, but for him it took hours to work up enough courage, to figure out exactly how to phrase it, and by that time he was usually such a nervous wreck that the girl sensed it and ran for the hills. How did everybody else manage it? he wondered. He wasn't angry, just hungry to know. He felt like a kid at a toy store, his face pressed up against the glass, looking in.

On the subway, Michael stepped over the rancid remains of someone's grocery shopping and retreated into a far corner of the car; as luck would have it, the last person to board was a bag lady, her breath reeking of gin, and she promptly sat down next to him. Michael recoiled a bit but did not have the energy to move. The train lurched forward, rattling in its tube like phlegm, and the bag lady dozed despite the noise.

Michael looked at the other passengers: a junkie trembled and twitched across the aisle, coldsweating, fitful, one hand holding the opposite wrist as if completing a circle of pain; a lonely-looking young woman with stringy brown hair and large, putty-like features staring into space; derelicts stretched out on the hard plastic seats. The vague unease Michael had felt last night suddenly crystallized; he knew now just why he hated these people so. He hated them because he was *of* them. A shy, homely twenty-nine-year-old man who watched other people return from places he would never visit, and fantasized relationships because he did not have the courage to initiate them. If anybody belonged here, he did.

He slowly became aware that tears were rolling down his cheeks. Embarrassed, he tried to stop them but could not; flushed and ashamed, he could only sit there as the fears and frustration of twenty-nine years finally broke loose. The bag lady beside him woke, saw the tears streaming down his face (but still he could not stop), and with a look of infinite compassion in her eyes, as though he were simply drawing upon some pool of common sadness, she placed a comforting hand on his knee and lay back again, eyes shut. Michael cried for her, for the junkie, for the woman with the sad, putty-like face—but most of all he cried for Tahiti, and Jamaica, and Hawaii, for all the places he would never see, for all the things he would never know.

2

Virginia Teresa Benedetti sat hunkered down in the main display window of Macy's, impatiently trying to eke out the last few ounces of artificial snow from her spray can; the last of the white flakes sputtered out with something like a sigh, clinging to the wrought-iron blades of the Christmas sleigh. The floor was covered by a quilt of white cotton batting, beneath which lay carefully crafted hills and drifts of polyethylene to simulate snowbanks. It had taken Ginny nearly three hours to get the contours exactly right, and the floor manager had kept nervously popping his head inside to hurry her along, but when he saw the results he was pretty well pleased, and so, for that matter, was Ginny.

She got up and adjusted the heavy winter clothing the mannequins in the sleigh were wearing. The female mannequin had on a dark red cashmere jacket, the male a suede coat with a white fur collar; their glass eyes stared out the window, mouths frozen in word-less smiles. For a moment, Ginny felt a pang of pride at what she had captured in the peaceful snowscene, then dismissed the thought as silly and proceeded to drape tinsel over the small Christmas tree in the corner.

If the holiday shoppers streaming past the window noticed her at all, they saw the young woman trim-ming the tree as a short, plump, somewhat skittish girl, about twenty-four, pretty in a waiflike sort of way, with short brown hair and large brown eyes. If they looked a little closer, they might have seen the reticence in her eyes, the way she avoided the tableau outside the window and preferred instead to concen-trate on the inanimate objects inside.

Ginny tried to keep her gaze down as she placed ornaments on the dry branches, aware suddenly, as she rarely was, that she was in full view of several hundred people. Of course, New York being New York, she could probably have been stark naked and no one would have given her a second glance—but maybe, she thought, that reflected more on her than on New Yorkers. The very thought made her blush unconsciously; the only person who had ever seen her naked, at least in recent years, was her sister, and that—well, she supposed that was probably all for the best.

But she couldn't help but look up occasionally from her labors to steal furtive glances at all the people clutching gift boxes as they passed—laughing, smiling, holding hands. Framed by the large display window, they looked almost as if they were on television, or in a movie, and that made it easier to watch them, somehow. When periodically she became aware that they were real, she returned her attention to the Christmas tree and redoubled her concentration.

"Ginny? Ginny, you in there?" Annie McGuire's voice preceded her into the window. Annie was a slim, black-haired, pretty woman a few years older than Ginny; she grinned as she surveyed the seasonal display. "Wow. Looks beautiful, Gin. Almost makes me forget Thanksgiving isn't due for two weeks." She hovered at the edge of the display, hand holding aside the curtain that separated it from the interior of the store. "You ready to boogie tonight?"

Ginny felt a cold sinking feeling in her stomach. "Uh, not really, Annie," she said, feigning a cough. "I'm not really feeling all that great . . . coming down with something, I think. Why don't you go by—"

Annie shook her head firmly. "Uh-uh, kid. You go into that tubercular routine every time you start having second thoughts. You made me a promise, Gin, and I'm gonna hold you to it."

"Annie, I haven't danced since high school. I won't know what to do. It'll be an ugly sight, Annie."

"I'm not listening to this," Annie declared. "Meet you out front in five minutes. Bye." And she zipped out before Ginny could say another word. Ginny sighed, a feeling of dread now hovering over the idyllic holiday scene. She went back to her trimming, though with less enthusiasm; the walls of the display window seemed to push in around her, ever so slightly.

Inside of an hour, Ginny found herself shoving her way through a mass of humanity as loud rock music assaulted her from all sides. The singles bar was crowded this Friday night, more crowded than even the subway Ginny took each morning to get to work; she hated that subway ride, the way people pressed against her, the vacant look in their eyes and the smell of their breath on her neck, and this was not much better.

Annie held her by the arm, tugging her along toward a table in the rear. "I hate this already," Ginny announced, to no one in particular. "It's a meat market. They're gonna hang us from the ceiling like slabs of pork."

"Ginny, *relax*. Hey, I think I see Bruce and Dennis." She guided her through the mob.

Ginny looked around at all the clean, shining faces, all the coiffed and permed hair and the slim, neat bodies wrapped in Jordache and Calvins, and wondered vaguely why everyone here looked like they'd stepped out of a Dr. Pepper commercial. She didn't have much time to consider, though, as abruptly she found herself facing two young men while Annie quickly made introductions.

"Bruce, Dennis . . . this is Ginny Benedetti. We work together at Macy's. Ginny, you know Bruce, and this is Dennis Mahoney."

Bruce, Annie's boyfriend, was a good-looking, muscular young man, while Dennis was a plain, diffident sort who nodded and smiled a bit shyly when Ginny looked at him—which wasn't for very long. "Hi," she said perfunctorily, dropping into a seat. Annie followed suit. There was a brief silence, filled largely with the pounding of a hard-rock beat from the nearby deejay's booth; then Annie broke the awkward moment. "I've, ah, been telling Ginny about this place for months," she said, "but this is the first time I've been able to tear her away from her work."

"Well, what do you think, Ginny?" Bruce asked with a friendly smile.

Ginny's frown deepened. "I think it's a meat—"

Annie's foot suddenly jabbed the calf of Ginny's leg, and Ginny quickly amended her sentence: "A *neat* place . . ."

"Uh, Bruce," Annie said quickly, "why don't we get some drinks? Margaritas, everyone?"

Ginny tried to protest, but Annie and Bruce were already rising. "Give me a hand, hon?" "Be right back, people." And abruptly they were gone, making their way through the mob of patrons toward a bar that seemed to Ginny as distant as Brazil; feeling exposed and helpless, she found herself alone with Dennis. Had she not been so intent on her own misery, she might have noticed that Dennis, too, did not look entirely comfortable. After a long silence, as Ginny studied the tablecloth intently, Dennis said, "So you, uh, work at Macy's, too?"

Ginny's heart pounded. Her eyes did not leave the tablecloth. "Uh-huh."

"So that's how you and Annie know each other."

Ginny glanced up, briefly. "Funny how that works out, isn't it."

Dennis uncertainly tried for a small laugh. "Uh. Yes." Silence again. Then, his voice a bit shaky (though Ginny did not notice that, either), he added, "You know, I . . . I don't come to these kinds of places very often myself."

"You looking for a merit badge or something?" Ginny said, unthinkingly. Dennis stiffened, ready to bolt right then and there but willing to give it one more try. Several uncomfortable moments later, he said, "Annie says you're from the Bronx? When did you—"

Ginny suddenly looked up, cut him off: "Look, if you don't mind," she said, tired and impatient, "I really don't feel like going over my whole life history right now, okay?" Dennis blinked. Ginny averted her gaze, more out of habit than anything else. "I mean, it's not as if you really care about where I was born, y'know? It's just what people are supposed to do on a date. You pretend you're interested in me; *I* pretend I'm interested in you. Next thing you'll be asking me who my favorite groups are, or what movies I've seen, or what I'm gonna do with my life. As if either of us really cared."

Ginny's gaze dropped again; she saw her hands twisting and pulling a napkin out of shape. She tried to focus on that and that alone. Dennis, stung, looked away. His voice, when he spoke, was quiet and trembling with hurt and embarrassment.

"I'm . . . sorry," he said softly. "I didn't mean to . . . bore you." He licked his lips nervously. "God damn it, I should never have let Bruce talk me into this. I always manage to screw up."

Something of his pain finally managed to seep through to Ginny. She looked up, beginning to realize what she had done. Her tone softened slightly. "Hey . . . I . . . I didn't mean to—"

Dennis stood. "Excuse me. You're right; this was all a bad idea. Give my apologies to Bruce and Annie. Nice . . . meeting you."

"Dennis—no—" But by the time Ginny was on her feet, Dennis was already elbowing his way through the crowd. "Dennis, please, I'm sorry—I didn't mean—I was being—"

No good; he couldn't hear her over the roar of the music. Or perhaps he could. Ginny stood there, guilt consuming her, feeling like shit; slowly she sank back into her seat, pounding the table with her fist in self-reproach. Oh God, she thought, why do I *say* these things? Why don't I ever stop and—

"Ginny?" Annie was behind her, a couple of drinks in hand, looking about puzzledly. "Where'd Dennis go?"

Ginny's voice was small. "Away. He . . . gave you his apologies . . ." The sentence trailed off. Annie's face darkened with recognition. She placed the drinks on the table angrily, turned to Ginny. "You did it again, didn't you?"

Ginny felt herself flush; she couldn't meet Annie's eyes. "I . . . I'm sorry, Annie. I'm just so damned stupid sometimes . . . I don't know what I'm saying . . ." She finally met Annie's gaze, saw the hurt in her friend's face, and rose. "I'd better go, too," she said, starting to move off.

Before she could take another step, Annie intercepted her, taking her firmly by the arm. There was more pain than anger in her tone, more confusion than recrimination in her manner. "Why do you do it, Gin?'' she asked, very simply. "I introduce you to my friends, and you insult them. You hurt them. You understand that, Ginny? You *hurt* them.''

Ginny's throat was dry as sandpaper. "I don't mean to,'' she whispered. "Honest to God, I don't. I just get flustered, and scared, and I . . . don't think about what I'm saying . . ." She knew that she sounded like a little girl and she hated it, but whenever she tried to assert herself—as she had just now—it backfired. Damn it, she couldn't *win*.

"Is it me, Ginny?'' Annie was saying. "I mean, I thought we were friends.''

Ginny was startled. "But we are,'' she said.

"Then why do you do this to me?'' Annie asked, trying to understand. "If you don't want to meet my friends, okay, tell me, but don't put me in the position of lining them up like ducks in a shooting gallery, for God's sake. How do you think I feel, seeing my friends hurt, however unintentionally?''

Ginny felt as though she had been dropped down a deep hole and the sides were closing in on her. Tears started to well up in her eyes, but she fought them back, fought to keep her dignity. She felt horribly guilty, aware for the first time of what she had done to Annie. "I guess,'' she said, ashamed, "I never really thought about it before.''

Annie put a hand gently on her shoulder. "Hey. It's okay. As long as you think about it now. Then, next time, maybe you won't make the same mistakes.''

No. She couldn't go through this again. She couldn't take the risk. She moved away, shaking her head. "Maybe there shouldn't be a next time, Annie,'' she said, on the verge of tears. "Okay?''

"Ginny, come on, don't—"

But Ginny was already running through the crowd, desperate to reach the exit. Behind her, Annie called out, but Ginny ignored her cries, pushing her way fiercely through the mob, hot tears streaming down her face. Only at the door did she stop for a moment, fighting back an urge to return to the table; she ached to go back, but knew she didn't dare. Angry and ashamed, she banged out the door, wishing she were dead.

After that, things were never quite the same between her and Annie. Oh, Annie was always friendly, always cordial, but because Ginny could not forget the shame and embarrassment of that night, she assumed no one else could, either; and so the nicer Annie was toward her, the more Ginny feared she was merely being polite. Soon, Ginny found herself going out of her way to avoid her . . . and slowly, Ginny's world began to shrink. Annie had been her one close friend, aside from her sister Margaret; now she wasn't there, and the store, even the windows, seemed lonelier than it had in years.

At Thanksgiving dinner, Mama looked worse than she had in a long while, her small body wracked with convulsive coughs even as she lit up one cigarette after another. Margaret was late, as usual, and Ginny found herself alone with Mama for nearly four hours in the small apartment on Mulberry Street she had rented these six years since Papa's death.

It was the same old routine. "Virginia, you meet any nice boys yet?" "Virginia, you're cute, you're pretty, what's wrong, why don't you go out more?" "You gotta learn to be more like Margaret, she's not afraid to go out, do things, meet people—you could learn from her, Virginia . . .'' Her black eyes shone as she recited the litany of Ginny's shortcomings, her wrinkled fingers curled around the burning cigarette, the smell making Ginny sick to her stomach. She wanted to run. She wanted to say, No, Mama, I haven't met any nice boys yet. I'm *not* cute, I'm *not* pretty, God knows you told me that often enough when I was little; why should I suddenly become pretty when all my life I wasn't? And she wanted to say, Damn it, Mama, I haven't met anyone, and I probably *won't* meet anyone, 'cause Mama, your little girl is fat and plain and can't keep her big mouth shut, and Mama, will you please *shut up* and leave me *alone*, will you, Mama, *will* you?

But she didn't say anything; she just sat and watched her mother drone on, not really hearing her, as if she were watching television with the sound turned off. She watched the way her mother's arms moved jerkily, like a puppet whose strings were tangled somewhere high above. She saw how the jet-black pupils of her eyes seemed to fade with the afternoon sun, becoming duller and grayer the longer she spoke. She listened to the voice, which had sung her to sleep in a distant dream, now raspy and grating, like a record worn down to the groove. And slowly, as the sunlight angled in through yellowed curtains, as the room went sallow and the smell of turkey mingled with that of cigarette smoke, Ginny knew that her mother was going to die.

Margaret arrived a little before five, sweeping in in a sexy red dress slit halfway up her thigh, which became a subject of conversation for what seemed hours ("Are you crazy? Mr. Pasquale down on the third floor, he plays with rubber dolls, and you dress like that in this neighborhood?") until, thankfully, it became time to eat.

Over dinner, Margaret and Mama talked and ate and smoked, not necessarily in that order, while Ginny picked at her food and wondered how long Mama had left to her, and whether or not Margaret knew. Probably not, she decided. Margaret didn't think like Ginny; they were as different as sisters could be. Where Ginny was plump and shy, Margaret was thin and outgoing; where Ginny's face was plain and soft, Margaret's was beautiful in a hard-edged, angular way. They had different interests, liked different people, laughed at different things. There was very little between them except, maybe, love. And Ginny wasn't even very sure about that.

"And how's your job coming, Margaret?" Mama stubbed out her cigarette and immediately scrabbled in her pack for another. Finding it empty, she reached out and took one from Margaret's. "Are you still seeing that boss of yours . . . what's his name, Roger . . . ?"

Margaret shook out her long black hair, blew smoke toward the ceiling. "As a matter of fact," she began, "I was going to tell you, I've decided to move on—I got a better offer from another company. Starting next week I'll be working for Metropolitan Insurance. Secretary to the regional sales manager," she finished, with a triumphant half-smile. Mama raised her eyebrows, properly impressed, and turned to Ginny: "You see the initiative your sister has? You could use a little of that, Virginia."

Ginny felt herself getting red with anger; she stood quickly. " 'Scuse me, Mama," she said, hurrying from the table, "I gotta go to the bathroom." Behind her as she ran, she could hear her mother say, in confiding tones, "You see? You try to give her advice, she runs away." Ginny felt even hotter as she slammed the bathroom door shut; she turned on the fan and allowed its rattle and hum to drown out her sobs. God *damn* Margaret, anyway. If Ginny changed jobs as often as she did, Mama would be berating her for being unstable, unable to hold a job; but if Margaret did it, it was just . . . career advancement! Damn it, why did she always have to—

A knock on the bathroom door dried Ginny's tears immediately. "Ginny? Can I come in?" Margaret's voice. Ginny felt guilty for cursing her, crossed herself more out of habit than any real religious conviction, and reluctantly opened the door to let Margaret in.

Margaret shut the door behind her as Ginny sat down on the toilet seat; she went to Ginny, squatted down beside her and held her hands. "I'm sorry, hon," she said with genuine concern. "She didn't mean it."

"Yes, she did," Ginny said flatly. "She always does. And why do you always . . . encourage her?"

Margaret looked stung. "Ginny, I do no such thing!"

"Oh? You don't say, 'Hey, Mama, I lost my job'; you say, 'I'm moving on to another company.' You don't tell her, 'Roger and me, we broke up'; you tell her, 'Oh, I met this *wonderful* man, his name is David,' and I'm the only one at the table thinking,

What the hell ever happened to Roger? Or Frank? Or Allen? My God, Maggie, you manage to edit all the awful things right out of your life! I wish to heck *I* could swing that, you know?''

A little surprised by her own vehemence, Ginny glanced away; Margaret's sharp features softened as she put her arms around her sister and rocked her gently. "God, Gin, I wish I could too," she said softly. "Good old Gin. You've always known how screwed up I am, haven't you? And I've always been so scared to admit it to Mama." She stroked Ginny's back gently. "I'm sorry, hon. I'll try harder. Honest I will."

Ginny smiled, sniffed back her tears, and hugged Margaret, who dabbed her eyes with a kleenex, then tried to apply a little makeup to hide the redness around them—a move which Ginny strenuously resisted. Margaret sighed. Minutes later, the two sisters emerged from the bathroom and returned to the dinner table.

Inside of twenty-five minutes, after Mama asked how Roger was getting along, Margaret began extolling the virtues of a man named Tony, a name which sent Mama's heart soaring, and Ginny sank a little in her chair, cursing to herself. The jaundiced light streamed through the dusty blinds, the air sulfurous with cigarette smoke, painting Margaret and her mother in shades of acid yellow, as the sounds of traffic drifted up from Mulberry Street—not so different from those on Arthur Avenue in the Bronx, so many years ago. Ginny watched the second hand sweep across the face of the kitchen clock, as she had so often before, in a different room of a different house, and cursed herself for a fool for thinking that it could ever change, that anything ever changed, or that anyone even cared if it did.

Mama died the first week of December. It was a big funeral, with relatives from as far away as Chicago crowded into Our Lady of Mt. Carmel Church and, later, into Uncle Sal's modest two-bedroom apartment on East 187th Street. They all expressed great dismay and shock, while simultaneously claiming to have seen it coming for a long, long time. They ate and drank and gossiped with an appetite which made Ginny retreat in disgust to a corner by the window.

Both Uncle Sal and cousin Dominick and his wife invited Ginny to spend Christmas with them, but she politely declined, claiming a prior invitation. As nice as Sal and Dominick and Therese were, they were really just strangers to her; the only relatives she had ever felt close to, outside the immediate family, were all dead now. Still, the thought of spending Christmas alone terrified her more than she would admit to herself, and so she was immensely relieved when Margaret took her aside and promised that they would spend the holiday together, maybe go for a drive to Connecticut, have dinner at an old country inn, and, as Margaret put it with such sentiment, "all that kinda crap."

Ginny continued to stand in her little corner, fielding sympathy from obscure relations, wondering vaguely what Annie was doing now, then pushing the thought out of her mind as too many bad memories came back to plague her. She stood hunched against the noise and the clamor, against the liver-spotted old men kissing her on the cheek with wine on their breath, and slowly she felt the walls of the room push in, constrict; she felt like a little girl trapped in a dollhouse growing ever smaller, and the smaller it got, the less she could breathe, the less she could think, and the more she wanted to scream, to cry out, before the walls finally closed in and pushed down and crushed her.

3

The trouble with Christmas, Michael decided, was that it was just so damned *consistent*. Every year around mid-November you thought, Well, maybe they'll forget this year. Maybe the world will be too preoccupied with wars and famine and economic depression, December 25th will roll around without any undue hype, and we'll all be able to get a little rest. But no; every year, two days after Thanksgiving, the turkeys and the pumpkins came down, the reindeer and the mangers went up, and Michael would have to start casting about for someplace to spend the dreaded day.

Each year he would be invited, it seemed, to the

home of a different friend, passed among them like an invalid cousin—and although he appreciated the invitations, in some ways they served only to accentuate his loneliness. Sitting in a room filled with somebody else's relatives, listening to the laughter of other people's children, with all those damned melancholy Christmas carols playing in the background . . .

He didn't think he could take that for another year. Already today, as he had mixed with the other wedding guests in the foyer of the Loventhal home on Staten Island, he had received his share of sympathetic glances and discreet inquiries as to what he might be doing on Christmas Day. Somewhat to his own surprise, Michael implied that he had plans . . . which, in a way, he might. Things were coming slowly together in his mind, and for the first time in years he was facing the holiday season not with panic or depression, but with calm and deliberation.

He was sitting in the third row of folding chairs that filled the Loventhals' living room, waiting for the ceremony to begin. Michael had never realized just how well off Shelley's parents were until he had stepped into the elegant Tudor home and seen the high, vaulted ceilings of the living room. The ceremony was to be a civil one, at Shelley's insistence, but as a concession to her more orthodox relatives, it would be sprinkled with some more traditional trappings: at the front of the room, for instance, stood the wedding canopy known as the *huppa*, and before the civil vows—which would have been called the *nissu'in*, or marriage proper, if this had been by-the-book—there would be a brief betrothal ceremony, as rewritten from the original by Shelley.

A sudden swell of organ music filled the room, and Michael turned to see Shelley, looking radiant in a light blue wedding gown, walk up the aisle on her father's arm. As she passed Michael, they exchanged quick, smiling glances, and then she was under the *huppa*, a nervous Josh standing there in a starchy tux.

The betrothal ceremony was short and to the point; Josh placed a gold band on Shelley's finger and recited the traditional declaration: "Behold, you are consecrated to me by this ring according to the law of Moses and Israel." Traditionally, it would have ended right there, but now Shelley placed another gold band on Josh's finger and repeated the same oath, doubtless sending some of the old-guard relations into cardiovascular shock. Michael smiled. Nice touch.

And then the civil ceremony began. "Dearly beloved . . . we are gathered here today . . ."

Michael studied Shelley as she stood expectantly beside her husband-to-be; he watched the way her eyes shone as she stole sideways glances at Josh, saw the touch of delighted disbelief which Michael liked to think only he could discern. It was an expression which seemed to contain all the years of blind dates and dead ends, all the angry, abortive relationships as well as the happy, all-too-brief ones; it contained the pain of nights alone, and the promise of no more nights alone; it held sad reflection on the past, wonder at the present, hope and trepidation for the future. It seemed to say: Maybe this time, God. Please? Maybe this time . . .

Michael felt a rush of gladness for her, remembering again all the nights they had talked away wondering if they would ever find that special Person, the one they wrote all the songs about. Listening to her recite her vows, Michael imagined that Shelley was finally hearing that song, and, distantly, Michael could almost hear it himself . . . being sung to someone else, true, but still he heard it, and that was the real hell of it. A snatch of poetry from college floated back to him, short and sweet and sad: *I have heard the mermaids singing, each to each; I do not think that they will sing to me . . .*

"Do you, Shelley Louise, take this man to be your lawfully wedded husband, to love and to cherish, for as long as you both shall live?"

"I do."

"Do you, Joshua David, take this woman to be your lawfully wedded wife, to love and to cherish, for as long as you both shall live?"

"I do."

The rings were already on their fingers, so they simply held hands and looked into each other's eyes. Michael smiled.

Goodbye, Shelley.

"I now pronounce you husband and wife."

And thanks.

On the ferry back to Manhattan, Michael stood in the bow of the boat and watched the whitecaps smash against the prow, the dull roar of the engines sounding like distant thunder. He stared out at the green-black waters of the Narrows and thought of the last time he had been on a boat like this, on an evening like this. Junior high; eighth grade. Three years of burning dedication to a girl named Karen, with whom he probably exchanged no more than two sentences a week. A sweet, sensitive-looking girl, not a wall-flower but no cheerleader either; they were casual friends and every time she spoke to him Michael's teeth ached. But he never did anything about it, a pattern that would recur in later years.

At the end of the school term, the entire class took a three-day field trip to Washington, D.C. (to this day, the farthest south Michael had ever traveled), one night sailing down the Potomac on a giant cruiseliner to an amusement park on the banks of the river. Michael wandered about the park alone, listening to the distant shrieks of classmates plunging down the roller coaster, too damn scared and stubborn to invite himself along.

On the way back, while everybody else was below decks, dancing, Michael went topside to wander again . . . and there was Karen, standing all alone in the bow of the ship, gazing out at the distant lights of the capital drawing slowly nearer.

And he wanted so much to go down, and stand next to her, and talk to her. And maybe, if he was lucky, he'd get to put his arm around her. All he had to do was take a few steps; a few lousy steps. But he never took them. Instead he stood there, frozen with fear of rejection, for long precious minutes, until Karen finally turned and walked away—oblivious to the fact that he had even been there.

Even now, fifteen years later, it still hurt. It hurt because it *was* fifteen years, and because it still *could* hurt him. Enough, he thought wearily. He wasn't depressed, or angry, merely tired. Tired of foisting his problems on his friends, tired of going to airports in the dead of winter, tired of being *him*. The aesthetics of his own life offended him: it wasn't tragic, or even pathetic, just—boring.

He stared out at the black waters and at the ocean just beyond the bay; he smelled the brine in the air, carried on a westerly breeze, and felt himself growing calmer. The sea, for some reason, had always calmed him—the rolling surface of the water extending as far as one could see, speaking of things greater, vaster, older than one could imagine. A million years ago, humanity had come from the sea, crawling up from cold depths to dark beaches; and when we die, Michael thought, it is the sea to which we should return, our bodies giving back nourishment to the ocean, becoming part of the great cycle of life, and death, and life. And in another million years, perhaps, another dark beach, and the cycle would begin anew.

When you looked at it that way, Michael realized, death wasn't so frightening; it wasn't very frightening at all.

Ginny woke feeling chilly, wondering, as she floated up out of restless dreams, if the furnace had gone out again. She opened her eyes and immediately squinted against the bright, diffuse light pouring in through her cramped apartment's single window; somehow, the shade had rolled up during the night. She wrapped herself in her blanket, stumbled blinking from the bed to go pull the shade down . . . but when she got to the window, she stopped, both startled and pleased by what she saw.

The window was covered with a crystal latticework of frost; touching it, even on the inside, Ginny's warm fingertips left small circles on the glass. Outside it was snowing, not an ugly New York storm but a gentle New England flurry, snowflakes falling from a white cotton sky. Ginny, eyes big, watched the flakes drift slowly down, then, caught by updrafts off warm pavements, bounce upwards again in random flurries and, finally, spiral gently down to earth. It reminded her of the Christmas she had spent in Vermont, so long ago it seemed like a part of someone else's life.

She had been eight years old; Mama had entered the hospital for heart surgery and Papa, an electrician, had to work on a construction site for most of Christmas week. With mysterious reluctance, Papa decided to take Margaret and Ginny (it was never *Ginny and Margaret*) to Vermont to spend the holiday with their grandparents—Papa's parents, neither of whom Ginny had ever met. For some reason, no one talked much about *nonno* and *nonna* Benedetti.

For Ginny, it was like entering another world. It was cold in Vermont, but a *clean* sort of cold, different from the dirty Bronx winters she was used to; Ginny remembered thinking how different the air seemed. Everything was clear and bright and loud as a bell; voices echoed from great distances, and there were no sounds of cars, or trains, or horns. When there was a sound outside the house, it was practically an event. There was room to walk, for miles and miles around her grandparents' farm, without encountering another human being if you didn't want to; you weren't forced into a confrontation every time you walked out the front door.

And the smells! Ginny was used to the thick, pungent smells of Arthur Avenue, the sausage-and-spices flavor of Italian delis and open-air markets and restaurants redolent with garlic and green pepper. And although she knew that flowers had fragrances, she had never realized before that you could also smell trees and grass. She liked to wander behind her grandparents' small, two-storey frame house and just lean into the wind, catching the pine scent of the forest a hundred yards away, somehow amazed that every time she did it, the smell was still there.

Nonno was a big, gentle, barrel-chested man with shaggy white hair and mustache who would take Ginny (and, sometimes, a pouting Margaret) on long walks in the woods, his fourteen-year-old dog, Teddy, sniffing out the path in front of them. Teddy was a Canadian husky, long past his prime and looking like a ball of puffy brown-gray fur, who nevertheless insisted on accompanying anyone entering the woods, routing out snakes and woodchucks, loyally creating safe passage for his masters. Ginny had never had a pet, and so fell immediately in love with Teddy; even at that age, though, she was pragmatic enough to realize that Teddy was dying, and sometimes she spent whole afternoons just sitting with the shambling, gentle dog, walking with him, feeding him, holding him, hoping to make things a little easier for him in his last days.

At other times, she and *Nonno* would play in the snow, or drive to town, or help *Nonna* with her cooking. Ginny's grandmother was a feisty, portly woman of German-Austrian descent who bustled energetically around the house; although she had lost her sense of taste years ago, she continued to cook and to eat with equal enthusiasm, perhaps the look and texture of the food summoning up memories of the taste, and Ginny loved the meals she would prepare, ones with funny names like *sauerbraten* and *spaetzle* and *kartoffelsalat*. (Later, Ginny would figure out that Grandma's lineage—and Lutheranism—probably had something to do with the way the rest of the family ignored them.)

Margaret, of course, hated everything about the visit. Her nose ran from the cold and she ate the food only with great shows of reluctance; eventually, to appease her, she and Ginny had to leave early, returning to the bustle and noise of the Bronx's Italian ghetto, and part of Ginny would never forgive her sister for that.

It had been the best Christmas Ginny had ever known, before or since, and although her grandparents assured her she could come back any time she wished, somehow that never happened. They died within three months of one another, when Ginny was twelve years old; she wasn't even allowed to attend their funerals.

Suddenly, watching the snowflakes fall onto Grand Street below, Ginny shivered. She pulled down the shade, pulled the blanket around her more tightly, and lightly touched the radiator. It was stone cold. Muttering to herself, she decided to skip her shower this morning; in the kitchen she heated just enough water to wash up (the stove, thank God, was electric), and was just starting breakfast when she noticed the time on the clock—7:24—and realized with a start that it was Saturday.

She fought back a quick surge of fear. It was not so much that she had gotten up earlier than she needed to; suddenly, an entire day stretched before her and she didn't know what to do with it. As usual, Ginny hated weekends—during the week she could busy herself at work, then come home and watch television until it was time for bed, but on Saturday . . . ? Four hours of "Creature Features" on Channel 11 was more than even she could take. Sometimes she liked to wander about department stores, just for the sake of having people around her, but there were only four shopping days left till Christmas and every store was likely to be a zoo. Ginny didn't feel quite up to that.

Forcing herself to remain calm, she ate breakfast and waited till nine-thirty to call Margaret, on the off-chance (more like a miracle) that she didn't have anything to do today. At the very least she could find out where and when they were to meet for Christmas.

But when she dialed Margaret's number, the answering service picked up and, flustered, Ginny hung up without leaving a message. She tried again in an hour, and an hour after that, but the service still picked up. The service operator didn't know where Ms. Benedetti could be, only that she hadn't picked up her messages yet for that day; resigned, Ginny left her name and didn't call again.

A certain foreboding hung over Ginny as she sat watching old movies on WPIX all afternoon and evening, waiting for a call, but none was forthcoming. She fell asleep in the middle of a Bowery Boys movie and didn't wake up till eight the next morning, by which time panic had consumed her. After calling one more time, Ginny felt the claustrophobia returning, felt it getting harder to breathe, and snapping up her

coat and scarf, she bolted the apartment. She ran all
the way to the bus stop, waiting fifteen minutes for
one to come along, and inside of half an hour found
herself pounding furiously on the door of Margaret's
apartment on East 81st Street, her heart beating almost as loudly as her fist hammered at the door.

Finally, after several minutes, Ginny could hear the
sound of locks being unfastened from within and the
door opened a crack to reveal a very pissed-off Margaret clad only—as best as Ginny could make out—in
a towel. "For Christ's sake," she snapped, "what do
you—"

When she recognized Ginny she stopped, anger
fading somewhat, brows knitting in annoyance. "Gin?
What's wrong, what are you doing here at"—she
glanced off to her right; her face fell—"nine o'clock,
for God's sake?"

"I've been trying to reach you all weekend,"
Ginny said, suddenly embarrassed. "I . . . uh, kept
getting your service."

"Well, of course. I'm having them screen all my
calls; guess I haven't had time to check in with
them." After a moment's hesitation, she opened the
door to admit Ginny. "Well, come on; no sense just
standing out there."

Ginny entered and Margaret, indeed wearing only
a towel, re-fastened all the locks, then pulled on a
robe which had been draped across a dining room
chair. Once again Ginny felt a mixture of envy and
disdain at Margaret's well-appointed apartment—
knowing as she did how Maggie got some of these
furnishings, but idly wishing that *she* were pretty

enough that men would give her paintings, television sets, furniture.

"Would you like some coffee? Sorry—orange juice?" Margaret offered. Ginny shook her head, about to speak, when out of the corner of her eye she saw someone emerge from the bedroom. She turned reflexively to find a dark-haired young man, muscular and wearing only a pair of trousers, blithely walk into the living room. He seemed as startled and embarrassed by Ginny's presence as she was by his. Margaret, unconcerned, glided past both of them to the dining room table and lit a cigarette. "Ginny, Tony DeSantis. Tony, this is my sister, Ginny."

The young man nodded, smiled politely. "Pleased to meet you, Ginny," he said. Ginny nodded dumbly. "Well, if you'll excuse me a moment, I'll just . . . put on something a little more appropriate for company." He smiled again, beat a fast retreat into the bedroom; Ginny looked after, once more in awe of Margaret's abilities. How in the hell did she *do* it?

"Earth to Ginny. Come in, Ginny." Margaret was waving a hand in front of her face; Ginny flushed, turned away from the bedroom. Margaret smiled wryly. "You, uh, had a reason for getting up so early on a Sunday morning?"

Ginny gathered her wits, nodded. "I—I just wanted to make sure you hadn't . . . I mean, I wanted to find out when we were supposed to meet on Tuesday." Margaret's eyes were blank. Ginny prompted, "Christmas, remember?"

Margaret went pale. Her face, not nearly as perfect this hour of the morning anyway, crumbled even further. "Oh. *Oh*," she said, guilt evident in her eyes. "Oh, God, Ginny, I . . ." She took Ginny's hand, instinctively. "You're going to think I'm terrible, but honey, I . . . I *forgot.*"

Tony had re-entered the room, now wearing a shirt, but Ginny barely noticed. Her heart pounded; panic rose within her. No. No. Please. "Maggie, you promised," she said, trying not to whine, not knowing if she succeeded.

"I know, hon, but . . ." Margaret glanced at Tony. "You see, Tony and I, we . . . we made these reservations, you see, for a . . . a holiday. In the Bahamas. We were going to leave tomorrow, after Tony got off work, and . . ." She must have seen the anger building in Ginny's face, because abruptly she stopped, trying to catch her breath and explain it all: "Honest to *God,* Gin, I thought we'd just *considered* getting together; I mean, it was only a few words at Mama's funeral. Last year you told me how your friend Annie always invited you to her family's for Christmas, and how you'd wanted to but couldn't because you couldn't leave Mama alone, and when I didn't hear from you this year, I just thought . . ."

She stopped, shrinking under Ginny's withering gaze. "You didn't even call," Ginny accused. "Just to make sure." Margaret put a hand on her arm: "Honey, I . . ." Ginny shook off the hand, turned, ready to leave. Margaret looked ashen. "Ginny, wait! Maybe we can work something out! I'll—I'll—"

Tony suddenly spoke up.

"We could change our flight to Wednesday morning," he suggested. Ginny stopped in her tracks. Margaret looked at her lover with relief. "Or maybe," he went on, gently, "Ginny would like to come with us. What do you say, Ginny? Seven days in the sun; it'll be great. I'm sure you can get off work."

Ginny was touched by his kindness, but she did not miss the brief flash of panic in Margaret's eyes. Studiously avoiding her sister's gaze, she turned to Tony, smiled sadly, and shook her head. "Thank you," she said. "That's very nice of you. But I'm not sure everyone likes that idea." She abruptly turned, headed quickly for the door; Margaret dashed after. "Ginny, I'm sorry, of course you can come, don't—"

Ginny slammed out the door, fighting back tears as she scrambled down the stairwell and entreaties from Margaret and Tony drifted down from above, racing faster than she could ever recall moving until, in a burst of pain, she ran out of the lobby of the apartment building, onto the street, and around a corner. She made for the 77th Street IRT, then stopped short of the entrance, already feeling the gray-white sky pushing down on her, making it harder to breathe or think; she couldn't ride in one of those tin cans for twenty minutes, not now. Instead she ran halfway home, her tears freezing on her cheeks, as yesterday's gentle snowfall turned into a cold, driving sleet; by 51st Street she was exhausted and, cutting over to Second Avenue, took the bus the rest of the way home.

Numb, emptied, Ginny shuffled into her apartment to find her phone ringing insistently. She ignored it, dropped onto her Murphy bed and lay there, the tears no longer flowing but her body heaving nonetheless as she tried to breathe. She thought of Vermont, of the snow and trees and the way she had felt loved and secure, and wondered if that had all been some cruel joke of God's: to show her what it meant to be happy, and then to take it away and never let her know it again.

The phone stopped ringing, then rang again five minutes later. Ginny waited for it to stop, then took it off the hook. She went back to bed, screwed her eyes shut, and tried to sleep. But the longer she lay there, the less sleepy she became, the longer the day stretched before her, and the more the walls pushed in from every side to claim her.

Monday was clear, bright, and cold, the skies holding the promise of light flurries later that night—perfect weather for Christmas Eve. Michael was up early that morning, at ten o'clock the first in line at Chase Manhattan as their doors opened; ten minutes later, he had withdrawn the entire contents of his savings account—a little over one thousand dollars—and converted them to traveler's checks. Ironic; this was the money he had been saving, putting aside a dollar here and a dollar there, for his fantasy trip, his long-dreamt-of voyage to exotic ports—at the very least, a week in the Bahamas. Perhaps, though, they would be put to better use this way. Michael felt no regrets, no sadness; he felt, in fact, calm, serene, and purposeful. For the first time in years, maybe the first time in his life, he felt at peace with himself, and he looked around him with a new perspective, with new eyes. For the first time since he was a child, he found himself delighting in the Christmas decorations strung across the street and in store windows; he stood and marveled at the beauty of the lights framing one display window, cool blue bulbs winking on and off, casting manger and magi in an almost heavenly blue glow. He craned his neck and looked up at the giant cardboard Santa perched atop a traffic light, in the very middle of a banner reading JOYEUX NÖEL, strung from one streetlamp to another. He listened to the Christmas carols blaring from P.A. systems of nearby stores, and with some amazement Michael realized that he was happy.

"Joy to the world; the Lord is come . . ." The music carried him from one store to the next, establishments he had heretofore seen only from the outside: Bergdorf Goodman, Saks, Bloomingdale's, B. Altman. The traveler's checks did not last long: a gold pendant for Shelley, a new video recorder for Bob and Susan, an enormous stuffed bear for little Alexandria. . . . His excitement and anticipation of Bob and Susan's annual Christmas Eve party grew with each purchase he made. Finally, after two hours, he was finished . . . but for one last purchase.

At a flower shop on West 29th, he used the last of his traveler's checks to send two large wreaths to his parents' graves in Plainfield, with enough cash left over to ensure placement of similar wreaths once a year for the next five years. The manager of the shop handed him a card, and Michael was momentarily nonplussed, uncertain what to write. Finally, his hands trembling a bit, he managed to sign his name and a brief note; handing it and the money over to the manager, he turned, gazed at the wreaths for several moments, then turned again and left the store. The manager did not bother to look at the card Michael had left behind, but if he had, he would have seen a short

note written in a shaky hand, half memorial, half
apology: *I love you,* it read, and then, below that: *I'm
sorry.*

Macy's doors closed at five o'clock sharp, the staff
quickly scattering—pulling on coats, laughing, wishing one another Merry Christmas as the lights were
dimmed and cash registers locked. Sitting in a corner
of her display window, trimming the Christmas tree
for the fifth time that day, Ginny listened to the
muffled laughter and the well-wishing carried back
through the curtain; she moved back a few inches,
behind a partition, as her co-workers began to leave
the store and hit the street, passing the window, not
noticing the concealed Ginny.

Nor did Ginny, staring at the small tree and its
blinking lights, notice Annie McGuire as she stopped
outside the window . . . glancing in all directions as
though looking for someone . . . waiting a full minute on the windy sidewalk, disappointment evident in
her eyes . . . then slowly turning and moving off,
into the night.

When they were all gone, Ginny came out from
behind the partition and looked down at her handiwork.
She looked at the brightly shining little tree, its multicolored lights, its frosted branches, the silver star at
the apex . . . and she kicked it over, her face twisted
with pain and rage. The tree's lights kept blinking,
winking, mocking her; Ginny yanked the plug out of
the wall, kicked the tree again, shattering several
bulbs this time—then, fighting back tears, she rushed
out of the window and into the store.

The whole floor was dark, deserted; the only illumination came dimly from track lighting overhead. Ginny walked through the store with a haunted look, her mind elsewhere as she absently examined the mannequins posted at regular intervals throughout, adjusting a sleeve here and a cuff there. She noticed for the first time that the mannequins were almost always paired, male and female. Their painted smiles looked down on her; their wooden hands entwined. Ginny felt suddenly embarrassed, as though she were intruding on lovers, lovers who would remain happy and beautiful forever.

In the evening wear department, Ginny stopped before a pair of mannequins in formal dress: the male in an elegant tuxedo, the female in a lovely powder-blue gown. Ginny stared enviously at the gown—it reminded her of the fairy tales she had read as a child, of magic and happy endings. She looked at the wooden woman—at her slender, delicate fingers reaching out to take the man's upraised hand; at the clear, chiseled face with exotic eyes and heart-shaped mouth—and Ginny noticed that the dress was, in fact, a bit too large for this particular mannequin, probably a mistake in shipping. The mannequin was a Size 9, and the dress seemed to be a Size 11. It could conceivably fit even . . . even . . .

Ginny glanced cautiously from side to side, making sure she was completely alone, then painstakingly began to remove the gown from its model. The rustle of cloth seemed loud to her, and she winced more than once, but the job was done before she could think better of it. Holding the gown carefully under one arm, she rushed into one of the dressing rooms.

She emerged minutes later, self-conscious but excited, in the powder-blue gown. It was a little tight around the bust and hips, but did not impede her movements much as she moved to a full-length mirror and took her first hesitant glance at herself.

What she saw astounded her: the woman in the mirror was almost pretty. The sheer blue fabric was diaphanous; it billowed gently as she turned around and around, surveying herself from every angle. Her image was repeated in each of the two adjacent mirrors. A smile came to her; the pale blue color seemed to lift her right off the floor, as opposed to the dark, earthy colors she usually wore and which made her seem rooted to it. For the first time in her life she felt tall, slender, light on her feet.

As she spun around, giggling despite herself, her eye caught the mannequins again, the female now shockingly nude. Ginny restrained a giggle at the featureless bumps that were the dummy's breasts: mine may not be all that terrific, she thought wryly, but at least they have nipples.

Then her gaze fell to the male mannequin, its hand still upraised in silent invitation. He stood in his tuxedo like a figure from one of those childhood tales, the knight or prince beckoning to his lady love, whose mere touch would right all wrongs . . . solve all problems . . . begin life anew. Ginny held her breath a long moment . . . then, as though mesmerized, took a first hesitant step forward . . . then another . . . then—

"Miss Benedetti! What are you doing?"

Ginny nearly screamed. The woman's voice froze her where she stood; fear, terror, a thousand different kinds of shame and horror washed over her. She turned slowly to find Mrs. Levitt, the floor coordinator, just emerging from a small office at the rear of the cosmetics department. The woman stepped quickly toward Ginny, who could only stare in guilt and alarm at her; when she finally found her voice, it was cracked, brittle, and she stammered helplessly.

"I . . . I was just . . . just . . ."

Mrs. Levitt stopped a few steps away, saw clearly the terror in Ginny's eyes, and her face softened; she waited a long moment before saying anything, and when she did her voice was quiet and not threatening.

"It's all right," she said gently. "But you'd better put it back now."

Ginny nodded mutely and ran into the dressing room, embarrassed beyond words. She stripped off the gown, put on her own clothes haphazardly, and rushed out again, thrusting the gown into Mrs. Levitt's arms, unable to look her in the eyes.

"I'm sorry," she said, already moving away. "I'm sorry." Before the woman could reply, Ginny ran out of the store, tears of shame and sorrow streaming down her cheeks, and onto the street. She did not stop running for a long time after.

At Bob and Susan's party, Michael's gifts were received with delight bordering on astonishment; he invented some eyewash about receiving a bonus at work to allay their uneasiness about his generosity, then joined in a chorus of Christmas carols with his friends. As he sat there, the sad, sweet strains of "Silent Night" filling every heart in the room, Michael felt good, as good as he had ever felt. He burst

with love and affection for these people who surrounded him, for all the caring and concern they had
showed over the years, and he knew that that love
was returned. He only wished that that could be
enough for him.

But it was not, and he hoped that they would
understand why. He left the party around ten o'clock,
amid much kissing and hugging and handshaking; if
this was to be his last memory of this earth, then he
could not have hoped for a better one.

The bus from Westchester deposited him at the
Port Authority, and as he had for more times than he
cared to remember, he boarded the IRT on 42nd
Street. But this time he did not get off at Houston
Street, instead disembarking at Delancey and Essex.
Feeling calm, enjoying the crisp evening, he headed
east on Delancey Street for ten minutes, until, finally,
he saw the lonely towers of the Williamsburg Bridge
thrusting above the skyline. Michael continued walking.

*Crybaby, crybaby, go home to Moma! What's
the matter, VirGINya . . . lost your bottle?*

*Is that your BLOUSE, Virginia, or have you just
been HOUSEpainting?*

*Didja see? Didja see? She licked the SNOT off her
mouth! GOD!!*

Ginny lay sobbing on her bed. The walls had
stopped moving when they touched the sides of her
bed, but she could feel the mattress trembling, the
frame buckling under the pressure, and she knew it
was only a matter of time before it gave, splintering
into a million pieces, and she would be dead. Why?
Why was this happening to her? All she'd ever wanted

was to be liked. Was that so wrong, was that so ridiculous?

You like HIM? Susie, can you beLIEVE it? Ginny likes TOMMY!

Look, she's got his PICture in her DESK!

I do NOT! You PUT it there! You—

GINNY LIKES TOMMY. GINNY LIKES TOMMY. GINNY LIKES—

Maybe it *was* wrong. Maybe she didn't deserve it. She looked up, gasping as she caught a glimpse of the ceiling pressing down, inch by inch. She looked away, but everywhere she turned there were angles in motion, planes intersecting, sharp edges to cut her, deep corners to swallow her.

Why do you do it, Virginia? Why you hurt your mother like that; why can't you be more like your sist—

Why do you do it, Ginny? I introduce you to my friends and you hurt them. You understand that, Ginny? You HURT them. . . .

Finally, as the air became too thick to breathe and the bed groaned under the weight of the closing walls and the floor rushed up to meet the falling ceiling, she decided to cheat them all of their victory. She ran into the bathroom, the floors shifting and slanting beneath her feet, trying to trip her up, trying to stop her, but she was too fast, too clever for them, and she tore open her medicine cabinet and threw everything into the sink and found the prescription Margaret's doctor had given her after Mama's death. The floor lurched and the wall twisted to knock the bottle out of her hand, but it was too late; she stuffed four of the sleeping pills into her mouth and downed them with water, then another four, and another, until she had emptied the small green bottle. As she made her way back to bed the floor shifted violently, trying to make her fall and spit up the pills, but she smirked as she fell onto the sheets, triumphant in her victory over the walls. She would cheat them, cheat them all. Slowly her eyes fluttered closed and she began drifting off to sleep, an odd, satisfied smile on her face—a smile of hard-won victory, but also of relieved surrender; a smile of bitter remembrance, but one, at last, of hoped-for peace.

It took the better part of half an hour, but Michael finally succeeded in scaling the bridge's chain-link guard railing; the Williamsburg was an old bridge, built around the turn of the century, its age nowhere more evident than in the way the rusted wire mesh bit into his fingers as he climbed, an occasional link snapping under his weight, flakes of rust sticking to the small wire cuts in his palms. Slowly he lowered himself down the other side—the river side—of the guard fence: one . . . two . . . three-and-a-half feet, until he had gained a tentative footing on a slippery length of cable. Carefully he turned himself around, keeping one hand enmeshed in the fence, until he was facing away from the bridge, looking roughly southward down the East River. He glanced down and fought back a wave of nausea at the dizzying fall below. Behind and above him, the occasional strobe of headlights came and went, the bridge rattling as each car rushed across, then was gone. Michael waited till the headlights became less and less frequent, the possibility of interruption more and more remote.

When he thought the time right, he bent his body to jump—then froze, suddenly terrified. He stared down at the dark waters, looking not like the peaceful, rolling surface of the ocean he so loved, but like a hard, solid, unforgiving length of steel. He fought to remind himself that it *was* water . . . that soon, very soon, he would be returning to the sea, his body carried downriver as the tide went out, into the bay and, from there, to the Atlantic. He would be one with the sea, and if he remembered any of this later, it would be as a dim, painful dream. Well, perhaps not entirely painful; he thought of his parents, his friends, of Shelley, and hoped that he would at least remember them. To his surprise, he found himself crying. He hung there, suspended in grief, for long minutes—until a sudden gust of wind buffeted him from behind, threatening to break his hold if he did not take action himself. All right, then. Taking a deep breath . . . tears still blurring his vision . . . Michael pushed himself forward, allowing the wind to help break his grip on the wire mesh . . . and he fell.

He plunged off the bridge—and screamed. The cry escaped him unbidden as the waters of the river fell *up* at him. Suddenly, once more, they were not liquid but solid, not water but steel, not the warm, beckoning arms of a lover but the cold, blunt fist of an assassin. He screamed and screamed and screamed, wishing more than anything on earth that he could undo it all, wishing he could go back, *go back*—and screamed again as he felt a horrible wrenching, as though he were being torn apart (though his body had not yet hit the water), and all at once he seemed to be watching his own body fall, arms flailing, legs spread-eagled, becoming smaller and smaller as it spiraled down to the black waters, tumbling end-over-end like a die thrown carelessly to the floor . . . until the impact, when it finally came, was almost anticlimax, and that was all Michael knew for a long time to come.

4

Christmas Day, 9:45 A.M.

As she slept, Ginny felt as though she were floating like a leaf on a warm updraft of air; rising up, as though through the ceiling which only moments before had threatened to crush her. She couldn't quite open her eyes, wasn't sure she wanted to, but she knew she was moving—moving as though held by the wind itself, faster and farther than she had ever traveled before. She sensed the motion, even as she sensed the city receding away below her. The sensation pleased her, she hoped it would never stop, but after several minutes she felt herself slowing, descending, and despite her silent protests, she found herself, soon, at rest, lying on some hard, cold surface.

She opened her eyes and immediately had to squint, raising a hand against the whitest, brightest light she had ever seen. She was standing in a field covered with snow for as far as the eye could see, bright with reflected light as the sun bounced off the glazed ground. Ginny gasped; it was purer and more beautiful than anything she had ever imagined. She took a step forward, the snow crackling beneath her heel. And then she saw them.

Farther down the snowy expanse, just before a tangle of pine trees, stood four waiting figures, their features obscured by the brightness. At least they seemed to be waiting, and Ginny had the strangest feeling that they were waiting, somehow, for her. She squinted again, took another few steps forward . . . and, her heart racing, suddenly recognized the nearest of the four figures.

It was Papa, his chubby frame clad only in shirtsleeves despite the cold, a great glowing smile on his warm, round face. He looked as he did when he was forty years old, in the prime of his health, when Ginny was just a little girl.

Beside him was Mama, and she was younger, too, and her face shone with the love and affection which Ginny had ached to see for so many long years. At first Ginny thought it was a trick, thought that this happy, loving woman she saw couldn't possibly be her mother . . . until she saw who stood behind her parents.

Ginny's grandmother and grandfather waited just a few feet in front of the forest—standing near a space between two tall pines that looked almost like the door to a cathedral. *Nonna* had on her plaid house-dress and apron, *Nonno* his workshirt and blue jeans; they had changed not at all since that Christmas in Vermont, and they were smiling, obviously happy to see her.

Ginny began running toward them, filled with a joy and a love she had never known before. Snow flew up as she raced forward, her heart pounding, taking in huge gulps of air as she ran—

But as she drew nearer to the four of them, one by one they turned away from her. First *Nonna*. Then *Nonno*. Then her mother. And, finally, Papa. As one, they began walking back toward the trees.

"Nonno! Nonna! It's Ginny—Virginia!" She ran faster, never so scared, so terrified of losing anything in her life as she was now. "Don't go! Please! Don't go!"

But they kept on walking, toward that cathedral-like space between the trees. Tears streamed down Ginny's face, freezing almost instantly; she struggled to get a better traction on the snow. "Mama!" she screamed, "Papa, *please,* it's me, it's *Ginny*—"

But first her grandmother, then her grandfather disappeared between the cathedral branches . . . next, her mother . . . and now only Papa remained, just a few feet from the trees. Ginny was sobbing now; she made one last desperate lunge forward, but her foot skidded on the snow and she fell, with a yelp of pain and longing and terrible loss, onto the cold, icy ground. She felt her face stinging from the impact, felt the pain of the ice-burn, but didn't care. She lay there, knowing she had lost them, and she cried . . . cried as she had the first time she'd lost them.

Suddenly, she felt a hand on her shoulder—and looked up to find Papa bent over her, his big, chubby hand brushing the snow off her. He reached down and gently helped his daughter to her feet. Tenderly he wiped the ice from Ginny's bruises, and Ginny, transfixed, could only gape in wonder at him, at his sweet, sad smile, at the love in his eyes as he brushed aside a lock of hair that had fallen across Ginny's forehead.

Finally, Ginny found her voice. "Papa. Take me with you. Please?"

But Papa only shook his head, sadly, silently. Without a word, he put his hands gently on her shoulders, leaned forward and kissed her on the brow. Tears sprang to Ginny's eyes, and in moments Papa had turned and was walking toward the trees, the branches closing up behind him as he passed through, and Ginny knew that she could not follow.

Resigned, she lay down on a soft snowdrift and shut her eyes. She cried for some time, then, slowly, felt herself floating once more—aimlessly, it seemed, drifting wherever the wind might take her. She hoped she would drift forever . . . hoped she might never land . . . but, finally, she did. She opened her eyes . . .

And had to close them again against the sudden brightness. Her heart skipped a beat with joy: they had taken her back, after all! She felt chilly, as though surrounded by snow; she opened her eyes again, calling out her father's name.

The window shade had rolled up again during the

night, and the morning sun was pouring in, making Ginny squint and sneeze as she sat up in bed. She shivered; the heat had gone out again. She cursed in frustration and disappointment. Not only had she been turned away, but she was right back where she started from.

She breathed in the chill morning air, and the disappointment was replaced by a sudden relief to be alive: the dream, if that was what it was, retreated to a hazy memory. Thank God—the pills must've knocked her out for the night, but she felt none the worse for wear.

Getting up, clad in the same furry green sweater and jeans she had worn the night before, she noticed that her front door was half-open. Had she been so upset last night that she'd left it ajar? What's more, it seemed so *still* out there in the corridor. What was wrong?

It was then she remembered that today was Christmas Day, and it was then that the sadness and fear came back to her. She had taken the pills because she did not want to face this day or any more like it, and here she was, facing it—alone—after all. She padded out of the apartment, desperate for the sight of another human face. The hallways of the apartment building were deserted; the worn carpets and floral wallpaper looked even bleaker than usual, somehow. Ginny trotted down the stairs until she heard the murmur of a woman's voice on the first floor; she recognized it as that of Mrs. Gibson, her landlady.

She stopped on the first-floor landing, called out to the matronly woman stepping quickly down the hallway. "Mrs. Gibson! Good morning. Merry Christmas!"

Mrs. Gibson kept on walking down the corridor, as though she had not heard.

Ginny called out again. "Mrs. Gibson? Mrs. Gibson!" The woman seemed not to hear. She turned and entered her own apartment, slamming the door behind her, ignoring Ginny's calls. Ginny was hurt and puzzled. Had she done something to offend her? The thought only made her feel more alone. Panic grew like a tumor. What was she going to do, where was she going to go? By now, Margaret must have been halfway to the Bahamas; Annie was almost certainly in Connecticut, with her family; even Uncle Sal or cousin Dominick would not have looked favorably upon her showing up on their doorsteps on such short notice. The walls started to close in again on her, but this time she caught herself; this time she would not allow it. She ran down the last flight of stairs, into the lobby. The lobby door was half-open; Ginny could hear the sounds of traffic from outside, the comforting sounds of car horns and people's voices, and she ran to them, out the door and onto the street.

Grand Street was not nearly as busy as it normally was, but there were enough passersby to ease Ginny's panic at being alone—even if none of those passersby even gave Ginny a glance as she stood, catching her breath, on the corner. It was enough that they were there. Calmer now, Ginny could deliberate as to what to do with the rest of her day. She couldn't spend it in her apartment, that much she knew; all the stores would be closed, and that left only—

The movies. Of course! Movie theaters were never closed; they were like soup kitchens or Salvation Army posts, always there for those who needed a place to stay. It was nearly ten A.M.; she could catch a morning show at the Trans-Lux, a matinee at the Ziegfeld or the RKO, a late show at the Paramount . . . by the time she was finished, the whole awful holiday would be over and she could go home, go to sleep, and, tomorrow, go back to work.

Delighted and relieved, Ginny ran to the curb to flag down a cab; she couldn't rely on the bus schedules on Christmas, and she didn't want to be late for the ten o'clock show. She didn't know what was playing, didn't care; as long as it moved, as long as it took her somewhere other than where she was, that was good enough for her.

A taxi was heading up the street toward her, its flag down, its passenger seat empty; Ginny waved her arm, called out, "Taxi! Taxi!" The cab continued to move, but the driver showed no signs of slowing; Ginny frowned, stepped off the curb into the street, waved again. "Hey! Read my lips: tax-i!"

The cabbie did not slow. Exasperated, Ginny took another step, figuring the only way to get his attention was to almost be run over by him. "Come *on*, for Pete's sake! Give a girl a break. *Taxi!*"

The taxi *still* did not slow; it seemed, in fact, to pick up speed as it ran a red light.

"For God's sake! Are you blind, or—"

Ginny never finished the sentence. To her utter disbelief, the cab was bearing down on her, racing forward at fifty miles an hour.

Ginny screamed, started to jump back, but it was

too late—horrified, all she could see was the yellow hood of the car as it loomed suddenly in front of her, and she braced herself, shutting her eyes against the terrible impact to come.

It never came.

One minute the cab was right on top of her, about to hit her head-on . . . the next, she felt an odd *tingling* throughout her entire body, and when she opened her eyes, the cab was *behind* her, continuing blithely down Grand Street.

Totally disoriented, Ginny turned and watched the receding taxi. What the hell was going on? It couldn't have had time to swerve; she had practically felt the heat of its engine as it bore down on her. Her relief was tempered by confusion. Something was very wrong here. . . .

So intent was she on her baffling escape that she did not notice—again, until it was too late—the second car heading toward her. She turned in time to see a '79 Chrysler with half a dozen people squeezed into it rushing straight for her, as though oblivious to her.

This time she kept her eyes open . . . and gasped in disbelief as the Chrysler roared right *through* her.

The bumper, the hood, even the winged hood ornament, all of it she saw clearly as it rushed toward her—and then seemed to be swallowed up by her *own body*. There were no words to describe what she was feeling, no concepts to explain what was happening; her body tingled again, not a pleasant feeling, like a limb that has fallen asleep and been shaken awake, rudely. In seconds, the entire car had seemed to passed right through her . . . and was gone.

Ginny screamed. She staggered, numbly, back onto

the sidewalk. *"No!"* she was yelling, but no one on the street seemed to hear her cries; *"No! No!"* Suddenly she felt weak, felt that she would fall without support. She reached out to lean on a mailbox . . .

. . . and her hand fell right *through* it. Ginny moaned softly. Oh, God, no. Please. It was all a dream, a very bad dream; Mary, Mother of God, let her *wake up*. She examined her fingers, one by one; they looked solid, felt solid. When she pinched them, she felt pain. But what she could not feel, she slowly began to realize, was the chill in the air, the nip in the wind. People all around her were bundled up in coats and scarves, and even at that looked cold, while she was standing in a brisk wind, wearing only a light sweater, and felt . . . nothing. She knew it was cold out, she recognized the feeling *as* cold, but she didn't actually *feel* it. It was a strange, disassociated sensation, as though everything were a step removed, like images on a television set . . . or a movie screen.

Cautiously she reached out to touch the mailbox again, praying that she had merely had some kind of drug-induced hallucination, some bizarre aftereffect of the sleeping pills. Her hopes died as the tips of her fingers simply sank into the metal like a knife into butter. She withdrew them quickly; they were tingling, but aside from that *looked* perfectly normal.

Tears streamed down her cheeks. Desperately she spun around, trying to grab onto a lamppost; her fist closed in on itself and vanished into the corrugated green column. She yanked back her hand, tried to pound her fist in frustration on the hood of a parked car; the car swallowed her arm up to the elbow, and she quickly withdrew it.

She started to run. Why, she couldn't say; she ran, perhaps hoping to wake up, but knowing in her heart that this was not a dream . . . even as the snowfield had not been a dream. The pedestrians around her were oblivious to her presence; she dodged and weaved among them, petrified to come into contact with any, not knowing what might happen. Abruptly she stopped in front of the local grocery store, searching the bright glass window for a reflection, some scant evidence of her existence.

There was none.

Ginny sank to her knees, covered her hands with her face and sobbed. Her worst fears were confirmed. The pills *had* worked, after all; she was dead. But because she had killed herself—a mortal sin; she crossed herself desperately—she was to be denied the peace and love her parents and grandparents had found. It was the only explanation she could fathom. Was this her purgatory, her private little hell? It didn't look like the hell she had read about in her catechism as a little girl, but in a way, it was worse. What could be more hellish than being lifeless . . . among the living? Not just to be dead and damned, but to be *reminded* of it for all time? She sat hunched over on the sidewalk, sobbing uncontrollably, feeling the chill of the wind only as a remembered thing, and she prayed to the God of her childhood to help her, to forgive her, to absolve her.

Christmas Day, 12:03 A.M.

Michael woke to the smell of salt air and the sound of seagulls crying somewhere overhead. Groggily he became aware of movement beneath him, the ground somehow rocking, swaying, shifting, and after a few moments he recognized the motion as the pitch and yaw of a boat.

He opened his eyes and saw the stars. He was lying flat on his back, staring up at the night sky—on the deck, it seemed, of a boat, perhaps a Coast Guard cutter. Distantly he heard the sound of engines revving up—but, oddly, felt no tremors, no vibrations in the deck as the engines fired up and the boat began to move; somewhere to his right voices were speaking urgently, but he was still too groggy to make out the words.

He propped himself up on one elbow, taking in deep gulps of the briny air, feeling it, as it always did, breathe life into him. As he began to think clearly once more, he suddenly realized just how impossible the simple action he had taken really was. His arms were strong and steady; he felt no pain, no pain at all. Even allowing for shock, he felt far better than anyone had a right to after a two-hundred-and-fifty-foot drop off the Williamsburg Bridge.

It hit him, then: he shouldn't, by all rights, have even been *alive*. He remembered the terror of falling, the sudden desire to live, but he remembered even more clearly the pain and the loneliness which had driven him to his actions, and he was ambivalent at finding himself alive.

Gathering his wits slowly, he looked down at himself. He was still wearing the windbreaker and corduroy pants that he had jumped in—but they weren't even wet. He felt his arms, his legs, his neck—not so much as a bruise. This was clearly impossible. What in the name of God—?

He started to get to his feet, marveling at the lack of any broken bones . . . then, as he glanced to his right, froze in horror and disbelief, the breath suddenly knocked out of him.

Not three feet away from him a team of Coast Guard medics in rain gear were working feverishly to resuscitate a broken, bruised body. Its skin was a deathly shade of blue; limbs protruded at odd angles from the torso, the legs broken in several places, a bloody rib poking out of the torn flesh of the chest cavity.

Michael's body.

Michael—the one who stood, unharmed, a few feet away; the one who watched in astonishment as the paramedics worked over the body—felt suddenly nauseous, felt like he wanted to vomit. He heard the voices of the medics, carried back to him as though from a great distance:

". . . cyanotic. We've got to ventilate . . ."

"Listen to that rattle. A diaphragmatic hernia?"

". . . least of his problems. Look at that chest cavity; probable pneumothorax. Tell 'em to have a respirator ready in the mobile . . ."

They inserted a tube into the nose; the body was breathing, albeit shallowly, but every time it drew a breath it was accompanied by a horrible, hollow rattling sound. Michael stared, tears coming to his eyes. He had never dreamed anything like this could happen, never imagined that he would not just die instantly, certainly never envisioned that he would find himself an observer to his own slow, agonizing death. He was immensely moved that these people should labor so to save his life, but he wished they would stop. He went numbly to their side, stood above them and tried to tell them, tried to make them understand.

"Let me go," he said simply. "I'm not worth the effort. Really. Why can't you just let me go?"

They did not respond, as Michael knew they would not; they continued their efforts, wrapping the body in thermal blankets, oblivious to the figure standing above them. Finally, unable to bear it any longer, Michael turned away, went to the starboard side of the foredeck and tried to lean on the metal guard railing. His hands passed right through it. He jumped, momentarily terrified, then forced himself to remain calm. What did you expect, anyway? he asked himself. His body—his real body—lay a few feet away, a broken pattern of blood and bone. This was merely . . . what? His soul, his spirit, the larger part of him? Of *course* it wouldn't be—substantial.

Whatever it was—whatever *he* was—he knew one thing for certain: he was simply marking time until his physical, corporeal body died. He wouldn't be here, like this, unless he were perilously close to death. Couldn't the medics see that? Couldn't they just let nature take its course?

But they wouldn't, and within minutes the Coast Guard launch had docked at Pier 73, where Michael watched as his body was transferred by stretcher— very gently indeed—to a waiting ambulance. Not quite knowing what else to do, Michael climbed inside the vehicle and sat beside his physical body as the ambulance shrieked up 30th Street to Bellevue Hospital. He looked down again at his body . . . at the bruised face tinged blue with cyanosis, a respirator clamped over the swollen mouth . . . and, bizarrely, he felt sorry for the poor bastard lying there, as he would for anyone in such condition. He had to remind himself that that poor bastard was *him*.

At Bellevue his body was wheeled into the emergency room, jabbed with syringes, connected to IV units, and examined by a phalanx of interns—all of it done on the move, as though the time could not be spared to stop. Michael's was not the only near-fatality here tonight; the room was a noisy jumble of activity as nurses, doctors, and residents performed triage on a startlingly large number of patients. Finally, Michael's stretcher came to a stop as a surgeon bent over his body, delivering hurried instructions to a frazzled-looking nurse. ''Seems to be stabilizing, at least,'' he said hopefully, his expression bleaker than his words. ''Landed on his left side—probable rupture of the spleen. Get me some X-rays on the spleen, the diaphragm, the chest, then prep him for OR. Keep him on whole blood. I'd like Jaarsma on anesthesia, if he's free.'' The nurse nodded, made the proper notations on her chart, and an intern wheeled Michael's body down the corridor to the OR—past burn victims, accident victims, people with wounds obviously *not* self-inflicted, and Michael, following, felt horribly guilty that he should be taking up time more rightly given to these people. Why in God's name couldn't they just let him *die*?

He tried observing the operation, but when the surgeon made the first incision in the thorax to repair the damage to the diaphragm, when Michael suddenly saw *his* flesh peel, *his* blood spurt out, he reeled with nausea and bolted. He ran, arms outstretched instinctively to push open the swinging doors of the OR, but before he knew it, his arms had vanished into the doors and the blond wood filled his field of vision. He felt a tingling sensation, and then, suddenly, he was on the other side.

Shaken and unsettled by both this and the operation, Michael wandered into the waiting area, filled with relatives and friends awaiting word on loved ones undergoing surgery, and Michael—not unaware of the irony of it all—joined them. Occasionally someone would sit in the same (to them, unoccupied) seat as Michael, and he would leap up, unaccountably repelled and horrified, as though he had been raped, and find another seat—until it would happen all over again.

What the hell had happened? How had he gotten into this bizarre situation? As near as he could figure, at that moment when he leaped off the bridge—suddenly consumed with fear, aware of his imminent death—something had . . . come loose. His spirit, soul, astral body, whatever, had been wrenched free by the trauma, and was now awaiting . . . what? Death, certainly, but *then* what? Transition? To heaven . . . or to hell? Michael had never believed in either, and wasn't about to jump to any conclusions. Perhaps this astral form of his was simply a biological energy force, and when his physical body died, he—his energy form—would fade and flicker like a candle being snuffed out, to become one with the other unconscious energies of the universe.

He rather liked the sound of that, but there was, of course, another possibility. If this *was* his soul, and there *was* a heaven—not the angels-and-harps number the Fundamentalists would have you believe, but some sort of beneficent afterlife—then perhaps there was a hell, too. Again, not the traditional fire-and-brimstone scene, but a hell, perhaps, of one's own making, a hell in which one's sins and shortcomings in life were continued in death.

The thought made him shiver. What could be worse than killing yourself, thinking it would put an end to your problems and pain . . . only to find that it really made no difference at all? That it was merely like taking your pain and anger and loneliness from one cold room to another?

Michael pushed the thought away. It was not something he wanted to consider—at least, not now.

Several hours later, Michael's comatose form was wheeled out of the OR and transferred to an intensive care unit at the far end of the hospital. Michael watched as an intern delivered his burden to the ICU nurse, who glanced at the new patient, winced slightly, and shook her head. "This has to be the jumper," she said, sighing.

The intern nodded, carefully lifting Michael's body, placing it gently in one of the ICU beds. "Merry Christmas," he said, grunting. "God, I hate this time of year. Everybody goes crazy."

Michael stared at all the various tubes inserted into his body—one in the arm, one in the nose, a third in the . . . well, he didn't even want to *think* about that one. He turned away, wishing that that damned sack of flesh on the bed would have a heart flutter, a respiratory failure, anything to bring this nightmare to an end. But somehow he knew he would not be so lucky. The body monitors beside the bed traced weak but steady lines; his EEG, EKG, respiration, and blood pressure were all relatively stable.

Suddenly, it all became too much; with an inarticulate cry he fled the ICU, rushing back to Emergency as though, somehow, he would retrace his steps, turn time backward, undo everything and start all over. He dodged and weaved among the myriad people filling the corridors, but there were too many, and just as the exit came into sight, just when Michael began to see some kind of light, his astral form was violated once more—this time by an intern wheeling a stretcher in from inside. Michael wailed like a lost soul as the stretcher, an unconscious young woman lying atop it, passed through his phantom body, causing it to tingle with pins and needles; he sank to his knees, sobbing uncontrollably, the words of the doctor examining the young woman coming to him as if from a great distance.

"Her landlady found her," the paramedic was saying, "apparently she left the door open and someone saw—"

The doctor grimaced, pushing back the woman's hands and feet, checking her pupils. "Gastric lavage," he sighed. "After that, I want her on Dopran—give to effect. Keep me posted on her BP. We can't do much more."

Michael looked up in time to see the woman being wheeled away. He pulled himself together, stood, and hurried out of the ER, away from the hospital, into the early morning darkness.

He wandered for hours, tired but afraid to go to sleep for fear of what new horrors might come. He walked numbly up First Avenue; around 58th Street he looked up to find the Queensboro Bridge on his right, and, shivering violently, he veered away, turning left on 59th, and headed toward Central Park.

It was Christmas Day, and there were more people on the street and more lights burning in distant windows at this hour than Michael had expected. He walked past laughing couples swaying drunkenly up the street, past brightly lit windows revealing chiaroscuros of families eating, laughing, singing. His loneliness was more crushing than ever. People walked past him without seeing him; he looked in puddles for a reflection even he could not see.

Finally, he found himself at the edge of Central Park lake, as the last stars dimmed in the distance and a far light crested the horizon. Almost dawn. He stood there, hands balled into fists, angry and hurting and frustrated because he could not take his anger out on anything, could not touch so much as a leaf. The anger grew and grew until he vented it with a blood-curdling shout, so loud that it would have echoed for hundreds of yards had it been composed of sound waves instead of . . . whatever.

"God *damn* it!" he screamed, hoping that the blasphemy, at least, might attract the attention of someone in charge. "What the fuck does this *prove!* Does it serve some kind of cosmic *balance*—I spent my life alone, I'll spend Eternity alone, is that it?" He trembled with rage, aching to hit something, to throw something, to make a single ripple on the still lake waters. "What kind of justice is that!" he yelled, tears springing to his eyes. "For almost thirty years I lived alone, slept alone, dreamt alone! Thirty years and I never—I never—"

Filled with a boiling, uncontrollable rage, Michael let out a guttural cry, swung down, snapped up a large rock, and hurled it with all the force he could muster into the lake, where it hit with an enormous splash.

"*God damn you all to—*"

Michael froze.

At the center of the lake, ripples were spreading out in widening circles, their strength diminishing with every inch they drew closer to shore, until all that was left was a tiny wavelet lapping the bank on which Michael stood. His mouth dropped open in astonishment, then delight.

He *did* it. He had *touched* something; had an *effect* on something. He didn't know how, he didn't know why . . . and he didn't care. All he knew was, in some small way he was still a part of the world. He began to laugh—wild, relieved laughter—the anger and the tension draining from him as he watched the last ripples on the lake surface fade in the dawning light. It was the best Christmas present he had ever received in his life.

Christmas Night, 10:42 P.M.

Ginny wandered the streets as she had for much of the day, torn between returning to her apartment for the night and not going back at all, not ever; she would never forget that horrible moment outside the apartment building, that terrible awareness of being *not alive,* and going back could only dredge up feelings best left alone. She had decided to go to the movies after all, anything to take her mind off thoughts of damnation and purgatory . . . but even sitting in the darkened theaters, attention fixed on Redford and Streisand and Gene Kelly and John Wayne, even then part of her could not forget. She was calmer than she had been, more resigned to her fate, but no more at peace.

She had learned during the day that she wasn't totally cut off from the physical world—that if she concentrated hard enough, became angry or determined enough, she could move things, touch things— but this was scant comfort to her as she headed uptown on Fifth Avenue, feeling somehow like the last person on earth. Perhaps she could go to Margaret's apartment. But what if she and Tony hadn't left for the Bahamas after all? The thought of sleeping, however invisibly, in the living room as Margaret and Tony went at it, gasping and panting, in the bedroom, made her queasy. She didn't need to be reminded of certain things. Especially not now.

Approaching 50th Street, Ginny looked up to see the ornate facade of St. Patrick's Cathedral looming ahead. She stopped, stared, debated a long moment, then—realizing she didn't really have any other choice—turned and walked through the great arched portal.

Christmas services were apparently over for the day; the great vaulted room was empty. Candles flickered everywhere; Jesus on his cross looked down at she padded silently up the aisle. She stopped a few feet from the altar, looked up at the figure on the cross, and cleared her throat.

"Excuse me," she said softly. "My name is Ginny. Ginny Benedetti. But maybe you know that already."

The figure, predictably, made no response, but Ginny went on: "I haven't been in a church in a long while. My mother used to take me to Mass when I was little, to show me off, but when I got older I guess I wasn't cute enough and she took my sister instead. So I'm afraid I don't have what you'd call real deep religious convictions. Except maybe when I'm scared."

She paused, feeling lost and helpless, the horrors of the day closing in on her; her voice nearly cracked.

"But I'm tired," she said, "and I don't have anywhere else to go, and . . . I understand if you don't want me here, but . . . I promise, I'll leave first thing in the morning."

She moved to the first pew, started to sit down—then turned and looked back at the altar, guiltily. Her voice was small.

"I just don't have anywhere else to go," she said.

She sat, folded her arms across her chest, lowered her head and slowly shut her eyes. For a long time she resisted sleep, afraid of what new terrors it might bring, then finally succumbed, falling into a tense, fitful slumber.

5

On the day after Christmas, Ginny discovered that she was not quite as dead as she thought she was.

She woke feeling—against all reason—*hungry*. Ravenous, in fact. She wondered idly how this could be; did ghosts eat? *Could* ghosts eat? If so, *what* did they eat—ectoplasm? And where did you go to get some? She wasn't certain about any of this, but quickly decided on one thing for sure: if it was possible for her to consume food, then by God she was going to do it. She was willing to give up a lot of things now that she was dead, but Sara Lee pound cake wasn't one of them.

Still feeling uncomfortable in the cavernous church,

she got up from the pew on which she had spent the restless night and headed for the doors—only to find that they were locked. Flustered, not wanting to spend any more time here than was absolutely necessary, she screwed up her courage . . . and walked right through the doors. It was the first time she had purposely used her ghostly abilities to pass through solid objects, and as her body tingled and she found herself on the other side of the doors, facing Fifth Avenue, she had to admit it wasn't entirely a bad feeling. In fact, it made her feel kind of—free. She realized, with a mixture of delight and amazement, that the walls which so often in the past had threatened to crush her could do so no longer—she would merely walk *through* them! For the first time in her life, she felt in control; she felt safe.

Then, as the word "life" passed through her mind, she was abruptly reminded once more that she was not, in fact, alive. Walking up Fifth Avenue, she became aware again of the brisk chill in the air—without actually feeling the cold. How? she wondered. She didn't feel any different from when she was alive, at least not inside; she felt her heart beat and her pulse race, and when she pinched herself she felt a twinge of pain; but when she touched other things, physical objects, she didn't *feel* them as much as *sense* them. In one of the movie theaters yesterday, she had, out of curiosity, touched the hot metal exterior of the hot dog broiler; she had recognized it as being hot but had felt no pain. She had run her hands over the soft velour seats, but felt no pleasure in the softness, only a sort of . . . awareness of its texture. It was as though everything out there in the "real" world were wrapped in some kind of invisible gauze, and even though she could affect things, move things, touch things, she still could not penetrate that gauze.

The thought of spending eternity like this, invisible and unfeeling, filled her with disgust and fear; it was too much like the life she had just given up. Better to concentrate on other things: like, for instance, food. From a few blocks away came the smell of roasted chestnuts; Ginny turned to watch a street vendor pouring a batch of them into a paper funnel. Her mouth watered, but she couldn't bring herself to pilfer one— she might be dead, but she was no thief. Finally, her hunger getting the better of her, she decided to brave the loneliness of her sister's apartment in exchange for the known rewards of her sister's refrigerator. She caught a bus up Madison Avenue, got off at 81st Street, and walked the few blocks to Margaret's place.

The sleepless night was catching up with her as she passed through the triple-locked door; the apartment was, of course, deserted. Ginny thought of Margaret and Tony sunning themselves on some tropical beach somewhere, then pushed the thought away and stumbled tiredly into the kitchen. When she reached out to open the refrigerator, her fingers slipped through the handle; she was more tired than she'd imagined. Screwing up her will power, she concentrated on grabbing the handle and opening the door— which, on the third try, she did.

Feeling a bit guilty at raiding Maggie's food—but only a bit—she picked out some butter, milk, eggs, and cinnamon, and proceeded to make herself some French toast. The ritual of cooking calmed her; for a moment she could almost forget where and what she was. She started whistling, the smell of the toast and the cinnamon tickling her nose, her mouth watering in anticipation.

She sat in the dining room, holding the toast with trepidation; she concentrated as hard as she could on biting into it, on chewing it, and then took the plunge. To her delight, her teeth bit into the toast with a satisfying crunch.

But her joy at being able to chew the food momentarily obscured its taste. Slowly she realized that something was not quite right. It tasted like French toast, all right, but had she not known what French toast was supposed to taste like, she wasn't sure she would have tasted anything. The food seemed as though it were wrapped in the same lousy gauze which surrounded everything else. Ginny finished it, but without much enthusiasm; the joy had gone out of eating. Dear God—this really *was* Hell.

She washed the dishes, putting them back exactly where she had found them, then collapsed on the living room couch, her body feeling like stone. Almost instantly she was asleep.

She drifted in a peaceful limbo for several hours, a slumber different from any which she had known before: where once she had frequently had dreams of flying, of floating above the clouds, now she felt peculiarly grounded, as though rooted to the earth. There were no colors, no shapes, no voices in her dream, only movement and texture; it was oddly soothing, peaceful, and Ginny almost resented it when voices from outside intruded on her.

". . . Maggie, it wasn't your fault . . ."

"Tony, if I'd only stayed home—"

"You offered to take her along . . ."

"No—*you* offered to take her along. I just stood there like a jerk and did nothing. Oh God, Tony, what did I *do* to her . . . ?"

At first Ginny thought the voices were part of her dream, but soon realized they were not. She woke, cleared her head, and looked up to find Margaret and Tony dragging their luggage into the apartment from the corridor.

"Maggie . . . ?" Ginny said softly, amazed. Margaret, of course, made no response. Ginny stood, startled by her sister's appearance; she had never looked so haggard, so worn, her aquiline face old and lined with worry. She looked a great deal like Mama.

Tony went to her, put his hands gently on her shoulders. "Maggie . . . honey . . . stop it. Maybe you made mistakes with Ginny, but now isn't the time to castigate yourself about them."

Margaret nodded dully. "I know. I'll be all right." She turned, made a bee-line for her purse. "God, I need a cigarette." She lit one, sucked in smoke, and seemed a bit calmer. Ginny walked slowly to her side. "Oh, God, Maggie, I'm sorry," she said with crushing guilt. "If I'd known . . . if I'd thought . . . I never would have—"

"C'mon," Tony said, putting a hand on Margaret's arm. "We'd better get to Bellevue before visiting hours are over."

Ginny started. What? *What* did he say?

Margaret's eyes were large with fear. "Tony, what if she dies?"

"She won't. Her doctor said her condition was stable. Don't you want to be there when she comes out of her coma?"

Margaret nodded and started gathering up her things. Ginny's mouth was agape: Bellevue? Stable? *Coma?* Her heart pounded wildly. Could it be? Just when she'd almost reconciled herself to the idea—was it possible she wasn't dead, after all? Part of her didn't want to believe it, afraid that it was another joke, another cruel curve the universe was throwing her . . . but another part of her was excited and hopeful for the first time in twenty-four hours.

Ginny was first out the door as Margaret and Tony prepared to leave; impatiently she waited for them in the corridor. "C'mon, c'mon," she said to no one in particular. "I've only got a few hundred years to spare." She giggled at her joke, sorry that no one but she could hear it. Margaret snapped up her purse and started out the door, then paused, something getting her attention; she frowned, sniffed the air. "Tony?" she said. "Do you smell something?"

Tony sniffed, blinked once. "Yeah. Like . . ."

"French toast?"

Ginny grinned and followed them downstairs to a waiting cab.

The first thing Michael saw upon waking was the familiar cracked plaster of his bedroom ceiling; the first thing he heard, the daily cacophony of groaning machinery as the garbage trucks on the street emptied the bins with a thunderous rattle. At first blush, there seemed to be nothing much to distinguish this morning from any other—except, of course, for the fact that this morning he did not happen to be inside his own body. A minor consideration, perhaps, but one which he found difficult to ignore.

He had spent the day yesterday wandering the city, from Central Park, where he had made the discovery that he could will himself "solid" for short periods of time, to midtown, the Village, and back again. Finally, exhausted from pondering his peculiar state of affairs, he had returned to his apartment on Houston Street, ready for a good night's sleep—then made the mistake of wondering, as he lay staring at the ceiling, why he had no trouble lying on the bed, why he didn't fall right *through* the bed, and the floor, for that matter, right down to the center of the earth? Why was he able to sit down on a park bench but unable to learn against a brick wall without actively concentrating?

So much for sleep.

Now, after more metaphysical ruminations than he had had since a philosophy course he had taken in college, he thought he had a handle on the situation . . . and as he got out of bed, clad only in his underwear, and began to get dressed, he examined the various points once more.

Point One. Obviously, the trauma of impending death had somehow torn loose his astral spirit from his physical body, and that was, in all likelihood, why his physical self was in a coma right now; there was nothing inside it but nerves and blood and autonomic functions, no life force, no essence. And unless Michael missed his guess, it would stay that way—either till those autonomic functions ceased, or Michael's spirit returned to it.

Point Two. Walking through walls, et cetera et cetera. It stood to reason his astral body had no material form—just pure consciousness, energy. It took the form of Michael's physical body because that was how he envisioned himself. Also, the clothes. The pants, shirt, socks, and shoes he was putting on didn't really exist; they were just convenient manifestations of his own subconscious, manufactured to make him feel comfortable. And this led right into . . .

Point Three. He didn't fall through the bed, or to the center of the earth, for the same reason he didn't fall through chairs. Gravity should have had no effect whatever on Michael's astral form, being pure consciousness, but since he had lived all his life in the material world, bound by its physical laws, through sheer force of habit he *allowed* his astral body to be affected by gravity—to stand on the ground or sit on chairs or lie in bed, even as he had done all his life—and not to, say, float away into the upper atmosphere. Anything that required conscious thought, however—leaning against a wall, picking up a dime—required conscious effort.

As for how he could become "solid" when he concentrated on it . . . well, if his astral body was made of energy, there was no reason he couldn't manipulate that energy to affect objects in the "material" world, was there? The same applied to food: he could eat because somehow, on some unconscious level, he was changing it into the same energy-stuff he was made of.

On the other hand, maybe none of this was real and he was lying on the bottom of the East River, having one last hideous nightmare for old time's sake. Who could tell?

Michael finished dressing and looked around the apartment. He knew he would not be returning here tonight—nor any night. The place had been depressing enough when he was one hundred percent alive; now it seemed almost like a tomb. Besides, if his body did not come out of its coma within a few weeks, the landlady would almost certainly contact someone about taking Michael's belongings, pack the stuff off, slap a new coat of old paint on the place, then jack up the rent and advertise it as a DELUXE EXECUTIVE SINGLE, UTILS, VU, DISCRIMINATING PROFESSIONALS ONLY.

Michael took one last look at his old French horn, knowing he could hardly carry it around New York with him in his present state, and bid goodbye to all the small possessions he had accumulated over the years. He willed his hand "solid" and ran his fingers over his record collection, the music which had been such good company for him on so many bad nights: his Debussy, his Delius, his Faure, his Satie. For a moment the melancholy but transcendant strains of Satie's *Gymnopedies* came back to him, giving him the courage to open a drawer of his dresser and, hesitantly, remove two photographs from within. One was a black-and-white enlargement taken fifteen years ago on a vacation in upstate New York, his smiling parents flanking a reticent Michael; the other was a strip of photo-booth snapshots of himself and Shelley clowning around, in each successive photo looking more gleefully ridiculous than the last. He smiled . . . then, slowly, his face hardened as he realized that, one way or another, live or die, something had to be resolved. He put the photos back in the drawer, almost tenderly, and, with one last glance back, left the apartment. Downstairs, he turned right off Houston onto Essex Avenue, and headed north—toward Bellevue.

Dr. Lambrose was a tall man in his mid-thirties, concise and efficient, not given to much preamble, but not unsympathetic to the pain Margaret was going through as she sat before his desk, Tony holding her hand. "Your sister consumed roughly two and a half grams of Amytal," he said, consulting his chart. "The bad news is that Amytal, like most barbiturates of intermediate duration of action, is metabolized by the body fairly rapidly. The good news is that your sister's landlady found her in time for the paramedics to prevent any cessation of oxygen to the brain and, therefore, any permanent brain damage. In that alone, Ms. Benedetti, you have a lot to be thankful for."

Lambrose was unaware that the subject of his diagnosis was also in the room, her astral self standing beside her distraught sister. Ginny listened with mounting shame and guilt at the litany of her stupidity.

"The unassimilated sedative was removed from her stomach," Lambrose went on, "but enough of it had already been assimilated to produce unconsciousness—the barbiturate inhibits transmission of nerve impulses in the midbrain, and despite the stimulants we gave her—I think we used picrotoxin—she lapsed into a coma. It's not unusual in such cases."

Margaret looked ashen. "It's my fault," she said, voice flat, eyes wide. She looked as though she would shatter into small, brittle fragments at the slightest touch, the merest breeze; it surprised and disturbed Ginny. "I should never have sent her to my doctor after Mama died," she continued. "If he hadn't prescribed those goddamned tranquilizers—"

"She would've overdosed on Tylenol, or Sominex, or even aspirin," Lambrose finished for her, gently. "Believe me, Ms. Benedetti, someone who wants to die will use whatever means are at hand—and practically anything, taken in large enough quantity, can produce a toxic reaction."

"But it *is* my fault," Margaret insisted, her voice thin, strained. "She . . . came over a few days before. I was supposed to spend Christmas with her, and I . . . I forgot. I'd made . . . other plans, and she must have been so lonely that she . . ." Suddenly, Margaret broke down completely, tears streaming down her face, body rocking back and forth in her seat, overcome with guilt. Tony went to her immediately, held her as he would a little girl in pain, as Lambrose looked away discreetly.

Ginny was stunned; she had never seen her sister exhibit any real remorse in her life. And now Ginny's own guilt assaulted her: this was *her* doing; she had never meant to cause anyone any pain, all she'd wanted was to end her own. She never thought anyone would cry for her passing—especially not Maggie, at least not like this. Tears came to Ginny's eyes as she watched her sister sobbing; she wanted to reach out, to lay a comforting hand on her shoulder, but she was afraid—would Margaret even feel her touch? And what reaction might she have to it? No; she couldn't chance it.

As Margaret calmed down a bit, Lambrose leaned forward, his voice soft. "Ms. Benedetti. I'm no psychiatrist, but I do know that people don't try to kill themselves just because they've been snubbed on Christmas. There has to be more to it than that . . . frustration, loneliness, something they keep inside themselves for too long. Maybe Christmas, for your sister, was a trigger; it is for many people. But it wasn't just your fault. Trust me."

"Listen to him, Maggie," Ginny said softly.

Margaret composed herself, wiped her eyes, and looked up. "I'd like to see her now, if I may," she said, rising.

Lambrose looked uncertain. "Are you sure you're—"

"I'm fine, Doctor. I want to see my sister." Her tone was calm and firm, with only the hint of a tremor. Lambrose nodded in assent, leading them out of his office and toward the ICU ward. "She's in ICU Number Three," he said, and Ginny followed them, feeling a mounting dread as she did—wanting to run, not wanting to see what lay in that ICU, but knowing that she could not turn back; that if Margaret could stand it, then she would have to, as well.

In ICU Number Twelve, Michael stood at the foot of a bed, staring at his comatose body. It lay with a sheet covering it up to the neck; what it looked like below that, he did not want to know. The legs were almost certainly broken in several places, and though the surgeons had repaired much of the damage caused to his internal organs by the fall, the body monitors still throbbed uncertainly. Clearly, things could not go on like this. Michael wasn't sure which he wanted— life or death—but decided he would leave that up to

Fate, or God, or whatever perverse entity was running this goon show. The only thing he knew for sure was that nothing would be decided until he was back inside that pathetic, broken body.

Michael took a deep breath and climbed into the bed, swinging his legs over until they passed through the legs of his corporeal form. He felt the familiar, pins-and-needles tingle of two objects sharing the same space—if not precisely the same dimension—then leaned back so that his entire body was similarly co-existing with his physical one. He shut his eyes and concentrated on merging, becoming one with the soulless husk in the bed; he imagined himself lifting a hand, moving a finger, opening his eyes; tried to feel the flow of blood, real blood, through real veins, the pounding of his heart as it pumped oxygen to the brain; and when he began to feel the physicality, as he felt something taking hold, he took another deep breath and slowly, cautiously, sat up.

He looked behind him to see his physical body still lying motionless in the bed.

Michael cursed. He tried the process over again—longer this time, five minutes—concentrating his will on the act of merging . . . and again it failed. Frustrated, he jumped off the bed. Dammit, that was *his* body, and he wanted it *back!* (But for what? Perhaps that was part of the problem.) He stood and stared at it for several minutes, angry, frustrated, anxious . . . and then, not knowing quite else to do, climbed back into the bed for another attempt—even as he suspected, deep down, that this one would end as the others. . . .

*   *   *

Lambrose led Margaret and Tony into ICU Three, a long, narrow room in which five patients, women of varying ages, lay sleeping or unconscious. Lambrose consulted briefly with one of the ICU nurses about Ginny's condition, while Ginny's astral self looked around with a mix of fascination and horror. Outside it was starting to snow, the gray sky bringing an early dusk; gray light sifted through the ICU's single window, illuminating dust as it slowly circulated around the room. There was a feeling of stasis here, of perpetuity and timelessness; it made Ginny nervous, reminded her of Mama's apartment on those long, static Sunday afternoons.

Lambrose led them down the length of the room, past patients with tubes in arms or noses, some with curtains drawn around their beds . . . until they reached the last bed in the room. In it lay the unconscious body of a young woman of about twenty-four, with short dark hair now awry and cheeks that seemed painfully thin and sunken, her skin nearly as gray and wan as the light from outside. A respirator mask covered her mouth, and her chest rose and fell in steady but shallow beats.

With horror, Ginny realized that the girl in the bed was herself.

She turned away quickly, not wanting to see, as from far off Lambrose's voice came to her:

". . . the pills, in effect, paralyzed her central nervous system for a while; the picrotoxin helped counter that, but we have her on the respirator for a few days more, just to be safe . . ."

No; no. Ginny felt the tears coming, unable to turn around, to face what she had done to herself. She stood there, hands covering her face, wishing it were all a dream, wishing that she could only *wake up*, praying that she would . . .

"Do you . . . have any idea when she'll come out of it?" Tony's voice. Tense, concerned.

"I really don't know, Mr. DeSantis." Lambrose again, blunt but sympathetic. "The fact is, she's going to have to *want* to come out of it, and the only one who knows that is Ginny herself—and she's in no position to tell us."

I want to! I do! Ginny screamed inside herself, but as she worked up the courage to turn and look at the body again—as she saw the myriad machines feeding into her like gross metal lovers—all she really knew was that she wanted *out* of there. The walls were moving in on her; she couldn't breathe. She saw the respirator mask and something inside her snapped; panic welled up and she ran, howling and crying, from the ICU, into the corridor.

She ran down one corridor, then another, not even bothering to dodge people or wheelchairs or stretchers but flashing right through them all, her body tingling as she raced through closed doors and patients alike. She ran, and ran, until finally she saw a door marked EXIT, way at the end of a final corridor; she picked up speed, rushing right through a nurse carrying a syringe, the only thing standing between her and escape being a horsey-looking young man emerging from an ICU. Ginny kept running, half-blinded by tears, toward the exit, straight toward the man—

But instead of passing effortlessly through him, she *struck* him, with point-blank force—sending both of them hurtling forward into the EXIT doors! Ginny yelped in pain—the first real pain she had felt in nearly two days. The man cried out, startled.

Sprawled on the cement floor a few feet from him, Ginny's anger took control of her. "You goddamn idiot!" she yelled. "Why don't you watch where you're—"

She stopped as she realized that the man was staring, dumbfounded, at her.

Staring. At *her*. The realization sank in, slowly.

"Can . . . can you *see* me?" Ginny gasped, part of her afraid this might be another cruel cosmic joke.

Michael nodded dully. He was no less astonished than she. "And you . . . *you* can see *me*?"

"My God," Ginny said, "you can *hear* me, too! Can't you?"

Simultaneously they realized that they were on the other side of the EXIT doors, but that the doors remained shut; they had not moved so much as a millimeter upon the double impact. There had been, in fact, no impact at all.

An awkward moment of silence as the two of them stared at one another, scarcely believing this was possible . . . and then Michael, getting nervous at the silence, took a deep breath, cleared his throat, and tried his best to sound nonchalant.

"So," he said, brightly. "You come here often?"

II

newly as from unburied which
floats the first who, his april touch
drove sleeping selves to swarm their fates
woke dreamers to their ghostly roots

—e.e. cummings

6

They got to their feet, regarding each other with a kind of wary optimism; Ginny in particular was skeptical as she sized up this young man in windbreaker and brown corduroy slacks. "Are you . . . dead?" she said, squinting as though she might detect some evidence of it in his face, his eyes, his manner.

The utterly deadpan way she asked that filled Michael with a sudden, perverse amusement. "Last time I looked, no," he said, a light, teasing tone in his voice. "Hold on, I'll go check." He took a step as though to leave, but Ginny stepped quickly in front of him.

"You know what I mean," she said, searching for

words to describe her peculiar condition. "I mean, are you a . . . well, *ghost* isn't exactly the right word, but . . ."

"What you mean is," Michael said, "can I do this?" Whereupon he reached out and inserted his arm, up to the elbow, into the nearest wall.

Ginny's eyes popped. It was true! A delirious laugh escaped her—a laugh of immense relief, a laugh contagious enough that Michael couldn't help but join in, the two of them standing there giggling like schoolchildren over a naughty joke, all their fears melting away, replaced with the giddy knowledge that they were *not alone*. Before either of them knew what was happening, they were embracing, laughing, crying, hugging a complete stranger for no reason but that they could *see* one another.

"Oh God," Ginny gasped, half laughing, half sobbing, "I thought I was the only one—"

"I know, I know," Michael said, "I never thought anybody would ever *hear* me again—"

"Oh *God!*"

"I know, I know . . ."

As Ginny stood there, arms wrapped around Michael, head pressed against his chest, she suddenly realized that for the first time in two days she was *feeling* something—not distantly, not as though through some gauze, but actually feeling something! Then, as she became slowly aware of *what* she was feeling— the warmth of Michael's body, the sound of his heart, his breathing, the feel of his arms around her waist as they held one another—she also felt the old panic, the old wariness creeping back. She didn't even know this man, and she was standing here *embracing* him?

For both of them, the giddiness was lifting at the same time; Michael, too, felt suddenly shy, embarrassed. Awkwardly they disengaged themselves from one another, looked at each other nervously. "Well. I guess we, uh, haven't really been properly introduced," Michael said, lapsing despite himself into the damned baroque-formal syntax he fell into when flustered by women. He extended a hand. "My name is Michael; Michael Barrett."

Fighting back an urge to bolt and run, Ginny warily took his hand. "Ginny Benedetti. Pleased to, uh, meet you."

A moment of awkward silence, then: "I take it you were visiting your, ah, body," Michael said, thinking as he said it that this was the damnedest small talk he had ever made.

Ginny nodded. "It was a short visit," she admitted. "I couldn't stand the thought of all those . . . tubes and machines. I had to get away." She hesitated. "Sorry for running into you like that."

"Are you kidding?" Michael smiled. "If you hadn't, we might never have met. God, I was getting so lonely I could talk to a rock."

Ginny bristled reflexively. "Gee, thanks," she said acidly.

Michael winced, cursing himself. "I didn't mean that the way it—"

"I mean, if you'd like to wait for a better talker to turn up, I'd be happy to move along," Ginny went on, not even knowing *why* she was saying what she was, the old reflex of striking out now back in control.

"Maybe you and the ghost of Dave Garroway can get together your own talk show. Think of the guests you could line up . . ."

Michael stepped forward, hands raised in a gesture of truce, feeling as though he were in over his head already. "Hey. I'm sorry. I don't blame you for being pissed, but I didn't mean anything—honest." He shrugged sheepishly. "Sometimes I try too hard to be . . . I don't know . . . clever. Kind of an insurance policy. If someone's laughing at you, they're that less likely to hit you. Know what I mean?"

Ginny allowed herself to relax somewhat. He didn't seem like such a bad guy, but still . . . "Yeah, well," she said. "I guess we're both a little tense."

"Can't imagine why," Michael said, and at that, Ginny had to crack a smile. Seeing her small grin, Michael breathed a sigh of relief. "Let's take it from the top, okay?" he said. "Would you like to go somewhere—get something to eat?"

Ginny wasn't really hungry, but nodded. "Sure. Why not?" And so, before either of them could open their mouths again to say something dumb, they began heading up Fifth Avenue toward midtown and a Chinese restaurant Michael knew of on West 48th.

Flurries fell through them like fairy dust as they walked, the streets relatively quiet, the twilight gray and still; Ginny held out her hand, palm up, to catch a snowflake, willing her hand "solid" to do so— then stared in wonder at the snowflake in her palm. "Look. Look at that," she said, softly.

"What?"

"The snowflake. It's not melting. Usually you catch a snowflake in your hand, it's gone in a few seconds, but . . . it's just *staying* there. Like that artificial snow I used to use to decorate the store window.''

"They melt from your body heat," Michael said, eyeing the white speck in Ginny's hand. "No body, no heat.''

Ginny felt suddenly sad. She turned her hand over, let the snowflake fall to the ground as they continued to walk. "The thing I hate most," she said, folding her arms across her chest, "is the way you can't really feel anything. I mean, sure, you can move things if you concentrate, but—if you pick up a flower, you can't even feel the petals; you just know that they're soft, somehow, like it's been radioed in to you.''

Michael blinked. He was ashamed to admit that till now, he had barely even noticed; even when he was alive, he had blocked out so much feeling, denied so much for fear of knowing what he was missing, that this had seemed not so very different. But as he thought about it, as he tried to feel the wind on his back, tried to smell the clean, crisp smell of winter flurries, he slowly realized that she was right—that it all seemed distant, somehow; removed—and worse, he realized with a certain sorrow just how long it had seemed so . . .

"Why is that, do you think?"

"Hmm?"

"Why can't I feel the snow, and yet I felt it when I ran into you?"

Michael considered for a moment. "Well, I guess because these are what you might call our astral bodies—our life-forces. And because they're made of some kind of . . . energy . . . we can't really feel in the same way we could when we had physical bodies."

Ginny thought of her grandmother, eating and enjoying food years after she had lost her taste and her smell, and it all seemed clearer to her; what little feeling they had, what small taste they could find in food, was largely memory—echoes of real life. "So we're able to feel each other because we're both made of the same kind of . . . energy?"

"I suppose. I really can't do more than give an educated guess about all this; I was a musician, not a metaphysician."

Ginny was impressed. "A musician? That's great. What did you play?"

"Uh, the horn. The French horn." His conscience prodded him to add, "Actually, I . . . haven't played professionally in years. I've been working in a graphics shop on Canal Street. How about you?"

Ginny shrugged. "I was a window dresser at Macy's. That snowscene in the 34th Street window, the one on the corner, that was mine." For some reason she was reluctant to discuss her life with this man; as relieved as she was to have someone to talk to, the old fears were still there, and she kept a discreet distance as they walked.

They were silent for a few minutes, until finally, his curiosity getting the better of him, Michael decided to broach the question he had thus far carefully avoided.

"Uh, listen . . . Ginny," he began, tentatively, "forgive me for asking . . . it's probably none of my business, but . . . did you . . . well . . . try to commit suicide?"

The word *suicide* made a chill run up Ginny's spine; coming from a stranger it seemed like a harsh accusation, a condemnation, and automatically she recoiled from it. She came to a sudden stop, stared daggers at Michael. "Well, you've got your nerve!" she snapped, eyes big with indignation.

Michael immediately regretted it. "I'm sorry, I just—"

"I mean, where do you get *off*, anyway, making personal suppositions like—"

"I'm sorry! Really! Please, forget I said anything!" He tried to move closer, but Ginny shrank back. After a moment they resumed their walking, keeping a cautious, tentative distance. Ginny kept her eyes fixed on the ground; her voice when she spoke was low, injured.

"It . . . happened to be an accident," she found herself saying. "I was . . . sort of depressed. All I wanted to do was go to sleep, so I . . . I took some pills." A pause as she contemplated her lie. "I guess I took too many."

Michael bit his lip. He felt like a fool. "I'm sorry. I shouldn't have jumped to conclusions."

"Well, I shouldn't think so." They walked again in silence for a while, then turned left on West 48th; this time, it was Ginny's curiosity that got the better of her. "Is that what you did?" she asked quietly. "Suicide, I mean?"

Flushed with shame, Michael could only nod wordlessly.

"How . . . how did you do it?" Ginny said. "That is, if you don't mind my asking."

Michael's stomach coiled. He saw again the black

waters falling up at him, saw again his own body plummeting toward them. "I was what they call in the trade a 'jumper,' " Michael said, his voice flat. "Off the Williamsburg. I guess the trauma . . . the shock . . . is what did *this* to me." He smiled ruefully. "Some luck, huh? Can't even kill myself properly. Other people walk in front of trucks, fall out windows, bam, that's it, goodbye yellow brick road; me, I jump two hundred feet into the East River and come out doing a road show of *Blithe Spirit*."

Ginny's voice was soft. "Do you . . . have any idea what happens now?"

Michael sighed. "I tried crawling back into my body, but . . . well, I guess I still don't know if I *want* to live, and without a reason to wake up . . ." He let the sentence trail off, but Ginny could figure out the rest and knew, deep down, that the same doubtless applied to her.

"Well, here we are." Michael had stopped suddenly and Ginny realized that they had arrived at the restaurant. She smelled the exotic odors of Chinese food wafting out from inside, but was indifferent to them. "You know," she said, "I'm not really all that hungry."

Michael smiled a lopsided smile. "Was it something I said?" he asked dryly.

A mantle of gray clouds obscured the moon and stars as a light snow fell across Central Park, carried at an angle by a warm winter wind; the snowflakes melted almost as quickly as they touched the cobblestones. The last of the holiday carolers sang on the periphery of the park as a solitary hansom cab glided regally up West Drive toward the lake. The horse shook its large brown head, snorting great plumes of frosty breath into the air as its hooves clattered on the cobbled path; inside the cab, an elderly lady with soft, Clairol-blonde hair sat wrapped in fur, staring out at the darkness, her eyes very far away. The driver, a stocky, good-natured man with a cigarette hanging from his mouth, kept one hand lightly on the reins while he unscrewed a thermos with the other.

"Coffee, Mrs. Gold?"

The elderly woman blinked, turned. "Oh, no, thank you, Richard," she said, smiling. "I'll be eating shortly, anyway."

"Sure." The driver took a swallow of coffee.

"Did you have a nice Christmas, Richard?"

"Very nice, Mrs. Gold, thanks."

Driver and passenger lapsed back into their comfortable silence, the man sipping his coffee, the woman staring out. Unknown to either of them, the cab held two other passengers seated immediately behind Mrs. Gold: a pair of invisible, disembodied, and very glum-looking astral spirits.

"It wasn't really a bad life," Michael was saying, "just not a very good one. I'd wake up in the morning and try to think of a good reason to get out of bed. Some days it'd take me hours. Then one day, I just ran out of reasons . . ."

Ginny squirmed uncomfortably, not wanting to hear this. "Uh-huh," she said noncommittally, eyes everywhere except on Michael's face.

Michael picked up on her discomfort, tried to shift the subject. "But, uh, what about you? You said you worked at Macy's?" She nodded. "Did you like it?"

Ginny shrugged. "It was a job."

"Well, did you have any other plans? Goals?"

"Not really," Ginny said.

Michael groped for some way to make contact. "You must've had some dreams . . . some—"

Ginny snapped her gaze around, voice sharp as a razor. "What is this, a game show? Do I look like a contestant on *Wheel of Fortune* to you?"

Michael's patience was wearing thin; this was the third time in the past hour he had tried to establish some rapport and the third time he had been slapped down. "I'm just trying to get to know you, for Pete's sake! We could be spending a lot of time together, y'know."

Ginny settled down, embarrassed by her outburst but still uncomfortable revealing anything of herself to this man. "Okay, okay," she said, softening a bit. She searched for something to say, at once personal and equivocating. "I really didn't have any . . . goals," she said. "I just sort of took things as they came. I was at Macy's for three years, at Woolworth's before that . . . those were my only real jobs. Except for a summer job in high school."

"Where was that?"

Ginny was reluctant to say, but there was no backing off. "I worked as a waitress at the Moonrise Ballroom—the one over on East 48th."

Michael smiled. "You liked dancing?"

"That was a long time ago," Ginny said, remembering the glow of summer evenings, the way the lights on the terrace cast halos in the evening mists, the people gliding two-by-two across the brightly colored dance floor. "I mean, I never thought I could really be a dancer—not at my weight—but I used to like to watch the customers dance. And sometimes I'd wait till the place closed, and I'd kind of . . . glide around the floor by my—''

She caught herself suddenly. Horrified that she had almost shared something like that, her tone became harder, defensive. "This is stupid," she declared. "That was all years ago."

"I don't think it's—"

Michael's thought was interrupted as the woman in the front seat, Mrs. Gold, leaned forward and spoke to the driver. "You can drop me at the edge of the park, Richard. It's such a lovely night, I think I'll walk the rest of the way to the restaurant."

Michael watched and listened as the driver turned around, a wry grin on his face. "High-stepping it a bit tonight, eh, Mrs. Gold?"

She smiled, almost blushed. "I have a gentleman waiting," she said, a bit embarrassed. "I'm told he's very nice." She laughed a little to herself. "My friend Mrs. Tiburzi arranged it; she says he has a beard—a beard, would you believe that? If poor Arthur could see me now." A moment as she seemed to reflect on that, then: "Actually, I don't think he'd mind."

The driver brought the hansom to a stop at the edge of the park, near Fifth Avenue. "I'm sure he wouldn't," he said. "Well, here we are."

Michael watched, fascinated, as the driver helped the elderly woman—obviously a favorite passenger—from the cab; Ginny, watching Michael, couldn't imagine why he was so interested in this. The lady opened her purse carefully, extracted a twenty and handed it to the driver. "Merry Christmas, Richard."

"Happy Hanukkah, Mrs. Gold."

The lady's gaze wandered back to the park, then off toward the restaurant a block away; her voice was soft, filled with expectation and fear, anticipation and dread.

"I do hope he's nice," she said, to no one in particular. Then she turned and, her bearing proud and strong, walked across the street toward the restaurant.

The driver went off for another cigarette, feeding his horse a sugar cube as he passed; Michael stared across the street, smiling, feeling good. "That's kind of beautiful, you know?" he said. "They never give up. They never stop searching." A wistful pause. "I wish I knew how they did it . . ."

Ginny had had just about enough of this; she finally exploded. "My God, you sound like Mary Worth! What *is* it with you, anyway? Are you trying to make me feel worse than I already do? Well congratulations, it's working!"

"I'm sorry, I wasn't—"

But the fears and the pain which had been building up for two days were at last bursting forth, and Ginny could not keep them in check any longer. "All right! All right!" she shouted angrily. "I admit it, okay? I was never loved, never needed, never taken on carriage rides in Central Park—you *satisfied* now? Is that what you want to *hear?*"

Michael was also getting angry. "For Christ's sake,

I wasn't talking about you, I was talking about me! What the fuck are you so paranoid about?''

"Watch your mouth, goddammit!"

" 'Watch my mouth, goddammit'?"

"There, you did it again!"

Michael's patience snapped and, true to form, he opted to throw in the towel. He jumped out of the cab in a fury, his right arm passing through part of the canvas top as he dropped. "That's it!" he announced. "I don't have to take this shit. I don't care if you *are* the only person in the whole damn city who can see me; it's not worth it!"

He stalked off into the park. Ginny suddenly saw in him all the people who had ever walked away from her—and knew that this one could very well be the last. "Where—where do you think you're going!" she shouted after him.

Michael did not turn, just kept on trudging through the melting snow. "Nowhere! Anywhere!" he called back. "Maybe I'll visit Grant's Tomb—he's gotta be better company than you!"

Panic started to take hold. Ginny jumped out of the cab, called after the rapidly dwindling figure. "Michael! No! You can't go!"

Michael kept walking. Ginny could already feel the clouds themselves pressing down on her. Her eyes were moist. "Michael! *Please!* Don't leave! I'm sorry!"

Michael stopped; turned; looked at her, and she at him: two lonely people in a cold park, with Christmas carols all around. Reason began to trickle back to him: where would he go, anyway? And would he ever find anyone he could talk to again? If ever there

was a time when he should not give up, this had to
be it. A moment's hesitation . . . and he took a step
forward, toward Ginny, who breathed her own silent
sigh of relief.

"Are you as tired as I am?" Michael asked. Ginny
nodded. Michael went to her side and the two of
them started out of the park, toward the street. Screwing up his courage, Michael raised a hand tentatively
to her waist; instinctively, Ginny shrank back, and
Michael quickly dropped his hand, kicking himself
for even thinking of such a thing.

To the night clerk at the Waldorf-Astoria, it seemed
as though a sudden breeze were rustling the pages of
his guest register—but a damned selective breeze at
that, one which flipped open a page at a time, as
though (and he knew this was impossible) someone
or something were reading what was written there,
the rooms occupied and the rooms left vacant, page
by page by page. Laying a paperweight on top to
keep the pages in place, he turned away . . . only to
find, upon turning back, that the paperweight had
somehow slid off the book, as though by itself, and
the pages were flipping open once more.

By now becoming flustered and impatient, the clerk
tried again—and watched as the paperweight did indeed slide off the register, as if of its own volition.
Angrily he grabbed the paperweight again, slammed
it down on the register . . .

. . . and watched, scared shitless, as the paperweight *floated* into the air, hovered there the briefest
of moments, then pitched itself over the desk, across
the lobby, to land with a thump on the lush carpeting.

The night clerk decided to let the pages of the guest register do whatever they goddamn well pleased. He was not a man given to belief in the supernatural, but on the other hand, he had seen enough movies to know that his was the character who got killed off by the end of the first reel for tempting the fates—the one who said "May I help you, sir?" as Jack Nicholson entered the room carrying an axe. No, the guest register could amuse itself in whatever ways it pleased, thank you; he was no fool.

Michael and Ginny passed through the locked doors into an unoccupied two-bedroom suite—and gasped. Even in the darkness they could feel the plushness, the comfort; Michael switched on the light to reveal an elegant, ornate sitting room with two sofas, a bar, a 22-inch Proton video monitor with stereo sound, video recorder, and cable TV. "Wow," Ginny said simply, and Michael saw no need for elaboration. On either side of the sitting room were two equally plush bedrooms; they wandered into the one on the right, and Ginny gasped again in delight. A canopied bed with blue satin sheets, a huge window overlooking Park Avenue, closets large enough to hold the gross national product of Bolivia, if not Bolivia itself, and royal blue carpeting as thick and deep as the sea. Ginny went to the bed, fell back as if on a cloud. "Ohhh," she sighed, "you have no idea how good this feels after spending a night on a wooden pew."

Without thinking, Michael stretched out beside her. "It'll do, I suppose. When we get tired of it, we can always move on to the Hilton. Or maybe the Plaza . . ."

Ginny, alarmed at Michael's proximity, bolted upright immediately. "Just what do you think you're doing?" she demanded.

Michael looked up, puzzled. "I thought I was resting."

"Here?"

"It was either here or the floor."

Ginny stood, hands on hips. "This is a suite, you know. That implies rooms—in the plural."

Michael remained where he was. "I know what plural means. I even know what a gerund is. Do you know what a gerund is?"

"I don't care what a gerund is," Ginny snapped. "I just want you to go to your room—"

"Singular."

"—and I'll stay here in mine, and we'll both get along fine!"

Sick and tired of this emotional seesaw, Michael suddenly bounded off the bed, consummately pissed; Ginny jumped back, startled by his intensity.

"For God's sake, lady," he said, voice rising, "I'm no ravisher of young women! I'm just a lousy goddamn *spirit*—how do you know I even *have* one anymore?"

Her gaze dropped involuntarily to his belt. "You mean you don't—"

"Well of course I do, I was being rhetorical! The point is—"

"The point is," Ginny said firmly, though a bit more gently, "that I . . . I just want to be alone. Please. I'm tired and I don't want to argue."

Michael realized that he was literally shaking with anger. Even when he *didn't* make a move, he got rejected. "Okay, okay," he said, voice trembling.

"I know the song by now. I heard it all my life; I know the words by heart." He turned on his heels and stalked toward the door.

Ginny saw the hurt in his eyes for the first time. "Michael, it's nothing personal—"

He spun around, glared at her. "Oh, it's *never* personal," he snapped. "Credit me with a little intelligence, for Christ's sake! I know that I'm not very . . . that I don't—" The words stuck in his throat; he felt as though he might burst into tears at any moment. "Oh, hell, forget it! G'night." Angrily, he tore open the door instead of simply walking through it and then, with great satisfaction, slammed it shut with all the force he could muster.

Ginny tried to sleep, but despite the soft blankets and satin sheets she could not; her guilt kept her awake. Damn it, she had done it again—allowed her fear to consume her, insulted someone who wanted only to be her friend. Scaring him off before he could hurt her. After an hour of tossing and turning, she got up and rummaged in the huge closet, finding only an old terry-cloth robe hanging in a far corner. She pulled it on, opened the door, and crossed the sitting room to Michael's bedroom.

After two meek raps on the door, she heard Michael's voice, sounding strangely distant. "Come in."

She entered to find the room—a twin of hers—empty, the window open; the curtains billowed gently in the cool night breeze. She looked all around; nothing. "Michael?"

His voice came from the direction of the open window. "Out here."

Ginny ran for the window. "My God," she gasped, "you're not gonna try it again, are you?"

Michael was sitting outside on the window ledge, wearing only an undershirt and jockey shorts, his legs swinging as he stared down at the bright tapestry of lights below. Ginny took one look down and felt dizzy. "What do you think you're *doing* out here?" she said, with genuine concern.

"Well, it's not as if I could break anything if I fell."

"Will you get back in here? Please?"

Michael noted the concern in her voice, sighed, and climbed back inside. He shut the window, then sat down on his bed. "Hope you don't faint at the sight of jockey shorts," he said. "The astral men's wear store was all out of pajamas."

Ginny almost retorted with something sharp, then caught herself. "Guess I deserved that one, didn't I?" she said with a pained smile. She hesitated, then, working up her nerve, sat down beside Michael on the bed. "I just wanted to . . . apologize. If I hurt your feelings. I've never been real good with people, you know? I talk before I think, sometimes." A moment, and then she shrugged, smiled. "A *lot* of times, actually."

Michael studied her. Part of him wanted to remain angry, to wallow in self-pity and a certain misogyny, but the larger part of him felt for Ginny and knew that she was as lost and frightened as he. He put a hand on hers, innocently. "Sure. I understand. Don't worry about it." He took his hand away. Ginny looked down.

"I've been thinking," she said after a moment. "About why we're here."

"We're here," Michael said, "because God is really Harold Pinter."

"Who?"

"Nothing. Go on."

Ginny took a deep breath. The horrors of the last forty-eight hours all tumbled in on her: the dream, Mama, Papa; Maggie crying as Maggie had never cried before . . . "I lied," Ginny blurted out. "About the pills. It . . . wasn't an accident." She felt her eyes getting wet. "I just got so *tired*, you know? Tired of wearing the wrong clothes . . . saying the wrong things . . ."

Michael was not really surprised. His heart went out to her, but, afraid of rejection, he hesitated to make any move to comfort her; instead he simply said, "I know," and watched as she began sobbing.

"I wanted it over. I wanted it to end," she said. "And now here I am, and nothing's changed, 'cause I can walk through walls and stick my head through doors, but I still can't figure out how the hell to make people *like* me. I still can't shut my stupid mouth, and I *hurt* people when I don't—I don't—"

"Hey," Michael said, gently. "*I* like you."

She looked at him in amazement. "How could you? After all the . . . crap I put you through tonight?"

"Well, it's not easy," he said, smiling, "but then I'm not exactly a Dale Carnegie graduate myself. Maybe I like that girl who would glide around the dance floor by herself, after hours. Is she still around at all?"

Ginny thought of that night in Macy's, the dress

and Mrs. Levitt, and smiled dolefully. "Oh, yeah," she said, sniffing back tears, "she's still around, all right."

Michael screwed up his courage, reached out and held her; it felt warm but somehow awkward. Ginny hugged him back, feeling the same awkwardness but hoping that it would go away, somehow. "Michael?" she said finally. "Do you think . . . maybe we were *put* here . . . for a reason?" A pause. "I mean . . . to do something in death . . . or limbo . . . *whatever* . . . that we never did in life?"

He looked at her, and she at him. He didn't know. He had never believed in a paternalistic God who answered prayers and managed human lives; but perhaps it wasn't God, at least not the traditional sort of God, that had brought the two of them together. Perhaps it was Karma, some unknowable design to the universe . . . did it really matter what, as long as it got them out of this mess?

He touched her cheek, gently. "Maybe," he said.

Wordlessly they moved apart and began undressing. Ginny dropped her terry-cloth robe to the floor, then, with a bit more trepidation, began unfastening her bra. She had never shown her breasts to a man before; she didn't know what to expect. She fumbled with the clasp, stalling for time. Michael took off his undershirt, feeling as self-conscious about his body as Ginny felt about hers—was it too late to build up his chest muscles a bit? Did he have time for a couple dozen push-ups? Ginny finally undid her bra and dropped it to the floor, then, before she could dwell on Michael's reaction, slid off her panties. Like players in a game of strip poker, Michael thought, sliding off his shorts. Ginny's gaze immediately fas-

tened on his penis, the first she'd seen since Tommy
Marcusi tried to get fresh with her in high school and
she'd put him in line (still one of her great regrets);
then she quickly averted her eyes for fear of seeming,
well, impolite. Michael noticed this, wondered if she
were disappointed (was it that small?). He moved
closer, tried to kiss her; Ginny moved her mouth at
just the wrong moment and he wound up kissing that
funny little indentation under her nose—what did
they call it—the filtrum. Gently, but scared out of
his wits, he guided her down onto the sheets of the
bed; Ginny responded stiffly, at best. One thing that
was not responding stiffly, however, was Michael,
and he couldn't quite figure why. Too late to turn
back, though; he decided to stall for time and, in
desperation, tried to recall every bit of foreplay he
had ever read about or known in his admittedly lim-
ited experience.

• • •

"What are you doing?"

"I'm touching your breasts."

"Oh. Do you have to do that?"

"Uh, not if you don't want me to."

"No no, really, if it makes you feel good . . ."

"Well, it's supposed to make *you* feel good,
too . . ."

"Oh. Well why don't you try again, then? . . ."

• • •

"You have a lovely body, Ginny."

"No, I don't. But thank you for saying so."

"No, really, I mean it. You're very—"

"Michael, please. You don't have to flatter me. I
know what I look like."

"Ginny, I swear—"

"Let's just drop the subject. Please?"

• • •

"Michael? Did I do something wrong?"

"No . . . no, not at all. I'm just a little . . . ticklish, that's all . . ."

"But isn't that supposed to be an erogenous zone? I mean, I saw this discussion on *Donahue,* and—"

"For Phil, maybe, but not for me! Can we move on here?"

• • •

"*Oh!*"

"Ginny? You okay?"

"Yes, I just . . . I mean, it's just that . . . nobody's ever touched me down there before . . ."

"Uh . . . nobody?"

"Tommy Marcusi came close. That's about it."

"You mean you're . . . uh . . . ah . . ."

"I'm about as 'uh, ah' as you can get, yes . . ."

"Well, for what it's worth, I'm not too far removed from it myself."

"Boy, we're quite a pair, aren't we?"

• • •

"Michael?"

"Yeah?"

"This isn't . . . working out, is it?"

"Damn it, Ginny, I'm sorry. I don't understand why I can't—"

"Not just that. The whole thing. I think maybe we're both a little—"

"Nervous?"

"Listen. You, uh . . . want to forget about this?"

"No, no, that's all right . . . I can still . . ."

"It's okay, Michael, really."

"I just feel so damn . . . You don't mind?"

"No. 'Course not. But maybe I could . . . just sort of stay here, with you, the rest of the night? Just sleeping?"

Michael put an arm around her; they nestled up against one another. Michael drew the soft satin sheets up around them and felt himself breathing for the first time in fifteen minutes. "You comfortable?"

Ginny closed her eyes dreamily, laid her head on Michael's chest. "Um. Fine." She felt relaxed; she wasn't used to sharing a bed with another person, sharing something as intimate as sleep, but had a feeling she could grow to like the sensation. "G'night, Michael," she said quietly.

"Good night, Ginny."

Michael shut his eyes, feeling relieved and unpressured.

He, too, liked having someone to snuggle with; already Ginny was drifting off to sleep. Peaceful, contented, warm, the embarrassment of a few minutes earlier already mercifully fading in his memory, he lay there, liking the softness of Ginny's shoulders, the smell of her hair touching his chin, the feel of her slow, rhythmic breathing on his chest. He smiled dreamily . . . and realized that he was suddenly hard. He sighed, looking heavenward. Some days, he reflected, you just couldn't win for losing.

7

He sat on the window ledge outside his room, looking out across Park Avenue, beyond midtown to the Hudson and, dimly seen in the pre-dawn darkness, the cold, flat shank of New Jersey. Behind him the sun was rising, turning the towering slabs of Rockefeller Center just ahead from black to slate to gunmetal-gray; on the streets beyond, taxis squeezed out from shuttered garages, buses rattled and thundered uptown and down. Lights clicked on in neighboring buildings, silhouettes moved and stretched behind shut blinds, radios snapped on and music played. Not the music Michael heard in his head, however; for him the city moved to a mournful blues number, saxophone wailing, strings sighing, a trumpet solo sounding like a bugle blown for a soldier lost in a cause he could not fathom. The taxis searched the morning dimness for prospective passengers, people caught at the ragged end of night: men or women who wake in strange beds, searching unfamiliar rooms for some trace of what had seemed so special and urgent the night before, and, not finding it, field awkward goodbyes and rush into the street, too many similar nights strung before and behind them, like beads on a necklace of regret.

Michael watched as the sun moved higher up the clear bright dome of the sky, watched the city as it fell into its morning rhythms, and wondered where he fit in, he and this unusual young woman who seemed as lost and as frightened as he. Why were they here? Was there some purpose to this—or was it all random chance, a toss of the dice?

Inside, Ginny woke to find herself alone in the wide bed. She sat up, momentarily alarmed, then saw the open window and, with a sigh composed of equal parts relief and amusement, padded over to it.

Sure enough, there he was, perched like a pigeon on the ledge, looking out at the city. Ginny had to admit it did look beautiful in the morning light. "There you are," she said, poking her head out. Michael shook off his reverie, saw Ginny smiling at him. "So," she said, "you coming in, or should I have breakfast sent out?"

Michael grinned. "Might be worth it to see how you place the order with room service. But no, I'm coming in." He climbed inside, and for a moment they stood awkwardly a few feet apart, the memory of the disastrous would-be tryst still embarrassingly fresh in their minds. "Uh, look," Michael began tentatively. "About last night—"

"It's okay. Really."

"No, it isn't. I've never . . . I mean, I guess I was so . . . scared, you know, so desperate to find some way out of this mess, that I didn't give much thought to—"

"Neither did I," Ginny said gently. "I guess strangers make pretty lousy lovers."

"Yeah," Michael agreed. "Who'd've believed it, huh? Sex *doesn't* solve everything, after all."

"I guess not." Ginny suddenly grinned mischievously, added, "My complexion did clear up, though."

Michael broke up, and Ginny joined in his laughter, pleased that she could make him laugh. He took her hand, gave it an affectionate squeeze. "You're an okay person, you know that, Ginny?"

Ginny beamed. "Thanks. You're okay yourself."

"Listen—we don't have to be strangers *or* lovers, do we? I could use a friend right now."

"Me, too," Ginny said. "I, uh, never had too many before, though. I can't guarantee I'll be any good at it."

"We don't have much choice," Michael shrugged. "I mean, if we can't relate to another human being now, when the hell could we?"

The thought made Ginny vaguely depressed, but she fought that back. Michael let go of her hand; they stood there, uncertain of how next to proceed, until Michael gave an elaborate sigh. "So," he said brightly. "What do you want to do today? Ice-skating, sleigh-riding, a picnic at Coney Island . . . ?"

Ginny considered for a moment, then got a wonderful idea. Her face glowed with enthusiasm; she clapped her hands together excitedly.

"How about a *movie?*" she said.

"Okay," Ginny announced soberly. "What do we have?"

A copy of the *Daily News,* filched from a room-service cart, lay spread out on the floor as Ginny, cross-legged, examined it with the serious purpose of a true film fanatic. Michael was somewhat underwhelmed by this whole idea, but was willing to go along with it if Ginny wanted to; he wasn't about to break the tentative truce they seemed to have reached. "Um, let's see," he said, scanning the first page of movie ads. "Great double-bill over on 42nd Street: *Vampire Cheerleaders* and *The Children of Bruce Lee.* Who says they don't make movies like they used to?"

"I can live without the experience. What else?"

Michael turned the page, caught sight of something interesting. "Oh, hey, there's a Bergman festival at the Bleecker Street Cinema—*Cries and Whispers, The Seventh Seal, Persona . . .*"

"Sounds great," Ginny said, without much enthusiasm. "That ought to take our minds off our situation, all right—six hours of people talking about death in Swedish."

Michael felt momentarily annoyed, then cleared his throat and turned the page. "Yeah. Right. Well." He scanned the page, finding nothing much of interest until he came to a small box advertising a double-bill at the Little Carnegie: "Hey," he said, smiling, "you must like musicals, right? How about *All That Jazz* and *Cabaret*?"

Ginny frowned sourly. "Call it a whim, but somehow I'm not in the mood for open-heart surgery, thanks. Besides, I like my musicals light and cheerful, not grim and depressing."

Her dogmatic dismissal of the film pissed him. "*All That Jazz* happens to be a very *uplifting* movie," he bristled. "At the end he experiences this epiphany, this realization; he finally comes to terms with himself, and then he—"

"He dies."

"Well, yes, but in an uplifting kind of way."

It took nearly twenty minutes, but they finally decided on a double-bill of *Silk Stockings* and *Singin' in the Rain* at the Cinema Village . . . and although the latter was one of his favorite films, as the hours rolled by Michael found himself growing increasingly restive, unable to focus his attention either on the charm and style of Gene Kelly, Donald O'Connor, and Debbie Reynolds or on the truly astonishing legs of Cyd Charisse. It all seemed irrelevant, immaterial; he couldn't even work up a good fantasy over Cyd Charisse. And it was then he realized that in the past forty-eight hours he had not had a single daydream . . . not one fantasized assignation with Dolly Parton, or airport check-in clerks, or anyone else, for that matter. Ironically, being thrust into this bizarre astral existence had rooted him more firmly to reality than he had felt in years.

Afterward, Ginny cajoled him into a triple bill, at the Embassy, of *Goldfinger*, *On Her Majesty's Secret Service*, and *Never Say Never Again* . . . and the day began to weigh heavily on Michael. But not on Ginny: she sat, as though in a trance, eagerly drinking in every image, every sound from the screen; Michael tried to ignore the way her eyes would particularly light up whenever Sean Connery would appear, which was often. Goddamn movie stars, he thought. If there were no movie stars, maybe the rest of us wouldn't feel so miserable for not looking like them. His anger grew steadily as he realized he had squandered an entire day watching shadows on a screen, flat and one-dimensional; he had wasted a good portion of his life on fantasy and daydream—he became determined not to waste this, too.

Back at the Waldorf, Michael, like a man possessed, drew up elaborate plans for the next several days. On Friday the 28th, they would take a walking tour of Lower Manhattan and the Villages, working their way up from Battery Park, through Chinatown and Little Italy, up to SoHo. "On Saturday," Michael went on excitedly, spreading in front of Ginny the map he had borrowed from the front desk, "we're gonna see all the sights jaded New Yorkers never get around to seeing: the Statue of Liberty, the United Nations, the World Trade Center, all the biggies. Sunday we'll hit Broadway. Nothing too much at first—a matinee, an evening performance, dinner in Sardi's kitchen . . ." After that, there would be the museums: the Guggenheim, the Whitney, MOMA . . .

"You'll love it," Michael burbled, circling points in red on the map as Ginny looked on, wide-eyed, a sinking feeling in the pit of her stomach. "I mean, this is the most culturally rich city in the world! Hell, this may be the best thing that ever happened to us, you know?'' He began flipping through *The New York Times* entertainment section. "Unless I miss my guess," he added, almost breathlessly, "the Bolshoi is due in town next month. Just think—all those other people will have to line up for days to get tickets, but we can just walk in and sit down on the damned proscenium if we want! Won't that be *great?*''

Ginny sank a little bit more into her chair. She was definitely starting to get a bad feeling about this . . .

True to his word, Michael showed her New York. More of New York, in fact, than Ginny had ever wanted to see. He showed her the Statue of Liberty— all 168 steps of it. He showed her Madison Square Garden, the Bronx Zoo, the United Nations, the Museum of Natural History. She got sore feet climbing the Statue of Liberty ("You gonna stop here, or do you want to go out and scale the torch?") and a stiff neck watching a laser light show at the Hayden Planetarium. ("It's all in your imagination. You're feeling discomfort because your mind thinks you *should* feel discomfort," he would tell her, and Ginny wanted to kill him, if only she knew how.) They ate, invisibly, in the kitchens of the best restaurants in town—La Grenouille, Windows on the World, La Caravelle . . . not only did the food still taste as though wrapped in gauze, but Ginny didn't know what half the stuff she was eating even *was*; after three days of coulibiac of salmon, frog legs Provençale, and caneton rôti aux pêches, she longed for a Sabrett's frank and an Italian ice.

They saw plays, mostly off-off-Broadway productions with very little scenery and titles like *split ends* and *Weeds*; and on Monday, Michael started on the museums.

In the morning it was the Whitney. Early afternoon, the Metropolitan. By late afternoon they were wandering the halls of the Museum of Modern Art, and Ginny's weariness and frustration was building to a high pitch. If she had to look at one more goddamn statue, she felt she would scream. So help her, she would.

Michael wandered over to a sculpture by Antoine Pevsner, turned to Ginny. "Now this is a pretty good example," he began, "of the constructivist school of—"

Ginny screamed. A long, high, curdling shriek that escaped her before she even realized it. Michael nearly went into cardiac arrest, leaping back half a foot.

"You don't like constructivism?" he asked, meekly.

Ginny screamed again. Since she did not seem to be injured or in pain, Michael found himself more baffled and annoyed than alarmed. "For God's sake!" he cried over her continuing howl. "We're in a *museum*, Ginny!"

"They can't hear us, can they?!" Ginny yelled.

"Well, no, but—"

"Michael, I can't take this any longer!" she went on, the weekend's frustrations pouring out at last. "Plays, museums, ballet, sightseeing—do I look so culturally deprived that I need you pounding this into my head, day after day, night after night, one weird French food after another?"

"I'm just trying to give us a common frame of reference, that's all!"

"*Your* frame of reference, you mean!"

"Oh, and yours is better? Shlock movies and junkfood?"

"I just wanna be *me!*"

"I knew it," Michael snapped. "I bet you even like Sinatra, don't you?"

Ginny's eyes widened. "That's it. That's the last straw, buddy. I can put up with a lot of insults to my tastes, but *Sinatra . . . ?*" Ginny spun around and began to run. They were on the third floor of the museum; she wound her way through the various exhibits, searching for a stairwell, but her mind was a jumble of conflicting emotions and every turn she made seemed to find her farther away from her goal. Behind her she heard Michael running and calling her name; she picked up speed, started running right *through* the paintings and sculpture. Michael, a psychological block preventing him from running cavalierly through the art, dodged and weaved between the pieces, giving Ginny the edge. She finally caught sight of the stairwell, looked back and saw Michael far behind, smirked to herself (a part of her wondering: what the hell are you so happy about? losing your only friend?), made for the stairs—

And suddenly stopped as she glimpsed a young male figure standing before a bizarre-looking metal sculpture, nervously studying a well-thumbed paperback on modern art, while beside him, a beautiful young woman in a black beret studied the sculpture, apparently oblivious to the young man's presence.

With a start, Ginny recognized him as her erstwhile date from the singles bar—Bruce's friend. What was his name again; Dennis? Seeing him once more, Ginny was filled with a crushing guilt, the whole embarrassing evening coming back to her. Hesitantly she approached him, wincing at the memory of the things she had said. Things like those she had said to Michael. She circled around him, wanting to say something, to apologize, but knowing that he would never hear her—and not certain, in any event, what to say.

"Ginny?"

She jumped, almost thinking that Dennis had addressed her, but it was only Michael, coming up behind her. He was out of breath and white as a sheet; there was genuine fear in his eyes as he came up and grabbed her hand, as if afraid she might otherwise run away. But Ginny found that her urge to run had vanished. "Ginny, I'm sorry," he said, panting. "I've been acting like a jerk. No—worse. I've been acting like somebody out of a Paul Mazursky movie."

She was startled but pleased. "You hate Mazursky, too?"

Michael looked contemplative. "I understand there were some remote tribes in Botswana that actually liked *Next Stop, Greenwich Village*, but fortunately, most of them have been eliminated from the gene pool."

She had to smile. "Y'know, there may be hope for you yet."

Michael's fears ebbed. "Listen," he said apologetically, "I'm not usually this bohemian. Really. It's just that I never went to any of these places 'cause I never had anyone to *go* with before, and I guess I just got a little crazed." He hesitated, then admitted, "And I guess I wanted to impress you a little, too. I'm sorry."

His eyes hungered for forgiveness, and Ginny, the memory of her past mistakes too fresh, softened quickly. "Don't worry about it," she said. On a sudden whim, she leaned over and gave him a friendly peck on the cheek. He squeezed her hand gratefully, and with that they both became self-consciously aware that they were still holding hands. Michael let go just as, a few feet away, Dennis cleared his throat to speak, causing Ginny to jump.

"It's, uh, not one of his best works, but it is interesting, isn't it?" He was addressing the young woman in the beret, who nodded almost imperceptibly; Dennis seemed to take this as a signal to continue and went on in a painfully nervous, halting voice. "Darnau can be erratic. I remember an exhibition of his at the Whitney, though. He did some remarkable things with clay that were really quite—uh—remarkable . . ."

Ginny winced, listening; Michael looked from her to Dennis and back to her. "Friend of yours?" he said.

"Not exactly," she said, circling Dennis invisibly. "I was . . . fixed up on a blind date with him. I sort of . . . hurt his feelings. Accidentally." Her eyes went opaque in a way Michael had never seen in her before. "He ran away as though he'd been bitten. Can't really blame him, I guess . . ."

Michael went to her, put a hand gently around her waist. He wanted to do more to comfort her, but it took all the nerve he had just to manage that much. He looked at the young, blond-haired man standing and talking before the sculpture. He recognized all too well the way Dennis lowered his gaze when he spoke, avoiding eye contact and, therefore, possible rejection; he winced as Dennis continued in his monologue, terrified to take his attention away from the sculpture in front of him, oblivious to the fact that the woman, obviously bored, began wandering slowly away halfway into Dennis' speech.

"I guess my favorites," Dennis was saying as though the woman were still there, "are, uh, Roszack . . . Hepworth . . ." He struggled as if recalling something from a book. ". . . uh, Manzu . . ."

Michael felt pained and embarrassed; Dennis' eyes were like mirrors, reflecting much that Michael had never wanted to see again.

"Who does he think he's talking to?" Ginny asked, puzzled.

Michael had to look away.

"Anyone who'll listen," he said.

Dennis finally turned—and saw to his horrified chagrin that the object of his monologue was gone. He turned red with embarrassment, glancing around to make sure that no one had seen him, breathing a sigh of relief when he saw that no one had. Except, of course, for Michael and Ginny.

Dennis moved off, continuing to glance behind himself furtively to make absolutely certain no one was watching, or laughing. He was not being careful about where he was going; too late he saw the slim, serious-looking young woman bustling toward the stairs. They collided amid an explosion of stationery. Michael and Ginny winced again.

A beet-red Dennis bent to recover the fallen papers. "Oh! I'm sorry! Here, let me—"

The woman also bent down, trying to gather up papers blown about by the breeze coming up the stairs. "Really, I'm fine . . . there's no need . . ."

He looked up to hand her a bunch of papers and saw her face for the first time. It wasn't a spectacular face, not what the media would even call pretty, but it was warm, open, and honest; her round-lensed glasses were slipping down the bridge of a thin nose, and her mouth was set in a tight line. It was only when she half-smiled in embarrassment that her true charm was apparent; she had a slight overbite, and when she smiled it was in a shy, rabbity sort of way that made Dennis smile in return.

That promptly made her so flustered she immediately looked away, concentrating on retrieving her papers. Dennis took this as a rebuff; he also looked away and picked up the pages, most of which were on museum stationery. "Here . . . I, uh, think you missed this . . ."

Finally they stood, and he handed the last of the pages to her. "I think this does it," he said, wishing he could think of something more to say. The woman took the papers, nodded, and smiled that same shy, strangely sexy little smile. "Thank you," she said.

"My fault," Dennis shrugged. "Better start looking where I'm going."

They stood awkwardly for another few moments, each—at least as far as Michael, watching, could tell—wanting to say something more, but neither making a move. Dennis finally started sidling away. "Well. Sorry again. G'bye."

"It's all right," the woman called after. But he was already down the stairs. She looked after him a moment, a bit wistfully it seemed to Ginny, then began ascending the stairs to the fourth-floor administrative offices.

Michael and Ginny were quiet for long moments, and then Ginny finally spoke, her tone softer, more pained than Michael had yet heard it.

"What do they call it?" she said to him. "Déjà vu?"

That evening—the last night of the year—they were drawn again to Bellevue, to watch the steady, unchanging beat of the monitors beside their inert bodies, which by now were stable enough to have been transferred to private rooms. Standing at the foot of his bed, Michael stared at his own body—the legs in casts; a respirator mask covering the swollen mouth; the skin pale, almost blue—and knew he had to get as far away as possible from this *thing* which had once been him. He had to place some distance between it and himself, as if only by so doing could he put behind the pain of his old existence. Ginny stood beside him, saying nothing, her breath on his shoulder, her presence making him feel safer and less alone than he had ever felt. She may have been a friend, and not the lover he'd always craved, but at least he would not have to face this alone, and he was grateful for her companionship.

As though reading his mind, Ginny suddenly said, "We have to get away," and Michael nodded silently. She felt it, too. As long as these bodies lay here, constant reminders of the fears and sorrows which had driven them to suicide, they would never be able to change, to grow—if that was even possible. They needed a second chance . . . and they would never have it, he knew, anywhere near these lumps of flesh. Or anywhere in New York, for that matter.

Outside, crowds gathered in the streets as the New Year approached; Michael and Ginny walked from Bellevue over to Times Square, passing absently through the throng of holiday celebrants. People laughed, shouted, drank, kissed; music played and the eyes of thousands were drawn to the ball atop the Allied Chemical Building. Michael and Ginny felt themselves getting caught up in the excitement, their pace increasing to a dash as they ran through unwary people to get a closer view of the building. Yes, he thought, a fresh start, a clean slate. The countdown began—ten, nine, eight, seven, each number repeated by thousands of spectators, thundering through the crowd—and for a moment they both felt a part of that crowd, not removed, not alone, but as though they belonged. The ball dropped. The crowd shrieked. Michael swept Ginny up in his arms and, to her astonishment, gave her a big, sloppy kiss. "Auld Lang Syne" seemed to come from everywhere at once, filling Michael and Ginny as completely as it did the rest of the mob. They parted, Ginny's smile wide and a bit dazed; she had never felt so giddy in her life. "Happy New Year, Ginny," Michael beamed. "Happy New Year, Michael," she replied, still in his arms. They held each other, not minding as the other people passed through their invisible, insubstantial forms, and Michael told her of all the places he had dreamed of going, the places he had seen in the eyes of the people at the airport, and asked her if she would go with him to see them. Now. Tomorrow. Before it was too late. Ginny took a deep breath and said yes. And, with a fleeting remembrance, hoped that auld acquaintance really could be forgot—at least for a while.

8

Michael and Ginny spent the next day and a half in their hotel room, poring over brochures borrowed from the travel desk in the lobby with barely contained anticipation. At first they could not agree on an itinerary, being for the most part at opposite ends of the world. Michael, of course, lusted to fly to one of the tropical paradises he had so long dreamed about—Tahiti, Jamaica, Hawaii, long-necked palm trees swaying in the wind, balmy weather, and coconuts filled with rum. Ginny, on the other hand, was immediately taken with pictures of places like Austria, Switzerland, Norway; their white Alpine villages nestled beneath snow-capped mountains reminded her of that Christmas long ago in Vermont. Michael agreed that they were beautiful, but argued convincingly that going from one snowbound city to another would be like traveling from Newark to Trenton for the change of pace.

Michael suggested the Caribbean; Ginny countered with Mexico. Michael pointed out the beauties of Italy and Greece; Ginny thought Japan looked kind of nice. Like union and management negotiators making slow, painful progress and concessions, they finally struck upon a compromise.

They would go everywhere.

Why not? It wasn't as though they had any more pressing commitments. Excited, they constructed an itinerary: they would fly first to Hawaii, specific island to be determined on arrival (though Michael leaned toward Maui and Ginny, Oahu). They would spend a few weeks there ("How many mai-tais can you drink, anyway?" Ginny asked, already restless) before flying on to Tahiti. From Tahiti it was a ten-hour hop to Japan, where Ginny was bound and determined to retrace Richard Chamberlain's journey in *Shōgun*, then a long, *long* flight to Athens, where, after the obligatory tour of the Acropolis and perhaps a few bus trips into the countryside, they would jump a luxury liner and enjoy a three-week cruise around the Mediterranean. Disembarking in Italy, they would take the fabled Italian trains north through Rome, Bologna, Verona and Belluno, then cross the northeastern border into Austria. They would go straight to Vienna, perhaps catching a plane in Klagenfurt, then, after a week or so in the capital city, take the train back through Salzburg and Innsbruck into Switzerland for several weeks. From Switzerland they would go to France; from France they would cross the channel to England, maybe Ireland; and, finally, they would catch a Concorde from London back to New York.

Michael estimated that, allowing for inevitable sidetrips, it would all take perhaps six, seven months. Maybe more, if they were lucky. Best of all, they did not have to make plane or hotel reservations; they could merely jump onto whatever flight they wished, transfer to the next available one heading in their direction, sleep in the best hotels in the world, and never have to worry about losing their American Express cards.

Even better—once the decision was made, they didn't have to waste precious time packing and preparing; they just *went*. It was mid-afternoon, and there was always a phalanx of taxis and limos outside the Waldorf, many bound for the airport—Michael and Ginny merely hitched a ride, invisibly, with one of them. "I can't believe we're doing this," Ginny said, very nearly giggling with excitement, as the limo pulled into traffic.

"But we are," Michael said, a tone of quiet satisfaction in his voice. "Finally. We are."

But as the limo unexpectedly missed the turn-off that would have taken them toward the Midtown Tunnel (the most direct route to the airport) and Michael heard one of the passengers make mention of picking someone up in Brooklyn, he had the uneasy feeling he knew the route the limo would instead be taking—a feeling which was uncomfortably confirmed soon enough when the towers of the

Williamsburg Bridge rose in the distance. Abruptly Michael's excitement paled; the guilt returned. He thought of the people he was leaving behind—of how, almost certainly, they were making periodic visits to Bellevue, hoping by some miracle for his comatose body to regain consciousness—and he felt a stab of conscience to think that while they grieved for a dying friend, that friend would be gallivanting all over the world, enjoying himself.

But no. Eventually, he told himself, they would stop coming. They had to. No one can grieve forever, after all; they all had their own lives, busy lives, and surely Michael could not have occupied more than a little part of those lives? No. Of course not. Eventually, they would forget about him; at least he prayed they would.

When she saw the Williamsburg looming ahead, Ginny glanced at Michael, not quite knowing what to expect; she hesitated a moment, but as the limo rolled onto the bridge and Michael's hand clenched unconsciously, Ginny put her hand gently on his, and slowly his fist opened, relaxed. He gave only a passing glance to the spot from which, only days before, he had taken his near-fatal leap . . . and in minutes, the bridge was behind them—as was Manhattan.

Ginny turned round for a last look at what had been her home for so many years. It was easier for her than for Michael, in some ways—easier to imagine that Margaret would, in time, recover from her guilt and sorrow; she always had. And she had Tony, of course; he seemed like a nice guy, better than most of Margaret's old boyfriends. She'd do fine.

And besides, Ginny told herself; she deserved this.

After twenty-four years of loneliness and pain she only occasionally admitted to, even to herself, she deserved a few months in faraway places, a few gentle snowfalls and a few tropical nights. Okay, maybe she'd never be like Maggie; maybe she'd never have a lover to go with her to the Bahamas. But she had the next best thing—a friend. And for someone who had never had many at all, that was enough. She couldn't count the times, in the last several days, she had almost said something dumb or caustic, then caught herself; she couldn't lose Michael the way she'd lost Annie, the way she'd lost all the people who had tried to be close to her. But God, it was hard! And so, rather than risk saying something that could inadvertently hurt him, she kept quiet, formulating her responses carefully, cautiously.

Was this what a "relationship" was? If so, no wonder they were so exhausting.

As the limo pulled into Kennedy, Michael's doubts were overshadowed by his excitement. He suddenly stood up in the back seat, thrusting his phantom head through the roof of the car, and grinned hugely as the car swung around the wide concourse toward the TWA terminal. "We're gonna do it, Ginny," he said, reaching down to take her hand; he pulled her up and, wobbly, she stood beside him, their heads and necks sticking out of the limo. "And you know what the best part of all is?" he asked.

"What?"

"*No baggage claim!*"

Laughing, they jumped out of the limo, raced inside the terminal, and consulted the display monitor near the check-in desk. The third line on the screen read FL 451, DEP JFK 5:04 P, ARR LAX 7:13 P, GT 23. It looked like Urdu to Ginny, but apparently it meant something to Michael, who grabbed her hand and ran with her toward the security checkpoint. "Come on," he said breathlessly, "we got three minutes before it leaves. We can catch a flight to Los Angeles, then transfer to one headed for Hawaii." They ran through the metal detectors without causing a single beep, raced along the moving sidewalk, through people and luggage with equal indifference (Ginny was almost getting used to the tingling) and up the escalator toward Gates 20 through 29.

Ginny's heart pounded and a chill ran up her spine as she realized all at once that they were actually going through with it, that in minutes she would be on a plane—only the second one she had ever been on—bound for parts unknown, with a man she had met no more than a week before! For an instant she wanted to break and run, out of the airport, back to New York, away from this madness . . . but when she thought where she could run to after that, her fear ebbed and died, and she allowed herself to be swept up in the thrill of the moment.

Michael navigated the crowds like the veteran of airports that he was. The clock read 5:02; two minutes to go. As he and Ginny ran for Gate 23, he saw a throng of travelers emerging from another gate, recognized the glow, the aura surrounding them, and with a rush of wonder and delight Michael realized that for the first time in his life, *he* would be the one leaving, instead of the one left behind.

They ran into the jetway just as the door was being shut; the door to the 747 was already closed and the jetway was being pulled away, but nothing was going to stop Michael now. Taking a deep breath and holding Ginny's hand, he vaulted the few feet between jetway and airplane and jumped right through the sealed door, into the aircraft. They landed, awkwardly, inside the first-class cabin as the flight attendants were demonstrating the use of oxygen masks to jaded businessmen who had seen it all a dozen times before.

"Michael, are you out of your *mind?*" Ginny gasped, picking herself up off the floor. "My God, we could've been—"

She caught herself, but Michael grinned, prompted, "Yes?"

Ginny grumbled and elbowed past him. "Never mind," she said. "Boy, take a guy outta his body and he turns into a regular daredevil."

She immediately headed for the coach section, but Michael held her back. "Where you going? There are plenty of seats right here."

Ginny looked aghast. "But this is first class."

"So what's the ethical difference between riding free in coach and riding free in first class?" Ginny still looked uncomfortable. Gently he added, "Ginny, c'mon. These seats would be empty regardless of whether we were here or not; we're not taking any money away from anybody." Ginny had to admit the logic in this, and soon joined him in the wide, comfortable velour seats.

In minutes the 747 was taxiing down the runway, and as it leaped into the air, Michael's soul felt as though it were soaring. God *damn*, it was really happening! He grinned like a fool, feeling giddier the

higher they climbed. Finally he would see it all—
Greece, Paris, Tahiti, the wonders of antiquity, the
beauties of the Orient; he could barely contain his
excitement.

For her part, Ginny looked around, spotted a flight
attendant handing out headsets. Her eyes popped;
adrenaline surged.

"Wonder what the movie is?" she said breathlessly.

Michael pinched the bridge of his nose, wearily.
This promised to be a very long trip.

As the plane banked over Manhattan and headed
west, Michael got up, went to an unoccupied window
seat a few rows behind, and peered down at the
landscape sliding away from them at a 45-degree
angle. The topography of New Jersey was still quite
distinct, a few wispy clouds scudding across its surface,
its western border clearly delineated by the Delaware
River. Michael had always thought it an odd-looking
state on maps, the top half resembling the head of an
old, old man, the bottom looking like the tail of a
fetus; a bizarre image, but strangely appropriate. The
beginning of life and the end of life, in one continuum,
with nothing in-between. How many relatives, how
many neighbors had Michael known whose lives had
no middle? How many family reunions had he at-
tended in which the main topic of conversation was
Uncle Freddie's new Cadillac, or cousin Lottie's new
house, or how the neighbors down the street put one
over on the IRS, how so-and-so had received a beautiful Christmas present from the Mafioso who ran the
numbers racket next door, a little thank-you for another year of polite silence? In New Jersey all the

myth-figures were named Guido. As a kid, Michael would sit in the back seat of the car as his parents pointed out houses belonging to people you never wanted to meet; they would tell stories of people who made the mistake of testifying against certain other people, only to have their remains shipped home in a Jiffy bag. The ethos was clear: Don't fuck around. Mind your own business. Settle for less. It was a state of bored housewives with bad henna jobs, of K-Marts and Korvettes, totems of cheap consumerism lining Route 46; life was merely a succession of sales at the Paramus Mall. Seeing his relatives, his old neighbors, Michael often felt a helpless anger, a conviction that life was not supposed to *be* this way, that somewhere along the path of eons a terrible turn had been made, and somewhere, in some alternate time, the true road still lay.

But even worse: his anger was mixed with a fierce, bitter envy. They came in pairs, most of them, the traditional American dyad, and even if their eyes were sometimes blank, and if at odd moments one could see the pain and bafflement in their faces, like shadows crossing the moon, they had still found something which had eluded Michael. Who the hell was he to judge them, anyway? He was alone; had always been alone, would probably always *be* alone. They, for all their dwindling horizons, had had no trouble fathoming the strange tribal courtship rites which had always baffled Michael. Perhaps he was the stupid one. Perhaps he had taken the wrong road. If so, how did you get back? How did you return to the turning point, how did you find your way?

Perhaps, he thought, by making a new turning

point. Like this. New Jersey disappeared beneath a blanket of cumulus and Michael turned from the window. A chapter of his life had closed; the rest of the world awaited.

He leaned back and suddenly realized how sleepy he was. It had been an exhausting week. He closed his eyes—and immediately, inexplicably, felt drained. His arms were leaden; suddenly he could barely raise them. He was even finding it difficult to breathe. What the hell was happening? He forced himself awake, leaned forward to grab onto the seat in front of him for support.

His hand went right through the back of the seat. He concentrated, trying to will his hand solid, but with each attempt his fingers merely sank into the fabric of the seat.

He stood, and nearly dropped from dizziness; he had never felt this weak in his *life*. He looked around for Ginny, saw her emerging from the aft lavatories. She looked about as terrible as Michael felt; wan, pale, unsteady on her feet. She wobbled down the aisle toward him, trying to brace herself on the seats as she walked, but, like Michael, failing as her hands passed through them. There was fear in her eyes. But that was not the worst of it.

With horror, Michael realized that the FASTEN SEAT BELTS sign at the aft of the cabin was shining right *through* Ginny's astral form. With each step she was becoming more and more . . . *translucent*.

Michael looked down at his own body and moaned as he saw the plush red carpeting clearly visible through his feet. Panic gripped him. He looked up at Ginny.

Ginny had stopped a few yards away and was staring at him, horrified and confused. "Michael—what—"

"I don't know," he said, terrified. "Something's—"

It all happened fairly quickly after that.

One moment, Ginny was standing in the aisle, sunlight streaming through her body, her features fading, like a figure etched on glass.

The next moment, she was hurtling away from Michael, her eyes wide with terror, her arms outstretched—and in seconds she had been wrenched through the hull and out of the aircraft.

Michael screamed. He tried to run after her, but his feet could not gain any traction on the floor; for half a second he seemed to float helplessly, and then the G-forces of the plane's flight ceased to have any effect at all on him. He felt as though he were rocketing back through the plane, but he knew that *he* was merely standing still and the plane, traveling at nearly six hundred miles an hour, was simply flying right through him. In moments the plane was gone and he was surrounded by blue sky and, far below, thick clouds. He was tumbling, head over heels, with no control and no guidance; weak, dizzy, he watched the earth roll first below him, then above, then below again. The roar of the wind filled his ears.

He extended his arms, hoping to gain some sort of balance, but all it did was make him tumble more slowly. In the distance, he suddenly saw Ginny—a lost, terrified figure falling away from him, hands and feet splayed in all directions—and he screamed, more for being separated from her than for his dizzying fall.

To Ginny, Michael was a small, blurry figure cartwheeling against clouds. She felt as though she were shrinking, falling, *dying*; the farther the plane had flown, the weaker she had become, and now she felt stripped of what little life had remained to her. Panic welled up inside her, but seeing Michael extend his arms gave her an idea. She fought back her fear, extended her arms and jackknifed her legs, like a skydiver. She knew the winds wouldn't have any effect on her, not really, but maybe she could fool her subconscious into thinking it would work.

She imagined an updraft buoying her up, catching her torso and lifting it up to Michael's level, a hundred feet or so above. To her astonished delight, she bobbed up—not by much, but some. He seemed closer. She twisted her body, picturing herself as a leaf carried on the top of a storm. She shot up, then over about three yards, then up again. She laughed, looked at her outstretched arms. They even seemed to be getting less transparent!

Michael saw what she was doing and immediately followed suit. He hit a downdraft, let it carry him to Ginny's level, but he undershot and wound up below her. He shut his eyes, imagining himself on Waikiki Beach, in the water. What did they call it, "body-surfing"? Yes, that would do. He opened his eyes, waited for the wave to roll in behind him, then hit it at its crest and let it deposit him next to the wave Ginny was riding.

They were level with one another now, calling out to each other. Ginny caught an updraft from the east,

Michael rode a seven-footer toward shore; they met somewhere in the middle of their metaphors. Their arms flailed; their fingers clawed at the air—

Their hands locked.

They laughed triumphantly, fingers entwined more tightly than they had held anything before in their lives. The ground was still almost twenty thousand feet below; it was far from over, and neither knew what would happen when they hit, but at least they were not alone. They couldn't hear one another over the rush of the wind, so they communicated non-verbally, Michael twisting his body when he wanted to catch a "wave," Ginny bending to complement him, and vice versa.

Then, at nineteen thousand feet, the sky vanished.

Just like that; one minute it was there, the next they were inside another plane, a small one this time, sitting side-by-side in two rear seats, hands still locked. The plane was a Piper Cub, and it was plummeting fast, nose pointed straight for the ground; Michael and Ginny could feel tremendous G-forces tugging at them, which moments before had seemed impossible. In the forward section a small child was screaming, a woman holding her while screaming herself. A man struggled at the controls, weeping, moaning, trying to pull the craft out of its dive; the cabin filled with a shrieking death-whistle as air buffeted the fragile hull.

Suddenly the nose of the plane exploded in a shower of flame and the cockpit window burst inwards. The man screamed, grabbed his head as a shard of glass sliced off half his face. The woman tried to shield the child with her own body, but as she lunged

toward the girl she fell against the starboard door—
which, weakened by the explosion, flew open. The
woman fell screaming from the plane. The little girl
screamed for her mother just instants before she was
decapitated by a pinwheeling fragment of glass. The
man, fighting gravity, turned round in his seat, virtually faceless, his blood streaming back into the cabin,
and clawed blindly about for his wife and child—
then he, too, was sucked out the starboard side. Only
the headless body of the child remained, pinned under a seat, trembling in the buffeting winds as though
weeping.

Michael and Ginny held on to each other, numb
with horror, unable to even think, as the hull broke
apart and the ground came spinning up . . .

. . . and they were floating again, lower than before,
but still falling at an angle to the ground, all trace of
the nightmare cabin suddenly, miraculously gone.
They looked at each other, tears streaming down
their faces, not knowing what was happening, wishing it would stop, knowing somehow that it would
not.

The dull roar of the wind was slowly supplanted
by a susurrus of voices, whispers, murmurs, all at
odds with one another, not a conversation but a
convocation, evoking a kaleidoscope of emotions in
Michael and Ginny; they seemed to *feel* the voices as
much as hear them. The faces came next, shadows of
all those who had ever passed this way, in plane or
glider or balloon—all those who had even known
anger, or fear, or envy, or love, or kindness, and had
left a little bit of it behind:

An elderly couple in a 747 passed by, filled with

anticipation at seeing their only son, now living in San Francisco; remembering the way he would cry as an infant, the days he would come home stiff-lipped and bloodied from fights with the class bully, the nights of flu and bad dreams. Ginny felt their love and their longing as they drifted past, and then they were gone. A beautiful woman in a Boeing 707 passed next, her long hair dyed platinum in the style of the 1950s, her ample body wrapped in cashmere and silk, but all Michael could feel from her was anger, and bitterness, and regret, for that was all she had felt at that moment, in this place, all she had left behind. A barnstorming pilot swung his Jenny past in a barrel-roll, all laughter and brash confidence, delighting in his freedom and in the awe of the yokels who stared up from the ground; he did another couple of loops, then roared away, tipping his wings in a salute as he went . . .

Three people in a brilliantly colored hot-air balloon floated into Ginny's field of vision, a pilot and his two passengers, a honeymooning couple gazing serenely down at the sloping farmland below. As they drew closer, Ginny felt their love, their hope, their faith in the future and their devotion to each other, more real and more beautiful than anything Ginny had known, and tears came to her eyes; she had never known it could be like this, didn't *want* to know. Go *away*, she wanted to scream, leave me *alone*. It only hurts more when you know what it's like, go away, go *away!* But the balloon, having no propulsion, drifted at a snail's pace across the sky, coming, it seemed, within a foot of her; the young couple laughed and held each other, and Ginny could

feel the warmth of their bodies touching one another,
the smell of the man's cologne as he kissed the
woman's cheek, the tingling in their groins, and the
raw, impossible desire to hold this moment forever.
Or was it impossible? They were still here, weren't
they, God knew how many years later . . . ?

Ginny was sobbing, unable to blot out the love and
contentment, unable to deny how much she wanted
it; Michael ached for her, feeling many of the same
things, though more concerned for Ginny's pain than his
own. His grip on her hand tightened—it was all he
could do—but she did not look up; he had no idea if
he was even getting through.

They passed through a thick cloud cover and for a
minute he could not see Ginny, knew that she was
there only by the touch of her hand. When they broke
through the clouds, they were falling at a 40-degree
angle to the east, picking up speed; the farther east
they fell, the stronger they felt and the less translucent their bodies became. Ginny's sorrow ebbed as
she saw that they were dropping faster toward the
ground; bare, wintry farmfields lay in checkerboard
patterns below them. She looked at Michael, managed a smile; he returned it, relieved that she was all
right. Their speed increased. The farm fields grew
larger, closer, frighteningly close. Their arms and
legs began to feel heavy—the ground loomed dizzyingly and they took deep breaths, hands still locked,
preparing themselves for impact. At a height of about
twelve feet, their transparent bodies turned opaque,
gravity grabbed hold with a vengeance (or seemed
to), and they plummeted into a wide, snow-covered
wheatfield, the snowdrifts flattening upon impact,
breaking their fall with a soft, welcome whisper.

9

There was, of course, no pain, but both Michael and Ginny were more than a little stunned by the impact; they lay a few yards apart on the snow-covered ground and wondered if it was all over, or if there were further nightmares to come. Overhead, crows circled and cawed, alighting on lonely phone lines; from somewhere else came the distant moan of a train whistle, growing fainter by the moment; the only other sound was the insistent barking of a dog, seemingly miles away. Michael propped himself up on one elbow, cautiously. Perhaps it was over, after all. Ginny sat up groggily, looking pale and shaken; Michael got to his feet immediately and began helping her up. "Ginny, you okay?"

She tried to dismiss the emotions still raging within her with a joke. "I'll tell you right now, Michael, I've had better vacations."

"I felt so helpless up there," Michael went on, as Ginny got unsteadily to her feet. "You seemed like you were in such pain—"

"I'd rather not talk about it if you don't mind, okay, Michael?" Her voice was sharper than she had intended.

"Ginny, we've *got* to talk about it," Michael insisted. "Do you realize what happened up there? We were picking up on some kind of . . . psychic residue! Do you understand how incredible that is?"

"You sound like you *liked* it," Ginny said with horror. She shivered at the memory of the crashing plane, the headless body of the small child pinned beneath the seat, the blood streaming back into the cabin. "That poor family, Michael! That little girl . . ."

Michael put a hand on her arm. "They died a long time ago, Ginny," he said, gently. "I know how you feel. It's just that . . . I can't help it, there's something exciting about the idea of catching the past in your hands, looking back into—"

Ginny began marching out of the wheatfield; she did not want to hear this. "For you, maybe," she said, her astral form passing effortlessly through the snowbanks. "Me, I never want to go through that again."

Michael sighed and followed her. Beyond the wheatfield was a small unpaved road; about a mile beyond that, a bright red silo and farmhouse sat placidly on the horizon. There were no sounds save for the crows, the dog's barking (from the farmhouse?), and the rustle of wheatstalks as Michael, willing himself "solid," pushed aside the stalks in his path, relieved that he could do so again.

Ginny sat at the edge of the road, feeling drained. Worse than the memory of the crashing plane was the lingering dream of love, passion, and longing she had seen/heard/felt; she tried to shut it out, tried to focus on other things, but the feelings would not go away, not entirely, and fearfully she realized that somehow things would never be the same for her again. *Damn* it . . .

Michael sat down beside her and idly began skipping pebbles across the road. "So this is the country," he mused, squinting into the distance. "Looks a lot like it does on television, doesn't it?"

"You're avoiding talking about it, aren't you?" Ginny said suddenly.

"Talking about what?" Michael said, heart starting to flutter.

"Why we fell out of that plane."

"Oh, that." Michael didn't consciously try to lie; he just didn't want to face the truth. "Nothing . . . mysterious about it. The plane banked, the line of acceleration shifted, we were pulled out the side. That's all."

Ginny fixed him with a knowing, accusatory stare that nearly made Michael flush.

"We were fading *away*, Michael," she said as gently as she could manage. "The further we got from New York—"

"No—" Michael began, suddenly frightened.

"—the further we got from our *bodies*—"

"*No!*"

"*Yes*. Michael, I'm sorry, but we can't kid ourselves any longer! God knows we've done enough of that already." She paused only a moment to wonder out of whose mouth that last remark had come, then went on, "The further we got from our bodies . . . our *real* bodies . . . the weaker we got! We would've faded away completely, I'll bet, if we hadn't gotten so weak our subconscious minds couldn't keep the illusion of gravity!"

"Where the hell," Michael snapped, "did you get all *that* crap from?"

"From you," Ginny countered, unyielding. "Remember? *You* told me all about your theories on gravity . . . how we 'allowed' it to affect us—"

Michael jumped to his feet, feeling combative, defensive, unwilling to lose his one last hope. "Then why the hell are we still *here*, goddammit? Why didn't we just hit the air like a couple of soap bubbles and go *pop?*"

Ginny considered that a moment, then answered calmly, "Because we floated back, toward the east. Toward New York. The further back we drifted, the stronger we got. Remember?"

Michael's hands balled into fists. Damn it—her logic was painfully cogent. He started pacing anxiously, up and down the dusty unpaved road; he could not bring himself to look at Ginny. Damn her, he thought. Damn her for being right. His joke of several weeks ago came back to mock him: Styx, indeed. Yes, Dante would have approved of this. There were circles of hell, after all, proscribed not according to sin or crime, but by the simple mortal demarcations of

state and borough. And he, he had ventured out
beyond the last circle and been cast back, and now
all he could do was return to the first circle, and
accept his fate.

And all the places he had never seen in life, he
would never see now, either. Tahiti, Japan, Hawaii,
they would all remain dreams to him—rumors carried
back to the damned. And those faces up there, alive
after all these years with love and hate and passion
and pain, were they also the faces of the damned? Or
just another of the tortures of hell, designed to remind him of all the things he had never known, and
would never know, not in this life nor in any other?

"Michael?" Ginny was looking at him worriedly.
"Are you all right?"

Michael stood there, his anger fading to a sullen
resignation. "Yeah, sure," he said. His hands were
no longer balled into fists and he suddenly could not
think what to do with them. They hung at his sides,
awkward and impotent.

Ginny approached, put a tentative hand gently to
his arm. "I'm sorry, Michael. I know how much it
meant to you." A moment, then: "Where do we go
now?"

Michael sighed. "Well, assuming that there's some
kind of safe radius within which we can travel, we
could probably go to Philadelphia . . . New Jersey
. . . upstate New York, maybe as far as Syracuse
. . . Connecticut, Rhode Island . . ."

Ginny was less than enthusiastic. "Not exactly the
Virgin Islands, are they?"

"Not exactly, no." Michael frowned, resigned himself to the inevitable. ''We might as well go back to Manhattan.''

The sun behind them, they struck up the lonely, unpaved road, heading due east—back to the city, their bodies, their pasts, everything they had hoped, in a moment of perhaps foolish excitement, to deny.

The farmland was serene, rolling, and unchanging, with only an occasional farmhouse or silo disrupting the peaceful rural landscape. It was very pretty for the first ten or fifteen minutes; thereafter, merely redundant. Occasionally a car or pick-up would rattle past, spitting up stones and pebbles which would bounce right through the two astral travelers trudging up the side of the road; Michael would sporadically attempt to run after one of the trucks and jump into it, but Ginny couldn't quite keep apace and he would have to fall back, breathless. ''Are you sure,'' Ginny would say, gasping, ''that this is how Gable and Colbert got started?''

At their first glimpse of macadam, they wanted to shout for joy. The horse-and-buggy road intersected with a real, honest-to-god four-lane highway—Route 76, according to the first sign they came upon. Ten-ton semis roared past, cars and vans and campers whipping up winds hot enough and fierce enough to have made Michael blink, had he been able to feel the wind at all. He finally began to realize what Ginny had meant about not feeling anything. Walking along the shoulder of the road, he expected to feel a trembling in the pit of his stomach as trucks thundered by a few yards away; but instead he felt nothing. He expected the gusts of wind from their

passing to knock him off-balance, but they did not;
he walked forward easily, without swaying. He did
not exist in the human world, he realized, and the
fact that it had taken him this long to realize it . . .
the fact that it had not seemed so very different from
his life *before* . . . made him wonder just how long
he had not been a part of that world.

They stopped at a Shell station, "borrowing" a
few quarters from the cash register to get a couple of
Orange Crushes from the soda machine. They drank
them inside the garage, careful to keep to a corner
cluttered with machinery and tools; against such a
backdrop it was less likely that anyone would notice
a pair of aluminum cans bobbing in the air by
themselves.

It was ten minutes before a large enough truck
pulled into the service station; as it gassed up, Michael and Ginny hopped in back and within minutes
were heading east on what they soon learned was
also known as the Pennsylvania Turnpike. The hours
dragged by, the scenery providing a numbing sameness;
afternoon slid into dusk, and Michael and Ginny
dozed. They woke with a start as the truck swung
around a curve; Ginny, heretofore curled up on the
floor, skidded sideways and nearly fell out of the
truck, her phantom limbs passing through the side-
wall until Michael grabbed her and pulled her back
in.

Poking his head out, Michael noted with alarm that
they were heading off the turnpike, taking the Mor-
gantown exit toward Route 23 West—away from
New York. The two spirits promptly jumped ship,
tumbling out the back, rolling ass-over-teakettle over

the concrete road. Again, Michael felt nothing, not a twinge of pain—just a sensation of pressure, an awareness of being jolted. It was starting to scare him; he longed for an ache, a bruise, a muscle spasm, *anything*.

They picked themselves up off the ground, Ginny brushing herself off more out of habit than necessity, as no dust could cling to them anyway. "Well," she said. "Where to now?"

Michael looked around. It was getting dark. About half a mile down the turnpike he saw the familiar orange roof of a Howard Johnson's Motor Lodge. He turned to Ginny, shrugged. "What do you think? You want to crash for the night?"

Ginny glanced at the orange roof, made a sour face. "Okay," she sighed, "as long as I don't have to eat the fried clams."

It was a far cry from the Waldorf. There was an empty double in the wing of the motel closest to the turnpike—entering, Michael and Ginny could hear the muted roar of cars drumming past less than a hundred yards away. The walls were bright green with a pattern of white-silhouetted trees, with matching bedspreads; the curtains on the single window were made of something with the same general texture as burlap, and the shag rugs (also green) looked as though they had been sheared off a dozen unlucky mops.

"Well," Michael said.

"Well," Ginny agreed.

"You, uh, want to get something to eat in the coffee shop?"

"Not especially," Ginny said. "I mean, it all tastes like cotton anyway, so what's the point?"

"Yeah. I suppose." Michael felt even more depressed than before, then realized that the Dayglo wallpaper was not helping. "Listen, why don't we go out and sit by the pool for a while?"

"In the middle of winter?"

"Yeah, but it's summer in Rio."

The pool, in the middle of the motel complex, lay empty and covered with a plastic tarpaulin; even the deck chairs and chaise longues were gone, locked away until spring. Michael and Ginny sat on the edge of the pool, feet sinking right through the tarp; it billowed softly as the wind moaned between the buildings. Something in that plaintive wail made Ginny smile, remembering Vermont and the way the wind shook the treetops, making music in the rustle of dry branches.

Michael noticed her smile. "Something funny?" he asked.

"Not exactly." She hesitated, wondering for a moment whether she should say anything; she had never told anyone about Vermont, not even Annie. But Michael was looking at her expectantly, and before she even realized it she was saying, "I was just thinking about my grandparents. About this place in Vermont they used to have."

Michael cocked his head. "Really? I hear it's beautiful up there."

"Oh, it is. Very . . . beautiful." Eyes shining, Ginny began to recount the details of her Christmas in New England, describing the smell of sauerbraten in *Nonna*'s kitchen on Sunday afternoons, the way the light made the frosted windows look like crystal, the sound of *Nonno*'s snowplow as it cut a path from their door to the narrow, winding road from town. She stumbled a bit in the telling, hesitating as she searched for words, but she didn't care, her excitement building as she spoke, and for a few minutes she almost forgot where she was, almost could imagine that that narrow, winding road was just outside, and that Vermont was not nearly as distant as it was.

Michael listened, pleased that she would share something so obviously dear to her with him, amazed at the way this diffident, halting young woman suddenly became so articulate in her evocation of another time, the tender way she had taken one moment out of her past and held it up to the light to show him. He wished that he had something equally treasured to share with her, but try as he might, he could not think of a time or a place that had ever made him as happy as Ginny's Christmas had made her. Shame and regret filled him; he suddenly felt inadequate, inferior. He realized that he had been thinking of Ginny as someone whose life had been even sadder than his own; he realized now that he had been a fool for thinking such a thing.

When she had finished, Ginny felt suddenly embarrassed at having talked so much, but Michael was smiling, looking at her somehow differently. "That's lovely," he said, and Ginny almost believed that he meant it. "Did you ever go back?"

Ginny shook her head.

"Didn't you want to?" he said.

"Of course I did. But *Nonno* and *Nonna* died a few years later, and . . . well, it wouldn't have been the same, going by myself. No matter how beautiful a place is, it's just another place unless you've got somebody there who . . . well . . . you know.''

Michael nodded. They lapsed into silence a moment, the tarp billowing below them, when Ginny suddenly spoke up: "That's what I don't understand, Michael," she said, and there was something in her tone which made Michael uneasy. "I mean, you had friends. You had lots of friends. Why did you do it?''

Michael considered carefully, trying to find a way to put it into words; perhaps this could be the thing he could share with her, and he wanted to get it right. Finally:

"Ginny," he said, tentatively, "having friends is wonderful, it's what kept me going as long as I did, and in a rational world, maybe that would be enough. But in this society, you're told from the day you're old enough to walk that you won't *really* be *happy* until you're part of a couple. One writer called it 'the eternal bliss machine'—the idea that all your problems, all your neuroses will just sort of melt away once you get married. I mean, my God, being part of a couple can be wonderful, sure, but the divorce rate alone should prove it's not Nirvana . . . yet we still go on, drumming it into our children's heads that it is, raising expectations and sowing desperation in the unlucky ones who *haven't* found anyone yet.''

He hesitated a moment, wondering how much he should say, how much he could share, then pushed aside his fears and went on. "I . . . I was a virgin until I was twenty-five years old, you know? And I felt like a freak. Like I wasn't a real human being at all. I shouldn't have felt that way, Ginny! I shouldn't have been *made* to feel as though all my thoughts, all my feelings, all my virtues were somehow invalid just because I'd never been to bed with a woman!

"Have you ever noticed . . . when people use the word 'love' . . . it's almost always 'love' as in *lovers?* I've loved a lot of people in my life, Ginny: I loved my parents, I loved my friends, but it's almost like that's not considered *real* love, you know? *Real* love is between a man and a woman, and not just platonic love, either; it's got to be romantic, sexual. My God, we've done more to devalue the word than any society in history."

Ginny was listening quietly, Michael's words and emotions all too familiar to her, a little bit amazed that someone had felt the same longings and frustration she had, and more than a little relieved that she had not been alone in them. Still, there was one difference. "You . . . did find somebody, though," she said softly. "You didn't feel like a . . . freak anymore."

Michael flushed with embarrassment, remembering. He didn't want to go on, but knew he had to.

"What I found," he said, very slowly, "was a prostitute with the good grace not to laugh at my fumbling. I was just so damn desperate to get rid of it, I didn't care how. And there's nothing wrong with going to a hooker, except that if you're insecure to begin with, it doesn't help thinking that the only way someone will make love to you is if you . . . if you pay them."

He shut his eyes to hold back the tears. Damn it, why had he started this? He didn't need to dredge all this up again. Ginny reached out and squeezed his hand, wishing she could do something more, but afraid he might interpret it as an act of pity. But Michael composed himself quickly; he stood, feigning a smile and a heartiness that he did not really feel.

"Well," he said. "I don't know how we got off on that, but . . ." He gave Ginny a hand up. "Getting late, I guess. Back to our little grass shack on the turnpike."

"Michael?" She stopped, looked at him with big eyes, voice small and uncertain. "You know, I . . . I've never talked to anyone like I've talked to you. It's kind of scary, you know?" A pause. "Right now I feel like a piece of china . . . like if you dropped me, I'd break, and I'd never ever get back together."

She suddenly smiled, filled with a warm glow. "But I know you won't drop me," she said quietly. "I *know*. And you have no idea how *good* that feels."

Filled with the same warm glow, Michael put his arm around her, and wordlessly they headed back to their motel room, where they went to their separate beds, each uncertain as to the other's feelings, neither wishing to risk shattering a valued friendship by making an overture. With a trace of disappointment, Ginny assumed that Michael wanted her as a friend, nothing more—why else all that talk about the value of platonic love?—and he assumed the same about her. Within minutes Ginny was sound asleep and Michael was staring pensively at the ceiling. His eyes closed slowly. He drifted in a kind of meditation for a long time, thinking again of the things he had seen in the sky—the plane, the balloon, the feelings. Warm

air escaped, sighing, from the heating ducts above
the bed; Michael listened, letting the sound lull him
deeper into his meditation.

Slowly, however, the sighing seemed to become
louder, and then Michael became aware, behind shut
eyelids, of other sounds growing out of the first—a
sudden intake of breath, a sudden release, a moan, an
inchoate cry, half a word lost in a swallow of air, the
slap of flesh against flesh, a wet, sucking sound.
Michael opened his eyes to find a man and a woman
making love next to him, oblivious to his presence.
They spoke in passionate whispers, the man gently
caressing the woman's breasts, the woman licking
the inside of his ear; the man kissed her breasts, then
her stomach, moving slowly down to her vagina. The
woman grabbed the man's head as his tongue began
massaging her clitoris and her hips began to move.
Michael watched, flushing with embarrassment; had
someone taken the room during the night? How could
they have entered without him hearing them? He
started to slide off the bed when he noticed that
despite the couple's activity, the mattress was not
moving by even a quarter of an inch, not even
trembling under the furious rhythm.

As soon as he realized what he was seeing—as
soon as his immense relief upset the meditative state
he had fallen into—the shadows dimmed and vanished.
The man and woman were gone, the bed unruffled.
They had been no more real than the images he had
seen/heard/felt in the sky that day.

And yet they *were* real, more real than anything in
Michael's own vapid life. He lay back down on the
bed, careful not to fall back into that meditative state

again. That was it, obviously; when they had been falling from the plane they had been weak, more receptive to the psychic impressions left behind by others, and that same state could apparently be recreated through pensiveness, meditation. Now he knew why Ginny wanted nothing more to do with this. He turned on his side, buried his face in his pillow, and tried not to think, seeking only the oblivion of sleep. But the mermaids, the goddamned bloody mermaids were singing louder than ever, and try as he may, he could not blot out their song.

The next morning they caught a ride with a moving van bound for Pompton Lakes, New Jersey, and soon enough were heading east once more on Route 76. Seated invisibly in the cab beside a balding driver, they watched as they passed through Philadelphia, crossed the Delaware River, and began heading north on the New Jersey Turnpike.

The ride was about as depressing as Michael had expected; were the earth to be engulfed tomorrow by nuclear holocaust, it would not, he thought, make much difference one way or the other in Central Jersey. Huge oil drums lined either side of the turnpike, the tanks' burnoff producing a foul, oppressive stench somewhere between the reek of ozone and an immense, lingering fart. Electrical towers straddled the dry, flat land, like robot sentries guarding the oil drums; the driver of a car passing in the shadow of these sentinels could not help but feel like an intruder, for clearly this place did not exist for human beings, but for the giant tools and machines of mankind, a kind of Brobdingnag of iron and oil.

It improved only slightly the further north they drove, the bombed-out landscape giving way to a more commercial sort of desolation, diners and motels and carpet stores all crammed side-by-side off the highway, as though they had not been built there as much as they had simply metastisized. These were the sights and scenes of Michael's youth, and seeing them again filled him with an odd mix of feelings, at both queasy and nostalgic; Ginny, however, was seeing all this for the first time. Michael noted her expression of amazement and horror, and couldn't help but smile. "Welcome," he said brightly, "to the Garden State."

But even Michael had to acknowledge that this was just a part of the state, and within half an hour they were passing through some pleasant suburban towns—and as he watched communities with names like Nutley, Montclair, Belleville, and Bloomfield roll past, he was lulled into a feeling of benign nostalgia. It wasn't until he saw the sign reading WILBURN, 3 MI that he suddenly sat bolt upright, filled with a cold dread at what lay three miles ahead.

"Michael?" Ginny looked at him with concern. "Something wrong?"

He tried to relax. This was silly. It was just a *town*. "No. Nothing wrong," he said to Ginny. "Just a bit startled. Didn't think we'd be taking this route." He nodded outside. "This town we're coming to—I lived there for five years. Went to high school there." He smiled sourly. "Nothing I want to press into the old book of memories, believe me."

Wilburn was a small community, a little over seven thousand in population, a town which for young people was virtually bereft of entertainment—with not so much as a single movie theater, even. Michael remembered how the local teenagers would congregate, out of boredom, in the parking lot of the McDonald's franchise—whereupon the local cops, also out of boredom, would duly disperse them, as though, over Big Macs and fries, they were plotting the violent overthrow of the United States government. Some would find relief from the unrelenting tedium of the town in things like pot, sex, and beer; Michael found his surcease in music, books, and television. To this day, he was not certain he had made the right choice.

Now, as the truck headed up Drummond Avenue into the heart of downtown Wilburn—a quiet commercial street with absolutely nothing sinister or forbidding about it—Michael felt increasingly pensive and depressed. They passed the bakery where you could buy the best black-and-white vanilla-cake cookies in town; the tiny record store which Michael had haunted as a teenager, buying up used copies of classical, jazz, folk, and soundtrack albums; and as he remembered, as his eyes glazed over with memories both good and bad, he began to think he was actually *back* here in every sense of the word—as though he had actually traveled back in time fifteen, twenty years; as though it might all be done over again, done *right* this time, with none of the mistakes, none of the wrong turns . . .

And it was then that he saw Karen.

She was walking down the street, books held to her chest, and she was still fifteen years old. Michael's breath left him. He reacted instinctively, without thinking, the lost opportunities of a lifetime ago seizing hold of him; he jumped out of the truck, right through the door of the cab, as it slowed for a light, and he began running after her.

"Karen! Karen!"

Ginny screamed after him as he leaped from the truck, but he did not stop. Without a moment's hesitation she leaped out after him, pursuing him as he ran down the street chasing—what? There was no one there; no one at all.

"Michael! *Michael!*"

Michael did not hear her. He heard only the pounding of his heart, saw only Karen's retreating figure as she headed down Drummond Avenue toward Wilburn Junior High. Her short brown hair looked as smooth, as soft as it always had—so soft he had to touch it, touch it as he never had in real life, in that *other* life, the one he would soon put right—

"Karen, it's me, Michael, Michael Barr—"

He caught up to her, reached out to tap her on the shoulder, his hand brushing close to her hair—

His hand passed right *through* her . . . and Karen popped out of existence like a soap bubble.

Michael stopped short, stunned, horrified . . . and then slowly realized what had happened, what he had just seen. More shadows. But, this time, familiar shadows. Ginny, huffing and puffing, came trotting up behind him, and suddenly he felt like a fool. "Michael, are you okay? What *happened?*"

Michael stared down the empty street. "I . . . I just thought I saw someone I used to know."

A chill ran down Ginny's spine; somehow, she knew exactly what he meant. She touched his arm, anxious to get him the hell out of here. "Come on.

There's a diner up the street with a lot of trucks in front. Maybe we can catch another—''

"Not . . . yet, Ginny. Okay?" He looked around him, at the stores, at the houses, at the people passing by. It was just a street, for God's sake, a typical small-town New Jersey street, and yet it evoked in him a volley of emotions ranging from fear to anger to regret. And it shouldn't have. He should've put this past him years ago; should've moved on to other things. But in a very real way he had never left this town, had never really put it behind him . . . and until he did, he knew, nothing would ever change.

Suddenly he knew what he had to do. He began walking down Drummond toward the now-closed-down red-brick building that used to be Wilburn Junior High, before the new, modern school had been built over on Lefcourt Road.

"Michael? Where are we going?"

"You don't have to come along, Ginny. I'll only be a . . . a few minutes."

"Where else am I going to go?" There was something in his voice, in his eyes, that worried her; she wasn't about to leave him alone. She followed him to the now-deserted school, its chain-link fence rusted and broken, its yard overgrown with weeds; Michael stood and looked out at that schoolyard, remembering how it looked fifteen years before . . . remembering the dust as it flew up during softball games, remembering the barking voice of the gym coach, remembering even the voices of his gymmates—

"Jesus, Barrett, can't you do *anything* right?" Suddenly, the schoolyard was alive again with teenage boys in gym clothes, with hoots and hollers and derisive sneers, with the piercing sound of Mr. Bockman's whistle as he gave it a short, shrill blast. A fly ball had just arced over the outfield and one of the boys, despite a leap at the ball, had missed it; now it bounced off the ground, quickly recovered by another outfielder, as the boy's teammates shook their heads in quiet disgust at the offending player.

The boy was skinny, uncoordinated, and looked as though he would rather be anywhere in the world—up to and including the base of an active volcano—than here. The boy was Michael, and looking at him standing there—arms hanging at his sides, shifting nervously from foot to foot—his older self wished he could communicate to him the fact that no matter how dismal and painful these days were, they would, in fact, *end*. No matter how many block-headed gym teachers would try to force him into competitive sports for which he had only disdain and contempt . . . no matter how much embarrassment he was forced to shoulder . . . it would pass.

"Michael?"

Ginny's voice broke the pensive meditation which allowed Michael to see the shadows in the schoolyard; he turned, continued on down the street. "Just one more stop, Ginny," he said, tonelessly . . .

They stopped again before a modest, two-storey frame house on a quiet sidestreet. The house was a different color than Michael remembered it—dark brown instead of leafy green—and the fence around it was new, but it was essentially the same house Michael had known years ago. His astral form passed through the wooden gate, into the front yard, and Ginny paced him as they circled round the house.

"I used to live here," Michael said quietly. "Lived here longer than any other place, as a matter of fact—about six years. Seems like we were always bouncing around from one town to another. My father was a salesman, with Xerox. We moved around a lot."

Ginny looked around at the backyard, replete with tool shed, jungle gym, and a set of swings, and her eyes widened. "Wow," she said. "When I was a kid it was a big deal if we could ride our bikes on Arthur Avenue on Sundays. You had all this room?"

"Yeah, plus a brook and some woods in back."

"Boy. Not bad."

No, he wanted to say, it wasn't bad. Not really. It just seemed like it at the time, and for some reason he had never let go of that, had allowed it to color his life in ways it never should have. He moved to a first-floor window, raised himself up on tiptoes and looked inside: it was a warmly furnished den, all mahogany and dark carpeting. But a long time ago it had been different. Michael shut his eyes, blanking out all awareness of his surroundings but for this room and the memories it evoked: the whisper of the brook behind him, waters caressing the mossy stones he had once straddled; the raspy sound of his $10.95 record player as it played over and over the favorite 45s of his adolescence; and when he opened his eyes, the alien den was now a familiar bedroom, messy as usual, books and records strewn all over the floor, a portable TV set at the foot of the bed. Scanning the bookshelves, Michael felt a pang of pleasure; as his gaze moved toward the bed, he felt a sudden rush of embarrassment.

On the bed sat a teenage boy, his pants rolled down to his knees, his hand grasping his penis; before him on the bed was a magazine. Michael felt mortified, not just at what the young boy was doing, but at the fact that even now, fifteen years later, Michael actually recognized the magazine, knew in fact what was on every page.

The boy pumped harder, and Michael, watching, wanted to break away, to run the hell *out* of there, but he couldn't take his eyes away; mixed with his shame he felt sorrow, pity for this poor kid living in borrowed dreams. For an instant, Michael forgot that the boy was himself—and the revelation struck him like a thunderclap.

That's not me any longer, he slowly realized. I'm not that kid anymore; I'm an entirely different person! Maybe not perfect, maybe not even close, but . . . *different*.

Just then the bedroom door—fortunately located up a small corridor, out of direct line-of-sight of the bed—opened, and a woman's voice called out. The boy desperately fumbled with his pants, pulling them up barely in time as he simultaneously tossed the magazine into a pile on the floor. The woman entered the room. "Michael, supper's ready. What do you want to drink? Milk, juice, soda?"

"Mom, I've told you a dozen times," the boy implored, "*knock* first, will you? *God*."

"Sorry. Didn't know you were entertaining royalty or anything. Milk okay?"

"Yeah, sure."

She exited, and the boy proceeded to zip up his

pants, hoping that she had not seen the open fly, and began getting ready for dinner.

Michael smiled.

Goodbye, Michael, he thought to himself—quite literally. I can't carry you around any longer; you understand? I've got to let go. It's not a betrayal; really it's not. I've just got to become the kind of person you never thought you could be. I've got to try, at least. You understand? I've got to try . . .

Softly, Michael said, "Goodbye," and the bedroom dimmed, faded, vanished; the boy winked out in mid-stride. The mahogany den returned. Michael turned—

And saw Ginny looking at him. With a start he realized that she, too, might have been able to see what had gone on in that room, so long before. The thought made him blush with embarrassment. "Uh . . . Ginny?" he said, quietly. "Did you . . . see all that?"

Ginny blinked, looked at him puzzledly. "See what?" she said. "I was looking at *you* most of the time. Are you all right, Michael?"

Immensely relieved, Michael took her hand. "I'm fine, Ginny. For the first time in my life . . . I think I'm going to be just fine." They started walking away from the house, toward the street. "C'mon. Let's go find that diner you mentioned . . . we can hitch a ride on a truck, if we're lucky."

Ginny breathed a sigh of relief. He seemed okay. More than okay, in fact—he seemed more at peace than Ginny had ever seen him. She didn't know what thoughts had gone through his mind, staring into that room—but she did know what *she* had seen in the room, even as she knew that she would never, ever let Michael know that she had seen it.

They caught a bus from Wilburn to Paterson, and from Paterson along Route 4 to New York. Traveling past Paramus, Bergenfield, Teaneck, Michael reached a kind of peace with New Jersey. It was no place he particularly wanted to be, but neither was it the hellhole of his adolescence; he would leave the hatred and the frustration for another Michael, a Michael living in shadows a long ways behind.

He didn't know what was going to happen now: whether his body in Bellevue would live, or die, or whether they would go on like this forever. He didn't know how he felt about Ginny, or she about him. But he knew one thing for certain. He had to *do* something, had to *touch* someone; he would not waste this twilight-life as he had wasted his real one. He had to leave something behind. And as the bus emerged from the dimness of the Lincoln Tunnel into Manhattan, he remembered a young man in a museum— awkward, gangling, much like the frightened boy back in Wilburn— and slowly that *something* took form in his mind.

III

Blow on the coal of the heart.
The candles in churches are out.
The lights have gone out in the sky.
Blow on the coal of the heart
And we'll see by and by . . .

—Archibald MacLeish, *J.B.*

10

"Michael, I hate this a lot. My mother didn't raise me to be a . . . a voyeur!"

"For Pete's sake, I'm not asking you to pick the lock on her diary, just find out what you can about her," Michael said. "Little things like her name, whether she's married, has a boyfriend, and if not, her hobbies, favorite kinds of food . . . you know, something we can use to plan a strategy."

Ginny frowned. "Sounds about as romantic as Rommel planning a raid on Africa."

"That's not fair. Rommel was probably a sweetheart of a guy once you got to know him. Just trust me, Ginny, okay?"

They were crossing West 53rd Street against the light, slowly and unhurriedly, unmindful of the cars and buses and taxis streaking through their astral forms. Ginny was still reluctant. "I just don't like the idea of butting into someone else's private life," she said. "Besides, aren't we making the same mistake you talked about back at that motel? Assuming that these two won't be happy until they're together?"

"No, we're not," Michael insisted. "You saw the way they looked at each other at the museum that day—they were obviously attracted to one another, and absolutely terrified to show it. I swear, Ginny, those two *want* to get together; they just don't know *how*. All we're giving them is an opportunity." He paused, then added, "Don't you wish someone had given you a little nudge like this, at least once in your life?"

Ginny thought of Tommy Marcusi, and her objections began to fall away. "All right," she sighed. "I don't think this is gonna work, but if it keeps us from seeing any more Ingmar Bergman films, I guess I'm for it."

They had by now reached the steps of the Museum of Modern Art; Michael grinned, pecked Ginny on the cheek. "Terrific. You're sure Dennis works at Keller & Ross?"

"That's what Annie said before we went out on that date."

"Great," he said, moving out into traffic again. "I'll meet you about five-thirty, okay? Rockefeller Plaza, by the fountains?" He didn't wait for a reply; he turned and ran into the street, through a large beer truck rumbling past, and was out of sight. Ginny sighed; she wished she could share Michael's enthusiasm, but the whole thing made her uneasy. Ginny hardly considered herself an expert on romance—what was she doing playing matchmaker?

On the other hand, she thought as she entered the museum, maybe the girl was already married or living with someone. Sure; that could explain why she was so fidgety around Dennis, why she made no sign of interest. Buoyed by the possibility, Ginny headed for the stairs and trudged up to MOMA's administrative offices on the fourth floor.

Since she had no idea what the woman's name was, she was forced to go about this trial-and-error, poking her head through each door she came to to see if she could catch a glimpse of the thin, brown-haired young woman with the slight overbite. On the fourth try, she found her: she was seated behind a desk in a cramped office, making notations in a ledger; the name plaque on her desk read PAULA VANDEN-BERG, ADMINISTRATIVE ASSISTANT. At the desk next to hers, a tall, beautiful black woman, also an administrative officer, was finishing up a phone call. Ginny took a deep breath, screwed up her chutzpah (as Michael would have put it) and passed through the door into the office.

As she stood there looking at Paula, the enormity of her task became apparent. What was she going to do, go up and ask, Hey, Miss; you married? Got a boyfriend? *Virginia, you meet any nice boys yet?* Her mother's voice came back to her, shrill and insistent, and she was filled with momentary horror: dear God, no, she didn't want to do to anyone what Mama had done to her! She had a sudden impulse to bolt the room, then caught herself. No. It wasn't the same. It wasn't . . .

The black woman swiveled in her seat to face Paula. "Hey, Paulie," she said, passing an invoice across to Paula's desk, "did you catch that new guy they brought in to replace Perlman? Are we talking hunk or are we talking hunk?"

Paula took the invoice, frowned, and glanced away, embarrassed. "I really hadn't noticed, Effie."

Effie's eyes widened. She slid her chair over and unexpectedly grabbed Paula by the wrist.

"What the hell are you doing?" Paula asked.

"Feeling for a pulse."

"All right," Paula laughed, "I saw him, I saw him. Very nice."

"He certainly seemed to notice you," Effie continued. "Or didn't you notice the way he kept looking over at us during the staff meeting?"

Paula flushed red. "If he was looking at anyone," Paula said, turning back to her work, "he was looking at you." She tried to bury herself in her paperwork, but Effie wouldn't let the subject drop.

"No such luck," she sighed. "I, uh, ran into him at the watercooler a while later. Didn't show a whole lot of interest, sad to say. Nope, it was you he was looking at, Paulie."

Ginny's interest was piqued; she wandered over and sat on the edge of Paula's desk, between the two women, who merely looked right through her, oblivious to her presence.

Paula was genuinely embarrassed. "Effie, please. Take my word for it. Men just aren't interested in me; never have been, never will be. Just one of those little facts of life you learn to live with—like cockroaches, or leaky faucets.''

Effie shook her head. "Girl, that's a real bad attitude you've got there."

That must have struck a chord in Paula, for she turned round again sharply to face her friend, her face stony, her voice measured. "Effie," she said, slowly, "I spent twenty-two years waiting for something to happen, for someone to notice me, and every time I got my hopes up, I got shot down. You know what it's like, growing up with so much metal in your mouth you pick up police calls every time you smile? Or watching while every girl in high school goes from an A cup to a C cup—and you're treated like some kind of lower organism because Walter Dixon, the class fat boy, has bigger boobs than you do?"

She shook her head emphatically, started to turn back to her work. "Every time I've fallen for a guy, Effie, I've come down in flames. I'm damned if I'll let them do it to me again."

Effie looked at her with a mixture of frustration and pity. "That's your problem, Paula," she said gently. "There *is* no 'them' . . . only a whole lot of people like *us*. But you're never gonna give yourself the chance to find that out, are you?"

Paula looked up, irritation flashing briefly in her eyes, then quickly steered the conversation back to business matters—specifically, a new lithograph from Hamburg which was overdue. Effie volunteered to go over to Shipping to check the freight delivery dates, and once she was alone in the office—alone save for Ginny, sitting invisibly beside her—Paula allowed herself to sink a little in her seat, then lean forward, elbows on the desk, rubbing at her eyes wearily. She looked like a tight, aching ball of pain, an injured bird hiding a broken wing. Ginny's heart reached out to her; without thinking, she willed herself ''solid'' and laid a hand, gently, on Paula's shoulder.

Paula promptly bolted upright in her seat, startled and afraid, and Ginny immediately cursed herself for her stupidity. Paula looked around, saw no one else in the office, and shivered; she turned back to her work and buried herself in statistics and shipping dates.

Ginny spent the rest of the afternoon in a corner, terrified at doing anything which might further upset her.

It was not what one would call an eventful day: by four o'clock even Ingmar Bergman movies were starting to look good to Ginny. At least people *talked* in those; after Effie's mild rebuke that morning, Paula pretty much kept her own counsel for the next several hours. Not that there was any acrimony between the two women—Ginny just got the idea that Paula was terrified at the thought of accidentally bringing up again topics she would rather avoid. Her defenses, Ginny noted, were like bear traps, sharp and swift.

Worse—there was something disturbingly familiar about them.

To Ginny's surprise, Paula started packing up for the day a little after four—leaving early? or did she start work at eight instead of nine?—and by 4:05 was running to catch a northbound bus on Broadway. Ginny was tempted to part company with her— Rockefeller Center was only a few blocks away—but Michael wouldn't be meeting her for another hour or more, and Ginny couldn't rid herself of the feeling there was something unfinished here. In a way, she didn't know Paula any better now than she did six hours ago. So, hard upon Paula, Ginny jumped through the doors of the bus as they hissed closed and the driver lurched away from the curb.

Rush hour was not yet in full horrific swing, and Paula was able to find a seat on the lefthand side of the bus. She sat, a study in fear and repression: arms folded across her chest, knees pressed together, newspaper in her lap. Ginny settled in beside her, her own arms folded as she studied Paula. For the first time, Ginny was beginning to understand what body language was all about; Paula looked as though her chastity belt was on too tight. Ginny's gaze dropped . . . and she realized that she was sitting in precisely the same position as Paula, arms crossed, knees locked! Flustered, she immediately dropped her arms and forced her knees apart, not quite knowing what to do with either for several minutes.

Her gaze wandered across the aisle, where a pleasant-looking young man was stealing an occasional glance at Paula. Paula caught his last glance, and the man offered a small, friendly smile. Paula immediately turned away, flustered; she whipped out her copy of the *News* with a great rustling of paper and fixed her gaze on the first page she came to. The young man looked away, taking the hint. Ginny studied him, then Paula, unable to understand.

"Hey," she addressed Paula aloud. "What's wrong with you, anyway? He didn't pull a knife; he just smiled at you. Looks about as threatening as a teddy bear.'' She sized up the young man, added judiciously, ''Kinda cute, too.''

Ginny leaned over, looked at the page Paula was reading. ''Transit subsidies? Nobody reads articles about transit subsidies. Nobody even knows what they are.'' She noticed Paula's eyes; they were barely moving, by no means scanning the page. ''You're not even moving your eyes,'' Ginny went on. ''Like when I didn't want to talk to someone on the subway, I'd stare up at the ads on the wall, but if you looked close, my eyes never—''

She never finished the sentence. The realization struck her all at once; she felt embarrassed, guilty, and, above all, dumb. She looked at Paula, burrowed deep within herself, and she wondered: Was that what I looked like? Like a scared little rabbit? She bit her lip, glanced over at the young man. The weight of her past pressed down on her; she felt a touch of the old claustrophobia return, wanted to dash out of the bus, into the open air. And then it suddenly occurred to her: she had spent the last couple weeks in small motel rooms and narrow jet cabins, in crowds and on buses—and not since that day in the hospital had she felt the walls close in on her. She'd be damned if she'd let them do it now. And, as soon as she decided that, the walls were gone, the pressure vanished. *Is that it?* she asked herself. *Is that all there is to it?* She expected the thought to trigger another assault, God or Mama or Maggie pushing the walls in from behind, but it didn't happen. Mama may have pushed the walls once, but only because Ginny had *let* her. That was the secret, wasn't it? They only crushed you if you let them crush you. And half the walls which had closed in on her, Ginny began to realize, were walls which she herself had pushed.

She stared at the young man across the aisle and felt tears coming to her eyes. How many guys like you did I look away from, she wondered . . . just because you smiled at me? And what good does it do me now . . . now that it's much too late?

Leaving Ginny at the museum, Michael walked the four or five blocks up Fifth Avenue to the offices of Keller & Ross. It was a small publisher specializing in how-to books and general nonfiction, taking up not much more than half a floor, so locating Dennis was not that difficult; Michael found him in the middle of the editorial bullpen, surrounded by other men and women at desks reading manuscripts, correcting galleys, and typing. The room was large, functional, and anonymous; it reminded Michael of the loft at Multigraphics. Dennis was sweating over a set of galleys, eyes down, back hunched, mouth set in a thin line, and Michael, approaching, wondered if that was what *he* had looked like when laboring over an album cover.

Michael sat down in an empty chair at the desk next to Dennis' and considered his options. What now? He knew nothing more about this guy than what Ginny had told him—he was shy, insecure, bright but self-deprecating—and from what he had observed that day in the museum. What was he like? Did he have any interests in common with Paula, something Michael could use to get them together . . . ?

Michael had a theory that you could tell everything you needed to know about a person from the contents of his or her desk drawers. While Dennis' back was turned for a moment, Michael inched open the leftmost drawer of his desk and peeked inside. He noted a clutch of paperback novels (not, pleasantly enough, the usual best-seller crap, but John Knowles, Thomas Pynchon, John Gardner), a copy of the *Atlantic Monthly*, and—ah hah—a hardback copy of *Writers Market,* two years out of date. Burrowing deeper, he found some typing paper, white-out, a manila envelope, and a—

Dennis turned, saw his drawer open, its contents rustling in the wind (though how could the wind carry all the way across the room?), and promptly shut it again. Michael yanked his hand away reflexively, though he could not, of course, feel any pain, and turned his attention to what was on, as opposed to in, Dennis' desk.

Unlike many of the other workers in the bullpen, Dennis had on his desk no framed snapshots of wife, girlfriend, whatever; instead of a rolodex, he had a small pad with a few phone numbers arranged alphabetically by name, most of the names paired (Jack and Bobbi, Nancy and Steve, Rob and Lynn); and where many of the other people had calendars marked up with dates circled in pen or pencil, Dennis' datebook was blank for weeks in a row, with only an occasional Saturday or Sunday circled with a notation like *Party at Rob & Lynn's* or *Dinner w/folks.*

As Michael winced with recogniton, a pretty young woman carrying a sack of mail approached Dennis' desk, dropping a nine-by-twelve manila envelope onto the blotter in front of him. Dennis' face fell; the mail girl eyed him sympathetically. "Sorry, Dennis. Was it the *New Yorker*?"

Dennis stared at the envelope. "No," he said. "*Harper's*."

"You want me to wait around so you can send it out again?" she added helpfully.

Dennis fingered the envelope, his expression turning bleak. He shook his head. "No. No sense to it." He smiled a bit ruefully. "All I'm doing is making the post office richer."

The young woman shrugged and moved off. Dennis eyed the envelope a long moment, then opened a desk drawer, dropped the envelope inside, and swiveled away from it, attacking the galley proofs with renewed vigor. For a moment, Michael was back in those sleepy coffeehouses and imposing concert halls of so many years ago, his horn in his hand, trying to work up the courage to play. He felt the parched mouth, the mounting fear; he heard the sour notes issuing from his instrument and he saw the looks of dismissal and amusement from the people in the audience. He looked at Dennis and felt suddenly sad.

"No, man," he found himself saying, as though Dennis could hear him. "That's how it starts, you know? You give up on the small things first, and that makes it easier to give up on the big ones. Take it from an expert."

But Dennis could not hear him. Michael sank into a seat, part of him wanting to run as he had wanted to run from that window in New Jersey . . . but now, as then, he did not, and he felt good about that. But whereas before he was a living person (sort of) looking at shadows, now *he* was the shadow, looking in at the living—and somehow would have to find a way of crossing that barrier which separated him from Dennis, and from the world which only recently he had tried to leave.

The afternoon passed quickly as Michael sat, pondering, a few feet from Dennis' desk.

"Hey, Dennis, you doing anything tonight?"

Both Dennis and Michael looked up within a heartbeat of one another. The speaker was a big, blond mesomorph of a man, good-natured and gregarious; he was pulling on a coat, and Michael noticed for the first time that it was close to five. "Larry and Sol and me, we thought we'd go over to that new singles place on 49th and Seventh. Want to come along?"

Dennis looked visibly leery at the suggestion. "Uh, no thanks, Chuck. My last experience in a singles bar wasn't exactly what you'd call emotionally enriching."

Chuck shrugged. "Who said anything about emotional enrichment? We're talking basically a few drinks, a few laughs, and who knows, you might get lucky."

Dennis recovered his coat from the chair over which it had been draped and was tactfully edging toward the door. "I don't get lucky, man. I get flustered, I get clumsy, I get torn up by blind dates who make John Simon sound like Mister Rogers, but I don't get lucky. Whenever I'm around women I turn into a total klutz. Thanks for asking, but I'd better save you the embarrassment."

Chuck shook his head. "Come on. You don't really—"

In his haste to leave, Dennis ran smack into the doorframe. He winced, turned, and shrugged at Chuck in a peculiar kind of vindication.

"See? A klutz. Thanks anyway. See you tomorrow."

And he was out the door before Chuck could say anything more. The blond man shook his head, sighed, and moved off, as Michael looked after Dennis, worriedly . . .

Rockefeller Plaza was cavernously empty by five-thirty, filled neither with the rush of workers hurrying home nor with people as yet passing through en route to dinner or the theater. The fountains were shut down for the winter, and although the giant Christmas tree was still up, to be taken down in a week or two, its presence already seemed oddly wrong, a lonely icon past its proper time.

Michael and Ginny walked the length of the plaza, under the mute witness of the Christmas tree; had they been part of the corporeal world, their voices would have echoed off the tall stone, but they were not (they were again reminded) corporeal, and so their voices sounded flat, hollow, and remote, to each other and to themselves.

"She's been burned so often she'd rather just throw in the towel," Ginny was saying of Paula. "Michael, I still don't like this. I mean, what if we screw up? What then?" She hesitated, then: "I did kind of a . . . dumb thing today. Tried to comfort her. Put my hand on her shoulder." She looked at her hand as though it were not part of her. "She was terrified—nearly jumped out of her skin. Can you imagine how *cold* . . . how *numb* we must feel to real people?"

Ginny shuddered. Michael took her hand in his,

squeezed it. "You're not cold," he said softly. "Not to me."

Ginny bit her lip. "I don't want to hurt her, Michael. Not like I hurt Dennis. Like I hurt every damn person I ever—" She didn't finish; didn't have to. Michael nodded, squeezing her hand again, and she was grateful for his touch.

"I understand," he said, quietly. "I'll just have to go it alone, then."

"*Why*, Michael? Why is this so important to you?"

He wasn't sure he understood it himself, but struggled to put it into words. "All I know is," he began, hesitantly, "is that what they want us to believe—in books, in movies, everywhere—is that everybody finds somebody. Everybody marries, love conquers all. But it just isn't true."

"What does that have to do with—"

"Ginny," he said, feeling the rush of emotion carry him now, "all over this planet there are people— too loud, too soft, too ugly, too *something*—people who go to work, come home, watch TV, and wonder what they're doing wrong, why can't life be the way it is on the tube. And they wonder, and they hope, and they wait for that Special Person to come . . . that one person who'll love them, the way they're *supposed* to be loved . . . and it never happens."

Ginny thought of Paula, hunched over like a wounded bird, and something inside her felt wounded, too. "And you think these two . . . Dennis, and Paula . . . they could end up like that?"

"Worse," Michael said. "They could end up like us."

Ginny flinched at the suggestion.

Michael went on, "They could get just as tired . . . feel just as hopeless . . . and take the same way out. I'm not saying they will, but they could."

Michael sat down by one of the stilled fountains and worked up the courage to face the real reason, the selfish reason why this mattered so to him. He averted his gaze.

"All my life, Ginny," he said, voice low, "I took the easy way out. I wanted to be a musician; I wound up laying out album covers. I talked about love and reaching out, gave my friends all this great advice about taking chances, taking risks . . . but I never took any chances myself. At least not for years. I'd get burned, I'd lose confidence, I'd give up.

"I blew every goddamn opportunity I ever had, Ginny. It kills me to admit that . . . but now maybe I've got a chance to make up for it, just a little. To do one thing . . . to prove that all those years I wasted weren't for nothing. And maybe help two people to find each other who wouldn't have before." He looked at her, and there was a resolve and a confidence in his eyes she had not seen before. "I can't give up this time, Ginny. I can't."

Ginny studied him, feeling a deep affection for this plain, sad-faced man; and she knew that, however much the prospect frightened her, however much she disliked the idea, she could not let him do it alone. For the first time in her life she realized that someone actually needed her . . . and when someone needed you, someone you cared for, what you liked or didn't like didn't matter. You helped them. It was as simple as that.

"So," she said, looping an arm through Michael's as they walked out of the plaza, "how do we go about this, anyway?"

In the small floral shop in the Waldorf lobby, papers rustled and drawers snicked open and shut, as if by themselves; a table lamp snapped on, casting a pool of yellow light across the sales counter. A sheaf of papers floated off a desk, the pages flipping of their own volition. A pen floated off the counter, began scratching at an order form.

"Okay. We fill out one of these forms, feed it into the teletype, and the florist's shop nearest the museum will send them over tomorrow."

"Make them roses, Michael. White roses. With long stems."

"Right. How many dozen?"

"Uh, Michael, no. *One* dozen will do fine. He's supposed to be asking her out for a date—not a wake."

"Okay, okay." The order form floated into a typewriter; the keys began chattering, like a player piano, then paused. "I don't know. I still like the idea of using that quotation from Goethe on the card—"

"*Michael*!"

"Just a thought. Just a thought." The keys chattered for another minute or so, then: "Okay, great. Now how do we sign it?"

"How about with his name?"

"No, no, we want to pique her curiosity. How about . . . 'An admirer from afar'?"

"How far? Ecuador?"

"All right. How about just, 'An admirer'?"

"Better."

The keys chattered, then fell silent—and in moments, it was done, and for Michael and Ginny, there was no turning back.

11

Ginny sat at the foot of the Christmas tree, a silver teardrop in her hand. The tree was a galaxy of winking lights, flickering candles, swaying ornaments; at the apex a chromium star revolved, catching in its faceted sides the glow of streetlamps outside the display window. Ginny placed the last teardrop on a dry pine branch and stepped back to admire her handiwork. There was a round of applause from those seated around her. Ginny turned and smiled at her friends. Annie was seated in the sleigh, one arm around Bruce, both of them grinning hugely; Margaret and Mama sat on one of the blankets covering the floor, each smoking and nodding their approval; *Nonno* and *Nonna* were piling Christmas gifts beneath the tree. They were all here, except . . .

"Merry Christmas, Ginny." Ginny turned to see Michael entering the window; at his side were Dennis and Paula, walking hand-in-hand. Michael kissed Ginny on the cheek; she blushed as her mother beamed.

"This is for you, Ginny." Dennis was holding a large gift box; Ginny stepped forward to take it, gratefully. She looked around at all these people, at all her friends, and was filled with joy. God, she was so lucky. Lucky to have them, lucky that they were all here. She had never felt so happy, so loved in all her life.

"Time to open the presents, isn't it, Virginia?" asked Mama, and Ginny knelt in front of the tree, eagerly distributing the gifts, lifting the brightly colored boxes from the bed of angel hair bunched around the tree. She reached over to grasp a particularly large one—

And lost her balance, falling into the tree. The branches shook; a candle tipped. Hot wax dripped onto a dry, flaky branch. Before anyone could move, the branch ignited. Someone screamed. Another candle flared, catching an upper branch, igniting the electrical wire crisscrossing the tree; the light bulbs popped like firecrackers, a ribbon of fire ran the length of the cord. In seconds the tree was a pyramid of flame.

Mama and Margaret pounded on the window, coughing and hacking, but the window refused to give. Annie and Bruce banged on the cloth curtain which separated the display from the rest of the store, but suddenly, inexplicably, the curtain was hard as steel.

Ginny's heart pounded. What had she done? How could she have been so stupid? The heat assaulted her in waves as she tried to smother the flame with her own body, but Michael pulled her back. "Let me go!" she screamed. "It's my fault!" Dennis and Paula ran for the window, but the fire spread swiftly from the tree to the blankets on the floor; in seconds the entire floor was a sheet of flame, and moments after that, Dennis and Paula were afire, sparks leaping up their legs, igniting their clothes. They stood there, transformed into living torches, their screams mingling with the spit and crackle of the fire. Ginny beat at their burning bodies with a blanket, but the fire refused to be quenched. She was hysterical now, screaming, screaming, as Michael continued to hold her. "It's my fault!" she shrieked. "I'm sorry, I'm *sorry*, it's my *fault*!" Michael was trying to pull her away, telling her it was his fault, not hers, but she knew better and would not let him pull her back; the flames were licking at her face now, at her arms, her eyes, and in a moment Michael's arms, too, were covered with fire and he was yelling—

"*Ginny!* Ginny, wake up! *Wake up!*"

Michael was holding her, trying to shake her awake, as Ginny's screams, hollow and echoless, filled her bedroom. The display window faded, became momentarily transposed on the bedroom, the flames seeming for an instant to lick at the blue canopy surrounding her bed . . . then they, too, faded, and the only remnant of the scene was Michael, holding her, comforting her. "It's okay," he was saying, his hand gently stroking the small of her back, and as he did,

Ginny came slowly back to reality. "You just had a nightmare, that's all . . ."

Nightmare? Yes; of course. Thank God. That would explain everything. Except . . .

Except she hadn't been able to dream in weeks. Michael thought it was because dreams were said to be memories of the soul, places it went, things it did while the body slept. *Their* souls were here, rooted to the earth, so they didn't dream. So what was it that she had just had, if not a nightmare? A fear? A dread? A premonition?

Ginny shivered violently, the fire and the heat still horribly vivid in her mind. She held on to Michael, tightly. "I'm all right," she told him, her tone belying her words. "Just hold me for a while please, Michael?" Part of her marveled at her ability to even say that—to ask for the affection for which she had been so starved for so long. She'd been through so many changes in the last few weeks . . . she couldn't go back, couldn't hurt one more person the way she used to; if she did, she was certain she would die. She shut her eyes, comforted by Michael's warmth, and in moments, the flames were fading in her memory, the screams dimming like the wail of sirens retreating into the distance; it was just a nightmare, after all. Nothing more. Just a nightmare.

By the time Paula arrived at work at eight the next morning, Michael and Ginny were already waiting for her, Michael sitting cross-legged on the floor, Ginny perched on Effie's desk as the black woman went about her morning routine. It wasn't until 9:43 that the messenger—short, stocky, and bluff—poked his head into the office, in his arms a long, slender white box with a red bow.

" 'Scuse me," he said, sounding about as bored as a human being could sound. "I've got some flowers here for—"

Paula did not look up. "She's over there," she said, nodding toward Effie. The messenger shrugged, approached the other woman, consulted his card. "You're . . . Paula Vandenberg?"

"Uh, no. That's her over there."

The messenger sighed. "You're sure, now?" He turned and placed the box on Paula's desk.

Paula looked startled and flustered. "There must be some mistake," she said. "Those can't be for—"

"Your name Vandenberg?"

"Yes, but—"

"Then these are yours. You gonna sign for them, or should we put this up to a vote of the General Assembly?"

Looking utterly baffled, Paula signed and tipped the man a buck; he made something halfway between a smile and a rictus and left. Paula just stared at the box for several moments as Michael and Ginny invisibly clustered around her, trying to gauge her reaction. "There must be some mistake," Paula kept saying. "I don't know who—"

Effie sprang to her feet and began opening the box herself. "Oh, shit, if you're not gonna do it, I will." She undid the ribbon and bow, tossed aside the lid—to reveal twelve perfect, long-stemmed white roses. Effie gasped. Paula gaped, disbelieving. Michael and Ginny exchanged satisfied grins.

"They're . . . beautiful," Paula said softly.

Effie had found the card and began reading it aloud, smiling with genuine pleasure for Paula—who, with each line, seemed more and more as though she wanted to crawl under the nearest desk in embarrassment:

> We make ourselves a place apart
>   Behind light words that tease and flout,
> But oh, the agitated heart
>   Till someone find us really out.
>   —R. Frost.

Paula was quickly dismissive. "I don't know any R. Frost," she said.

"The *poet,* dummy," Effie said, and Paula shrugged sheepishly. "It's signed"—and here she paused for dramatic effect—" 'An admirer.' " She grinned. "Talk about still waters running deep. You leadin' a secret life on me, Paulie?"

Michael winced as he saw Paula's face first blush red, then cloud over defensively. Damn it, when would people learn that was the *worst* thing you could do with shy people—*Wink wink, nudge nudge, know what I mean, know what I mean?* Paula swiveled in her seat, trying to return to work. "It's just a joke, Effie. It has to be. Just a stupid joke."

"Somebody went to all this trouble and expense just for a joke? Come *on*." She considered a moment. "Maybe it was that new guy in Shipping . . . the one who was looking at you in the meeting the other day?"

Paula's mouth was a taut, hard line. "He was *not* looking at me. Don't be ridiculous. I bet he could have any woman he wants—why would he send flowers to someone with all the sex appeal of boiled cauliflower.''

Effie was becoming exasperated. ''Paula, for Christ's sake—''

Paula turned in her seat and looked fixedly at her friend, her tone measured but with a tremor of remembered pain creeping in now and then. ''Effie, *it's a joke.* Like when I was thirteen, with braces and stringy hair, and all the guys in my homeroom got together and sent me this Valentine's Day card, you know? Only I didn't know it was a plot, see, and I get this card, with hearts and curlicues and all that, and it's signed, 'Love, Jeremy.' Jeremy was the class brain, and everybody hated him, except me, and so I thanked him for the card.'' She looked down. ''Of course he didn't know what I was talking about, and the two of us stood there like jerks while the other kids nearly busted their guts, giggling behind our backs at these two . . . gimps.''

She pushed the flowers away, toward Effie. ''You can take these home if you want. Be a shame to waste them.''

Effie sighed, took the flowers from Paula's desk, and returned to her own work, while Paula began sorting invoices, doing her best to ignore the sweet scent of roses. Michael and Ginny looked at one another despairingly.

''Well,'' Ginny said, a bit of the old cynicism creeping back, ''if this is your idea of breaking the ice, I can see why your social life was so depressing.''

Outside, Michael's determination was undiminished.

''Okay, the anonymous card was a mistake,'' he admitted as they struck up 53rd Street. ''I'd planned two or three bouquets, you know, each one bigger than the last, and by the time she got the last one, she'd be bursting with curiosity, and that would've been the one we'd sign Dennis' name to.'' He sighed. "I guess some people just don't like being tantalized.''

"Do you?'' Ginny asked.

"Well, no, but I thought women were supposed to like that sort of—''

He caught himself, looked sheepishly at Ginny. "I, uh, guess that's kind of a dumb generalization, isn't it?''

"Kind of, yeah.''

"Well I've never done this before. Bear with me, okay?'' He considered a moment, then nodded, looking determined. "All right. One more bouquet of flowers, and this time none of this 'admirer' stuff. How does this sound? 'Yours in anticipation—Dennis Mahoney.' ''

Ginny frowned. "Still sounds an awful lot like 'Love, Jeremy.' ''

Michael shot her a sour look and said nothing all the way to the florist's.

The second bouquet, arriving the next morning, was a lovely assortment of white, yellow, and pink flowers that was waiting for Paula when she came to work. The office was empty—not even Michael and Ginny's phantom forms were present—as Paula entered, saw the flowers, and stopped short. Not *again*? She approached them cautiously, as though they might bite, and despite herself she smiled at their clean, heavy scent. Then she saw the card.

She picked it off the wire retainer which held the

bouquet together, and read with growing amazement; no joke this time, no anonymous name, no group of giggling boys laughing at you behind your back, just a simple, straightforward, and—to Paula—immensely flattering note:

Dear Ms. Vandenberg:
Hi. Remember me? We had a minor collision in the MOMA lobby last week. Hope there were no broken bones. I thought maybe we could meet again, under less jolting circumstances—say, lunch or dinner, at your convenience? My number at work is 253-8000; I look forward to hearing from you.

Yours in anticipation,
Dennis Mahoney.

Paula stared at the card, disbelieving . . . but slowly, the ghost of a smile came to her. She sat down, staring at the flowers, then at the card, then the flowers. Even if the flowers were partly sent by way of apology for the "minor collision," it still sounded—incredibly—like this guy was interested in her. Idly she rearranged a few of the orchids as, invisibly, Ginny's astral form popped through the office door.

Ginny's annoyance at being late was quickly forgotten when she saw the look of cautious pleasure on Paula's face. Ginny sat down on Effie's desk as Paula put Dennis' card in her address file and tried to get down to work . . . but her gaze kept wandering to the orchids. She glanced about, afraid that Effie would burst in at any moment and make her feel self-conscious about the flowers, but it was ten after nine and her office mate was nowhere to be seen. Impulsively, Paula snapped up the phone, took the card out of her file, and began dialing—then the fear set in, she stopped after the third digit, and hung up hurriedly. What if someone came in and saw her? To her surprise, a voice inside her countered: So *what* if they see you? She started screwing up her nerve once again—

And the phone rang. Paula's heart nearly stopped on the spot; on the second ring she regained her composure and answered it.

Ginny leaned in as Effie's voice came over the line. "Paulie? Me. Listen, I think I'm coming down with something. I won't be in today, okay?"

"Uh, sure, Effie. It isn't anything serious?"

"He sure is," Effie said, and Paula had to smile at the wink in her tone. "No problem," Paula laughed. "I'll cover for you. I, ah, hope the condition worsens." It was Effie's turn to laugh. They exchanged a few more words; then Paula hung up, looking at the receiver thoughtfully.

She felt suddenly, inexplicably free—no one around to make her feel self-conscious; no one to see if this all turned out to be a colossal mistake. The only one who would see her come down in flames, if that was what happened, would be herself, and God knows that was nothing new to her.

Still (a part of her wondered, afraid), did she really want to take that kind of risk again? Her last date had been over six months ago, and while not an unqualified disaster, it had been awkward and boring enough to put her on social sabbatical ever since. Did she really want to go through that again?

She glanced at the flowers again . . . and found herself picking up the phone once more, dialing de-

spite her better judgment—and feeling an unaccus-
tomed giddiness.

Less than ten blocks away, the phone on Dennis'
desk rang, and Michael, slumped in a nearby chair
while Dennis corrected galleys, jumped up, suddenly
alert. He leaned in as Dennis picked up the phone on
the second ring, even as Ginny, in Paula's office,
leaned closer to hear her end of the conversation.

"Dennis Mahoney. Can I help you?"

Paula screwed up her courage, cleared her throat.
"Uh—Dennis? This is Paula Vandenberg. From the
Museum of Modern Art?"

For a moment Dennis went blank, then the voice
triggered an image of Paula's face and he remembered the pleasant, attractive young woman with the
rabbity smile. He smiled, startled but pleased to hear
her voice. "Oh . . . yes. Of course. How are you?"

"I'm fine," Paula said, too nervous to notice the
edge of bafflement in Dennis' tone. "I was just
calling to . . . that is, I just received the flowers you
sent; they're beautiful. I . . . just wanted to thank
you."

Dennis blinked. Flowers? What flowers? Michael
moved forward, fully prepared to step on Dennis'
foot should he start to protest, but—

"This may sound silly," Paula went on, before
Dennis could say anything, "but . . . well . . .
nobody's ever sent me flowers before. I'm very
flattered."

Dennis didn't know what the *hell* was going on
here, but he did know that she sounded so pleased,
so vulnerable, that he couldn't bring himself to tell
her the truth. Besides, he rationalized, he would have

liked to have sent her flowers, if only he'd had the nerve; what was so wrong about taking advantage of some sort of misunderstanding?

"Well, I'm, ah, glad you liked them," Dennis said, hoping that this was not the set-up for some elaborate practical joke.

"Well, I do. Very much." A moment of silence, then, as both Michael and Ginny made frantic and unseen *c'mon, c'mon* motions to, respectively, Dennis and Paula; finally, Paula broke the silence with a tentative, "On the card you, uh, mentioned getting together—"

"I did? Oh. Yes. Of course I did. Well, look, if you can't make it—"

"Oh, no," Paula said quickly, "I'd love—I mean, I'd like to, very much. When did you, uh, have in mind?"

Dennis may not have known what the hell was happening, but he damn well knew an opportunity when he saw one. He cleared his throat. "Well, maybe . . . Friday? Dinner and a movie?"

Paula fought back a moment of panic as she realized she was plunging into the dating fray once more. "That sounds fine," she heard herself say. "About . . . seven o'clock?"

"Uh, great. Great. Where can I pick you up?" He half-winced at that; *pick you up* sounded somehow tacky, but . . .

"I'm on the Upper West Side," Paula said. "Chilton Terrace, about two blocks up from Zabar's. Apartment 6-N." Another awkward moment, then: "Well. I'll . . . look forward to seeing you again."

"Yes. Same here," Dennis said, relieved that this

conversation was drawing to a close. "I'll see you Friday."

"Right."

"Well . . . have a good day."

"You too."

"Bye."

They hung up, both immensely glad that they had lived through the conversation. Paula found herself beaming as she went back to work, while Dennis sat at his desk, his excitement tempered by utter bafflement. What had just happened here? How did Paula know his name? Who sent her the damned flowers? He stared out the window, as though a sudden epiphany might burst forth from the overcast sky—

And one did, in the form of his co-worker, Chuck. Of course. Who else? Confidently, Dennis got up, strode toward Chuck's desk, stood there and smiled knowingly. "Cute, Chuck," he said as the blond man looked up. "Just tell me—how the hell did you find out? Were you there in the museum that day?"

Chuck blinked in confusion. "What?"

"The flowers. The girl's name. How did you find out?"

"Dennis," Chuck said pleasantly, "what the fuck are you talking about?"

Dennis' certainty began to erode. "Uh . . . you mean you don't—you didn't—?"

"Is this multiple-choice or essay?" Chuck asked with a bemused smile, and Dennis realized that his friend really didn't know what he was talking about. With an embarrassed "Never mind, it was nothing, really," Dennis turned and went back to his desk— now more confused and baffled than ever.

For his part, Michael could barely contain his delight. He ran jubilantly toward the door. Somehow, despite all odds, it had all fallen together. Now all he had to do was ensure that it would not somehow fall *apart* . . .

They were little things, but they began to add up. Paula would be rummaging about the office, searching for a voucher or a piece of promotional material, a pamphlet on a new exhibit by Roszack or Manzu, and suddenly she would find a newspaper clipping advertising some new romantic comedy playing downtown—or an article from *Cosmopolitan* provocatively titled "Dating: Do's and Dont's!" At first she feared that Effie had somehow found out about her date and was "seeding" these around the office to get her psyched up, but somehow that didn't seem like Effie's style—and when Effie found a couple of the damn things, too, and seemed just as baffled as Paula, Paula's confusion only increased geometrically . . .

As for Dennis, more than once he returned from lunch to find a phone book open on the desk next to his, usually to the "Restaurants" section at the back of the yellow pages, with the better establishments circled in red felt pen. Occasionally there would be a notation outside the circle, an appraisal of food or service (*"Excellent food, intimate atmosphere"*; *"Service exceptional, ask for table w/view of garden, highly romantic"*), and whoever it was seemed to have a particular fondness for French restaurants like La Caravelle and La Crêpe. The maddening thing was, Dennis was familiar with the handwriting of nearly everyone in the office—and this belonged to no one that he knew of.

This, and the fabled flower incident, made him wonder whether it was possible for a publishing house to be haunted—by the ghost, perhaps, of some deceased author seeking revenge for some botched job of copyediting, or for a particularly hideous cover foisted on his book by the art department.

When they were not providing such subliminal support to Dennis and Paula, Michael and Ginny found themselves waging an unexpected battle against boredom. Michael was suddenly without any desire to go to plays, museums, or restaurants, and Ginny, much to her astonishment, actually walked out of the first movie they went to since their abortive vacation. They became acutely aware that all of these were little more than distractions—distractions from the business of life, from the things that mattered. And yet they couldn't really be a part of life, either. More than any other time since their attempted suicides— and despite their efforts with Paula and Dennis—they felt isolated, exposed, as the things they had used to distract themselves, the ways they had developed to avoid thinking about what they *should* be doing with their lives, all were being stripped away one by one, leaving them with . . . what?

Finally, inevitably, they were drawn back to Bellevue, and their bodies.

Michael left Ginny alone for the moment with her own comatose form and headed down the long corridor to the room where his body lay. It was early evening; those patients who could eat solid food were being served dinner, the halls full of the familiar smell of chicken, tomato soup, and rice pudding. Michael perceived the odors dimly, wondering what the food tasted like. It had been so long since he had really tasted anything, in any way other than the strange, detached sensation of this unnatural state, that he began to wonder if food tasted the same as he remembered it. He allowed himself a brief paranoid fantasy that perhaps the entire structure of things— food, drink, touch, sex—had somehow been altered in the weeks gone by, and he would never again know what it was like to taste, smell, and touch as he once had . . .

He passed through the closed doors of the ICU, headed toward the bed where his unconscious body lay—and stopped short, stunned by what he saw there.

Clustered around the bed were Shelley, Josh, Susan, Bob, Val, and Morrie. They stood awkwardly at Michael's bedside, grief in their eyes as they looked down at Michael's unconscious form, unaware that Michael himself—his real, conscious self—had just entered the room and was slowly, hesitantly approaching them. To them, Michael was that broken body on the bed, that fragile shell so tenuously connected to monitors and machinery. For an instant, Michael hated that shell, because *it* had his friends, *it* was the object of their love and their grief, and all *he* could do was stand here, gaping, longing to reach out, unable to be heard or seen.

Shelley was placing a bouquet of flowers on the table beside the bed; she addressed Michael's body as though it could hear her. "Hello, Michael," she said. "Look who I picked up off the streets."

The others tried to smile, but they were clearly ill-at-ease, and Michael could hardly blame them.

But Shelley went on talking. "Dr. MacKenzie says the CAT-scan was negative," she said softly, "no neurological damage . . . so you should be out of those casts inside of a few months . . ."

Josh touched her arm, gently. "Shel—"

She ignored him, continued to address Michael's comatose form. But her voice trembled just a bit more. "It looks like a replay of the Christmas party in here. There's Morrie . . . Val . . . Bob . . . Susan . . ."

"Shelley, he can't hear you. This is crazy."

The speaker was Bob, looking pained and guilty for even having said it. But his discomfort was mirrored in the faces of everyone else in the room, save Shelley, who glanced irritably at him.

"He could be in that coma for two weeks or two years," Bob continued, sadly. "This won't help."

Shelley's tone was defiant. "How the hell do *you* know he can't hear us?" she snapped. "How do you know what he's feeling—locked inside his own head like that? How do you know he's not lying there, hearing every word we say, unable to do anything about it?"

Michael, listening, felt tears welling up in his eyes.

"I don't," Bob said helplessly. "But neither do you."

Shelley straightened. "Maybe not," she said, her tone becoming slowly more vehement, her eyes more fiery. "But I think I know how he felt before he tried to kill himself—he felt alone! And now he's alone again, and maybe the only way he's going to pull himself out of it, the only reason he's got to wake up, is *us*! Did you ever think of that? What does he have to wake up to *except* us? We're supposed to be his friends, God damn it! That's supposed to *mean* something!''

Her voice was getting hoarse, ragged; Josh put a hand to her back, comfortingly.

"All I know," she went on, the tears starting to come now, "is that he's my *friend*, and I'm going to come here as often as I can, for as long as I can, talking as *much* as I can, and if I'm wrong, well, the worst that'll happen is that some people will think I'm being a jerk, and that's their problem! But if I'm right—if I'm right, maybe he'll know that someone's *here*, that someone *gives* a shit, that *some* of us *care* about whether or not he wakes up! And if that's crazy, Bob, then fine, I'm crazy, I'm a jerk, whatever you want to call me, think whatever the hell you want to think and *leave me alone with my friend!*"

She broke off, sobbing, as Josh held her, and the others—heads bowed—said nothing more. Michael, watching, stumbled closer, stopped within several feet of Shelley; he wanted to reach out, wanted to touch her, to thank her, but he did not dare. "Oh God, Shel," he said, "I'm sorry. I never meant—I didn't want to . . . to . . ."

He couldn't continue. He turned away, stood there crying for several long minutes . . . and then, slowly, he became aware of voices behind him. He turned.

One by one, almost in alternation, Bob and Susan and Josh and Morrie and Val began speaking to Michael's unconscious body—chatting about nothing in particular, just talking, letting him know they were there. They talked about the weather, about sports, about mutual friends and television and books and music . . . and if any of them wondered whether or not he could hear them, whether their words were being wasted, they did not show it.

Michael sank into a chair, smiling through his tears at them. What on earth had he done to deserve such fine, gentle people as these? How could he have done what he did? And how in God's name could he undo it? He sat there for the better part of an hour, listening to their voices, their stories, the jokes they told . . . until visiting hours ended and one by one they began filing out of the intensive care unit. Shelley was the last to go; she stood alone in the room, bent over Michael's body, and gently kissed him on the forehead. She straightened, looked down at him with sad eyes. "I love you, Michael," she said, her voice very thin, very fragile.

"I love you, too," Michael whispered . . . and, to his astonishment, Shelley looked up; looked around, oddly, as though at a breeze grazing her cheek, or a light seen distantly and quickly gone; and for the first time that evening, she smiled, though not quite knowing why. And then she, too, left the room, leaving Michael alone with his corporeal self . . . and with every fiber of his being Michael wanted to lie back into that body and make it move again, to open his eyes and see the relief and delight on his friends' faces when he did. And he might have tried, right then and there, had it not been for one thing: a still-frightened, still-uncertain young woman sitting in an ICU much like this, not a hundred feet away. He knew now that he wanted to live—but did Ginny? And if not, how could he possibly leave her behind?

12

Friday turned out to be a gray, depressing day: not warm enough for rain, not cold enough for snow, the result a bleak compromise of sleet and hail. At midday Michael and Ginny went their separate ways, he to shepherd Dennis through to the evening, she to Paula. As might have been expected, both Dennis and Paula were jumpy and apprehensive all day; Paula snapped at Effie more often than not, necessitating an apology and, later, letting her in on Paula's "secret." Effie's response was predictably enthusiastic, embarrassing Paula to the point where she almost found herself hoping the date would be a bust, just so she could show Effie up. Dennis, meanwhile, spent the day stumbling into open doors, and the more shins that he bruised (Michael could have sworn that human beings only had two), the worse he seemed to get. By five o'clock, as he ran out of his office building and went skidding across an icy sidewalk, keeping his balance only by the grace of God, he doubtless could have qualified for federal disaster relief.

For both Michael and Ginny, the litany of horrors was all too familiar.

Ginny stood in Paula's bathroom, watching her frantically applying mascara with the finesse of someone who had not had to do this in several decades. Ginny empathized as Paula's hand quivered and, in one stroke, the mascara brush undid ten minutes' careful application of eyeshadow. Paula cursed, grabbed a kleenex, tried to repair the damage as best she could, then went on to the eyeliner. "Only in America," she muttered into her mirror, "would a grown woman stand around outlining her eyes in crayon."

She looked at the thick black circles around her eyes and realized to her dismay that she resembled nothing so much as a giant panda. "To hell with it," she sighed, wiping away the eyeliner. "One more tribal custom bites the dust."

She started toweling her still-damp hair, frowning as she examined the wet strands dangling down her neck. She was still wearing her bathrobe, her dress carefully laid out in the bedroom; she turned, about to flee the bathroom, when Ginny, alarmed, purposefully knocked over the lipstick she had forgotten to apply. It clattered into the sink, reminding Paula; she quickly snapped it up and began applying it.

The doorbell rang and Paula nearly jumped out of her skin, leaving a thick line of coral pink zigzagging across her left cheek. Ginny looked heavenward as Paula hurriedly wiped the lipstick off her cheek, yelled out to the living room. "Coming!" Good God, *now* what? She only had half an hour before Dennis arrived; who the hell could *that* be?

She padded into the small but well-furnished living room, looked through the peephole of the door and was horrified to see, standing in the hallway—Dennis, in suit and tie. My God, was it seven already? No; glancing at the clock, she saw it was only six-thirty— what the hell was Dennis doing here so early? The bell rang again, shaking Paula from her panic; drawing her bathrobe around her a bit more tightly, she opened the door.

"Dennis. Hi," she said, her hair wet, her makeup awry, trying to forget that she doubtless looked like the Wicked Witch of the West. "You're . . . early."

Dennis entered, his overcoat dripping water. "Uh, yeah, I'm . . . sorry about that. It was raining, and I thought it'd be hard to find a cab, but it wasn't, and . . . uh . . ." He realized he was dripping, abruptly jumped back onto the plastic welcome mat inside the door. "Listen, I can wait downstairs if you—"

Paula waved a hand. "Don't be silly. Come on in. Let me take your coat."

As Paula put Dennis' coat in a closet, Michael followed him into the apartment; Ginny, leaning against the doorjamb between living room and bedroom, smiled sourly. "Couldn't you have held him up, for Pete's sake?"

"I tried," Michael insisted, joining her. "I did everything short of locking him in a closet. If it hadn't been for me—turning on the stove, breaking an occasional dish for him to pick up—he'd probably have shown up here at *six*."

Paula was trying to get her bearings as she guided Dennis to a seat in the living room. "Would you, uh, like a drink? Some wine, maybe?"

"Oh no, I'm fine, thanks."

"Oh. Okay. Well," she said, trying to beat a delicate retreat toward the bedroom, "if you'll excuse me, the Revlon SWAT team should be arriving any minute, so . . . there's some Coke and RC in the fridge; feel free to help yourself."

"Thanks. Take your time; I'll be fine."

Paula nodded and hurried past Michael and Ginny into the bedroom. Michael looked after her, then back to Dennis, who sat drumming his fingers on the arm of the sofa. "Jesus," Michael said, shaking his head. "Maybe we should slip some Valium into their coffee."

"I already looked in her medicine cabinet," Ginny sighed. "I don't suppose a few dozen Bufferin would do any good?"

"Not much, no."

"So much for drugs, then."

Dennis' nervous energy finally got the better of him; he stood, paced a few moments, taking in the apartment, then headed for the kitchen and pulled out a can of Coke from the refrigerator.

"Terrific," Ginny observed. "Just what he needs—twelve ounces of caffeine."

Michael was starting to get a headache.

Unthinkingly, Dennis bounced the can up and down in his hand as he looked through Paula's cabinets for a glass; upon finding one, he put it down on the counter and popped open the tab of the Coke. The soda, whipped into a carbonated frenzy, promptly spurted out of the can, foaming all over Dennis' hand, down his pants legs, and onto the floor.

"Does he do this often?" Ginny asked, eyes wide.

"Often enough," Michael winced.

Frantically, Dennis grabbed some paper towels and began wiping the Coke first off the floor, then from his pants. He had just about reached his left thigh when Paula, now fully clothed, entered the living room. "By the way," she called, "glasses are in the third cupboard on the—"

She stepped into the kitchen and came to an abrupt halt as she saw Dennis trying to wipe something off his trousers. He looked up, turned red, coughed. "I, ah . . . just had a little . . . accident," he said, and then, hearing his own words, added quickly, "With the *Coke*, I mean." Paula smiled weakly. . . .

Michael said, "He's just nervous. He'll get over it." But already he could see the distance growing between the two already-shy people, the tension as each was thrust into a social situation they had not dealt with in too long. "Look at it this way," Michael said, trying to make his tone sound cheery. "It can't get any worse than this."

That night, Michael learned the meaning of the word *hubris*—Greek for "It can *always* get worse."

*   *   *

The cab ride was spent in mostly tense, awkward silence, punctuated by occasional attempts at conversation—most of it concerning the weather, the restaurant, or the time—while Dennis and Paula sat several feet apart, eyes rarely meeting, both feeling unaccountably warm even in the chilly cab. Michael and Ginny sat up front, next to the driver, feeling every little pause in the conversation as much (if not more so) than the couple in back. Now Ginny was starting to worry. This was no longer funny. She prayed things would improve once they reached the restaurant.

The cab deposited them at a posh French restaurant— one of the ones Michael had circled in red in the phone book—on Central Park South. Entering, Dennis gave his name to the maître d', who scanned his reservations list and, forehead wrinkling, professed no prior acquaintance with Dennis' name. It took Dennis a few moments to catch on, then he reached into his wallet and slipped the man a five-dollar bill.

The maître d' glanced down at the fiver as though someone had just dropped a live snail in his hand; the corners of his mouth turned up in a tight-lipped smile, and he consulted his list again. "Oh . . . yes," he said in a tone which made Michael, listening, immediately flinch. "Here we are—*Mahoney*." He milked the surname for all the commonness he could, then led the couple to a table, more or less, at the far end of the dining room, approximately five feet from the ornate and constantly swinging doors which led to the kitchen.

Before Dennis could say anything, the maître d'

had placed menus on the table, mumbled something about their waiter being with them shortly, and left. Dennis sighed inwardly, settled into his seat. Immediately the kitchen doors swung open behind him, thudding into the wall; Dennis jumped, felt like a fool, gave Paula an embarrassed smile. "Looks like we've got the only table in the place equipped in four-track Dolby," he joked. Paula laughed nervously. Dennis wanted to die.

Michael and Ginny found an empty table a few feet away and settled in for the duration.

The waiter who was to be there shortly was apparently coming by way of Iceland, forcing Dennis and Paula to make awkward, self-conscious small talk—talk punctuated either by long, tremulous silences or by the periodic thudding of the kitchen door.

"So," Paula said. "You work for a publisher? That must be interesting?"

"Well . . ." Dennis searched his memory for some witty anecdote, some publishing *bon mot* to enthrall her, but this was not, alas, the Algonquin, and he was by no means Alexander Woollcott. "To tell the truth, it's really kind of dull," he admitted. "Most of the books I copyedit are pretty dry stuff: mathematics texts, sociology, stochastics . . . the kind of books no one would buy if they weren't on some assistant professor's required reading list."

"Ah. I see," Paula said. They lapsed into silence again, then:

"Your job must be exciting, though," Dennis said. "Working at MOMA, you must meet a lot of contemporary artists."

"Well," Paula said, "it's not exactly as if you run

into Jackson Pollock every time you go to the bathroom. Frankly,'' she added guiltily, ''I've never really been much into modern art except as it relates to my work. I'm mostly just an administrator.''

''Ah,'' Dennis said. ''I see.''

The silence was longer this time. Then, in a burst of inspiration, Dennis asked, ''Are you, uh, from New York originally?''

Paula seized gratefully on the question. ''No, as a matter of fact, I'm from Pennsylvania. Just outside Harrisburg.''

''Ah,'' Dennis said, with illumination. ''Harrisburg.''

Paula brightened. ''Have you been there?''

Dennis coughed. ''Well, no. Not really. I mean, I know the name.''

''Oh,'' Paula said.

By this time, Ginny was lying with her face down on the neighboring table, afraid to look up. ''Maybe it just *sounds* bad,'' she said to Michael, who was observing the whole fiasco. ''Tell me they're smiling, Michael. Tell me there's electricity in the air, laughter in their eyes. Tell me that, would you?''

Michael looked disconsolate. ''There were more laughs aboard the *Andrea Doria*.''

For the next several minutes Paula played with her silverware as Dennis studied the lace designs in the tablecloth until, finally, a reprieve arrived in the form of their near-mythical waiter. ''Are you ready to order?'' Ready and eager: drawing out the process as long as they reasonably could, they ordered paté, soup, salade niçoise, and, for a main course, duck à l'orange. Dennis fumbled for a few moments over the wine, then, at the waiter's suggestion, ordered an expensive Bordeaux . . . and then the waiter left, and Dennis and Paula lapsed back into dull, spasmodic conversation.

Dennis knew how badly it was going, but could not think for the life of him how to turn it around. He knew what he wanted to know about Paula—what were her interests, her passions, what made her laugh, what made her cry?—but had no idea how to draw that out in conversation. Now he remembered why he hadn't been out on a date in months, not since that awful night with that sharp-tongued little Italian girl. He could never figure out how you connected, what you said, how much of yourself to reveal: did women want to see a man's vulnerable side so early on, or should he try to project a stronger, more assured image? He hated playing a role, but at times he thought that that was all that dating really *was*. Damn it—why had he gone through with this, anyway?

For her part, Paula felt nearly as uncomfortable physically as she did emotionally; her dress was cut lower than it had seemed in the store, and with a body like hers, she felt like a fool wearing it. And if that wasn't bad enough, the restaurant itself was intimidating as hell; she almost wished Dennis had taken her to a Burger King, where every little pause and stammer in their conversation wouldn't take on such mammoth proportions. She felt skinny and plain and awkward and boring; why had she even tried this again? Sitting at home watching *Odd Couple* reruns on Channel 11 couldn't have been worse than this.

Finally the waiter arrived with a bottle of St. Emilion, nestled in a wine cradle, for their inspection;

Dennis nodded his approval, then tried not to seem too surprised when instead of opening the bottle at the table, the waiter returned to the kitchen to decant it. Another few awkward minutes passed until the waiter came back, decanter in hand, ready to pour— when Dennis, desperate for something to do, announced, "I'll take care of it, thank you," and took the decanter from him. The waiter gave Dennis a small condescending look, nodded, and moved off. Michael and Ginny exchanged worried glances as Dennis took the wine, but to their relief he poured it expertly, spilling not a drop. Paula looked as relieved as Ginny and Michael. Dennis, grinning, raised his glass in a toast; Paula followed suit.

Dennis thought for a moment, then proposed, "Well. To . . . chance meetings."

"To chance meetings," Paula agreed.

They extended their glasses, made contact with a gentle clink of crystal . . .

. . . the door behind them banged open with a sound like a gunshot and Dennis jumped, spilling half his Bordeaux onto the tablecloth. What did not sink immediately into the cloth splashed off the table and onto Dennis and Paula, speckling his shirt and her gown with little red dots.

Michael's head sank to the table and he buried it in his arms. Ginny stared, horrified, fear gripping her.

Dennis stammered helplessly: "Oh God, I'm *sorry* . . . here, let me—"

He snapped up a napkin, handed it to Paula; she made a couple of swipes with it before seeing that it was just as sodden as her dress. Dennis saw and went pale. "Oh, shit," he said. "Paula, I'm so—"

"It's okay," Paula said, using the corner of the tablecloth to blot up most of the wine. People were staring at them from other tables; their waiter was doing his best to avoid seeing them. "I'll just . . . go to the ladies' room for a second. If you'll excuse me . . ."

She got up, flushing with shame and anger, and as she passed Michael and Ginny's table, Ginny's worst fears seemed to be coming true; she saw again the burning Christmas tree, heard again the screams, the wails of anguish, felt the awful *heat* . . .

Michael was still sitting with his head on the table. "It's over," he kept saying. "It's a disaster. Irwin Allen could make a movie out of this."

Ginny looked at Dennis, his head hung low, his eyes stinging with embarrassment, pain and self-loathing written on his face. Again. Again she'd hurt him. Damn it, no. No! Not this time. She wouldn't let it happen again!

She stood abruptly, grabbed Michael by the arm, and pulled him to his feet. "It's not over," she cried in sudden inspiration. "Not yet, anyway. Come on!" She hauled a puzzled Michael through the dining room, out the restaurant, and into the night.

The sleet had stopped, thank God, and the air was brisk and cold. A crescent moon hung above Central Park to the east; Ginny ran toward the park, Michael yelling at her a few steps behind. "Ginny! Ginny, where the hell are we *going?*"

"All we've gotta do," she called back, "is establish a romantic mood! Give them someplace where they can talk, where they don't have to worry about snotty waiters or pouring wine!"

"*Where*, for crissake? Guatemala?"

"You'll see!"

Ginny ran into Central Park, and Michael, having no better idea, followed. She dashed up, down, and along winding cobbled paths, her astral form streaking through bushes and walls and trees, until, after ten minutes, she found what she was searching for. There, a few hundred yards from the lake, its driver sitting on the edge of the front seat and smoking a cigarette, was the hansom cab they had ridden in so many weeks before.

Ginny came to a momentary halt, beaming happily. Michael trotted up behind out of breath. "Jesus," he gasped, "I never knew you could *run* so fast."

Ginny laughed, gasping for breath as she did. "Neither did I. Come on, we gotta hurry!"

She ran toward the hansom with a burst of renewed energy.

The driver sat on the edge of the seat, scanning a racing form and not noticing as, behind him, the horse's reins floated up off the seat by themselves, hovering in midair for just a moment.

"Uh—Gin? You ever done this before?"

"What's the big deal? A horse is a horse. I've ridden plenty of carousels."

"Oh, great."

The reins flicked themselves against the horse's flanks and the startled animal whinnied and took off at a gallop, the sudden lurch nearly toppling the driver off the seat. He grabbed onto the nearest support, struggled to keep his balance . . . then gaped as he saw the reins jiggling in midair. He lunged forward, straining to grab them, but the cab hit a bump and he was pitched backwards into the seat, end-over-end.

"See?" Ginny said. "Nothing to it."

The reins flicked again as the horse was prodded to go faster. The hansom hurtled through the park, its dazed and baffled driver rattling around in the back seat, then careened around a corner and out of the park, heading east down Central Park South.

Dinner seemed to arrive very quickly; Dennis suspected that the maître d', who had observed the entire fiasco with narrowed eyes, was trying to get rid of them as soon as possible, and Dennis could hardly blame him. Paula returned from the ladies' room, the stains on her dress only slightly faded, and they were kept thankfully busy eating for the next forty-five minutes. Skipping desert, they were on their way out seconds after Dennis signed the credit card chit.

Dennis stopped off at the men's room to stuff paper towels under his arms and to try to regain some of his composure; Paula waited just inside the lobby. She caught her reflection in the wide glass doors, and was immediately sorry she did: she looked utterly at loose ends, her dress speckled with wine stains, her hair awry, her eyes dull and sad. She couldn't even bring herself to fully blame Dennis; he had been as nervous as she. It was just all wrong. She simply wasn't cut out for this. She turned away from her reflection in disgust, just as Dennis ambled sheepishly out of the men's room. Wordlessly, they left the lobby.

Outside, they stood, bedraggled and embarrassed,

neither certain what to do next. Finally, Dennis spoke up. "Are you . . . ah . . . still interested in the movie?" he asked, a bit sheepishly.

Paula looked decidedly skeptical. "We're not exactly off to the most auspicious of starts, are we? And I would like to get out of this damp dress."

"Of course," Dennis said. "I'll just take you home. Let me find a cab." He raised his arm to hail a taxi, when suddenly he heard the whicker of a horse, not far off. He glanced around to find, parked just across the street, a hansom cab—its horse whinnying as though it had been slapped, exhaling plumes of frosted breath from its sleek brown head.

Dennis raised an eyebrow. "Say, how about taking a hansom instead? We could cut across the park . . . probably be faster than finding a taxi, anyway."

Paula glanced at the horse and carriage standing calmly in the glow of a half-moon, and the thought of a quiet, peaceful ride through the park appealed to her, particularly after the carnage of the last few hours. "Sure," she shrugged. "Why not?"

A delighted Michael and Ginny proceeded to pour a thermos cup of coffee into the still-dazed driver; by the time Dennis and Paula crossed the street, he was alert and very, very confused—though not so confused that he could turn down a fare. In minutes they were entering the park via East Drive, past the pond, heading toward West Drive and Paula's apartment on the Upper West Side.

As the cab glided through the park, Dennis found his voice and, in halting tones, tried to formulate an apology for everything up to and including the weather. "I had it all planned so carefully, see," he said ruefully. "Then it all started to unravel like a cheap suit."

Paula nodded, feeling herself sink slowly into depression. "It's not just you," she said gently. "I'm not much good at this sort of thing, either. I was stupid to even try it."

Dennis gazed down at his feet, awkwardly. "I know how you feel," he said quietly. "Funny, isn't it. When you're a kid in school they teach you algebra, geometry, geology, stuff I haven't had to know about since twelfth grade. But they never teach you how to get along with other people, do they? I guess they don't think that's very important, for some reason. Or they think that somehow you'll pick it up as you go along, like osmosis or something. They'd never try that with history or English, though, would they?"

His words struck a responsive chord in Paula. "You did all right with the flowers," she said softly. "That was very sweet."

Dennis felt a jab of guilt. He turned red, frowned. The one thing he did right—he didn't do at all. Behind him, in the rear seat, Michael shut his eyes. *No. Dennis. Don't . . .*

"I . . . didn't send those flowers," Dennis admitted. Paula's eyes widened. Michael covered his face with his hands. Ginny wanted to cry.

"Not that I wouldn't have liked to," he added quickly, "but I . . . I would never have found the guts." He looked away from Paula's stunned expression. "I don't know who sent them . . . don't know who signed my name . . . but it wasn't me. I only wish it had been."

Paula felt tears coming to her eyes. "You . . . didn't send them?" she said, her voice so small and hurt it tore open Dennis' heart. "It was all some kind of a . . . joke?"

Ginny, horrified, stood up and yelled. "No! Paula, it wasn't a joke! It wasn't a—"

"I didn't say that," Dennis said quickly. "All I said was—"

"All a lie," Paula was saying, the tears flowing freely now. "Just like the card. Just like—"

Ginny was crying now, too. "No! No, it wasn't *like* that—"

Michael had to hold her back for fear she would grab Paula—the last thing anyone needed right now. "Ginny, for God's sake, she can't hear you!"

"God *damn* it," Paula whispered vehemently. "It isn't fair! I'd gotten used to it. I wasn't going to let myself hope anymore—"

Dennis reached out to touch her arm; she jerked back, angry, indignant. "Leave me alone!" she snapped. "Who the hell asked you to come into my life, anyway! Who the hell asked for your flowers and your poem and your goddamn cards!" She leaned forward urgently. "Driver! Stop here."

The driver blinked. "But ma'am, we're not out of the—"

"I said *stop here*." The driver obliged; he brought the cab to a halt on the western edge of the park, and as soon as he did, Paula jumped out. Hitting the ground, she twisted her ankle and winced as the pain shot up through her leg.

Dennis leaped out after her, followed by Ginny, then Michael. "Paula, please, let me take you—"

"Haven't you done *enough?*" Paula demanded. "*All* of you?"

By "all" she obviously meant men in general, but to Ginny it seemed as though the remark was aimed right at her. The tears continued to roll down her cheeks.

"L-Let me pay for your dry-cleaning bill, at least," Dennis stammered out, unable to think of anything else.

Paula wiped at her eye, saw a smudge of mascara on her fingers. Wonderful. She straightened, fighting to keep her tone measured and calm. "That—won't be necessary," she said flatly. "I . . . kind of doubt I'll have any use for this dress again."

She turned and ran out of the park, each step she took sending blinding spikes of pain up her calf; Dennis stared after, feeling like shit—feeling like *less* than shit. After a moment he took out his wallet, handed the hansom driver a twenty, and trundled out of the park himself, wishing he were dead. Wishing he had never been born.

But Dennis' guilt was as nothing compared to Ginny's. She saw the two lonely people rushing brokenly away, and she wanted to hide, wanted to run, but there was nowhere to run to, no way to escape her own guilt. "No," she whimpered, the old Ginny creeping back, taking hold, "no . . . please . . . not again . . ."

Michael reached out to comfort her, but, to his shock, she recoiled from his touch even as Paula had recoiled from Dennis'.

"*Damn you!*" she shrieked at him, and, stunned

and hurt, he shrank back. "You *made* me do this! I didn't want to, but I did it for *you!*"

Michael didn't know what to say. "Ginny, I—"

But Ginny's rage was not about to be cooled. "All my life, I hurt people—without meaning to, without knowing how or why or even when I did it, not until it was too late! I hurt Annie, I hurt Dennis, and when I tried to *end* it all, I hurt *Maggie!* And now—"

She started to run off. Michael grabbed her by the arm, firmly but not at all violently. "Ginny, I'm sorry—don't you think I feel like—"

"Let go of me!" Ginny screamed in a voice Michael had never heard before; she wrested free of his grip, twisting Michael's wrist in the process. He yelped in pain, and within moments Ginny was racing out of the park, sobbing. Michael stood by, as helpless as Dennis had been, fear and shame and guilt growing within him like a cancer.

He walked all the way back to the Waldorf, keeping within a couple of blocks of Ginny as she ran ahead of him. He passed through the doors into their suite, but Ginny was not in sight and the door to her bedroom was shut. After debating a moment, he stuck his head through the bedroom door for just an instant, long enough to see that Ginny was lying face-down on the bed, her body heaving as she cried herself to sleep. Michael considered entering, then decided against it. Damn it—hadn't he done enough already? He poked his head out again and shuffled disconsolately back to his own room.

He fell onto his bed and felt like crying himself. How, how, how could he have been so stupid? How could he have thought that *he*—a failure at everything he had ever tried—could possibly have known more about life than Dennis and Paula? What the fuck made him think that he could help?

It took him hours to fall asleep, and when he did sleep, it was brief, restless, and troubled. It was his turn to dream tonight—if that's what it was—and he dreamt of one of the lush tropical islands he had so often longed to see . . . but the island was barren, deserted, beautiful but utterly empty, with only the stars and the whisper of the surf to keep him company. He woke coldsweating, trying to shake off the full horror of that dream; afraid to go back to sleep, he lay awake in bed for two hours until a dusty dawn light filtered through the curtains.

He got up a little past six, hoping that Ginny was all right, wondering if he should go to her. Finally, working up his nerve, he crossed the sitting room to her bedroom, took a deep breath, and passed through her closed doors. He stood inside her bedroom and felt the fear take hold again, cradling him in its cold, dank arms.

Ginny was gone.

13

Michael,
I'm sorry I yelled at you. It's not your fault, it's just me—I can't seem to do anything right. You'll be better off without me. I didn't mean to hurt you. But then I never do, do I?

Goodbye
Ginny

The note was scribbled on Waldorf stationery. Michael's hands were sweating. He sank slowly onto the bed, feeling numb. This couldn't be happening. She couldn't be serious. Could she?

He looked again at the note in his trembling hand,

and he knew somehow that she meant it. He saw again the anguish and the guilt on her face last night, and he cursed himself for not doing more. If only he'd gone into her bedroom last night, if only he'd talked to her— But no. He pushed the recriminations aside; they wouldn't help him find Ginny.

His first thought was the hospital. He didn't know what would draw her there, but it was the only thing that, in his clouded state of mind, occurred to him. He couldn't seem to gather his thoughts, couldn't fight off the crushing fear; blindly he tore out of the room, dressed, and dashed down twelve flights of stairs, running through walls, doors, any and all obstacles in his path, seeing nothing in front of him but Ginny's tortured face, hearing nothing but her anguished voice. *How?* How could he have done this to her? As he ran into the subway station he castigated himself for wrong turns and errors in judgment about which he could do nothing; not for the first time he wished he could turn time backwards, somehow. But of course he couldn't. Time existed outside his grief, a vessel for the world's sorrows, nothing more; as he rushed through the turnstile in the IRT, he felt himself passing through each moment of time in a way he never had before, each instant falling away behind him, never to be regained, and he felt a passing melancholy for each moment lost and squandered. He jumped onto the moving subway car, acutely aware for the first time of how precious time truly was; the thought that Ginny could exist now only in his past, in moments scattered behind him, filled him with terror.

Twenty minutes later he was in Bellevue, but as he

burst into Ginny's intensive care unit, his heart sank;
only Ginny's body was here, breathing shallowly,
unhearing and unseeing, the body monitors attached
to it able to document the presence of biological life,
but little else. Michael looked down at the sweet,
round face, the pale skin framed by a crop of un-
kempt hair; it resembled Ginny only in the way a suit
of clothes resembled a person's physique, reflecting
the cut and shape of bones, muscles, tendons, but
unanimated, without form, or breath, or substance.
He would not let this be his last memory of Ginny.
He would *not*.

Looking up Ginny's address in the nearest phone
book, he went to her apartment on Grand Street—but
found nothing. He searched Macy's, first the display
window she so often worked in, then each floor and
department in rapid succession—and again, nothing.
He even went to Margaret's apartment, admittedly a
long shot but worth a try, and found only Margaret,
preparing to leave for work, looking haggard and
worn and worried, chain-smoking Virginia Slims.

He searched the Hilton, the Plaza, the Park Lane,
and St. Regis hotels, checking all suites listed as
unoccupied on the guest register; Ginny was in none
of them. He was running out of ideas. Exhausted,
discouraged, he left the hotel district and trudged
wearily into Central Park, to take stock and consider
his options.

It had snowed during the night, dusting the frozen
pond with a white, virgin powder; Michael sat at the
water's edge, staring out at the wide expanse of what
seemed like nothingness, feeling frightened and alone.
It was cold, but he felt no chill; the ground he sat on

was hard and brittle with winter, but he felt no discomfort, only pressure and a dull awareness of cold. Physically, he might've felt no pain, but inside he had not hurt this badly since the day three years ago when his parents had died and he'd realized that he would never be able to tell them now how much he loved them. And now Ginny would never know, either, because up until now, Michael had not known himself. Once again he wanted to cry, and once again he held back: that would not help find Ginny. That was all that mattered now. Once, perhaps, he would have been content to wallow in his own pain and pity, but now all that concerned him was finding his friend.

Where? Where could she have gone? Where could someone like Ginny, who had tried to kill herself because she had had nowhere to go on Christmas Eve, where could she possibly *go* when everything else fell in on her? There was no place left to—

He stopped, ran back that last thought, turned it over in his mind. Christmas?

Pushing aside his pain, he searched back, connecting words, phrases, snatches of conversation. Christmas; snow. Snow; field. Field; farm. Farm; *Vermont* . . .

Was it possible? Could she even *get* that far without starting to fade away, as had happened on the plane? He scrambled to his feet, ran out of the park and into the nearest stationery store. Not caring about the stunned reactions of onlookers, he grabbed a fold-out map of the Northeast, a pencil, and—in a burst of inspiration—one of those tiny compasses they gave you in fourth grade while teaching you about diameters and radii. He ran out of the store, clerks running after the merchandise bobbing through the air; halfway across the street they gave up the chase and Michael took the material to a secluded bench in the park.

Somehow he had to figure out exactly where above Pennsylvania they had begun to lose their strength and fade away. The wheatfield might have been a starting point, except that he had no idea where it was located (road signs had not begun to appear until they hit the turnpike) nor of how far they had fallen before that. No, the wheatfield was no help; scratch that.

He searched his memory for any little detail of that trip which might prove useful, finally remembering how he had looked out the window of the plane and seen a long, winding river passing beneath them. Yes! Consulting his map, Michael determined that that was probably the Susquehanna. It was roughly ten minutes after that, he recalled, that they had begun to fade away.

Good; now he was getting somewhere. Assuming the plane was traveling at maybe six hundred miles per hour, ten miles per minute, then they could have flown perhaps a hundred miles in those ten minutes. Michael took the compass, put the metal tip squarely on the eastern flank of Manhattan—specifically, Bellevue—then brought the pencil to a point approximately a hundred miles west of the Susquehanna River. That was the radius within which they could travel safely.

He swung the compass around, creating a full

circle with Manhattan at its very center, its radius not more than about two hundred miles across.

The circle cut a swath right through the middle of Vermont, the lower half of the state comfortably within the radius of safety.

It *was* possible. Michael tried to contain his excitement; there was, after all, no evidence that Ginny had even gone there. But now, at least, he had somewhere to look. The next step was to find out exactly where her grandparents' farm was, or had been—and whether it was within the circle.

Returning to Ginny's apartment, he began pulling open every drawer, examining every address book or scrap of paper he could find, in hopes of finding some clue. He felt vaguely guilty, as though he were invading Ginny's privacy—which he supposed he was—and hoped the invasion was not for nothing. Finally, after half an hour, he stumbled onto an old trunk tucked away in the back of a closet—a trunk that looked as though it had been there for years, its handles broken off, its lock rusted and, more to the point, sealed tight.

Taking a deep breath, Michael tried something he had not heretofore attempted: he stuck his hand inside the trunk, then willed *only his fingers* to become solid, careful to keep that part of his arm which was passing through the trunk ephemeral; God only knew what would happen if he suddenly became substantial inside a solid object, and he didn't care to find out. He fumbled around, blindly, inside the trunk, feeling about for some sort of spring or catch which might release the lock mechanism. Finally, his thumb seemed to trip something—he heard a soft click from inside—and, allowing his fingers to become insubstantial again, he pulled out his hand. The trunk opened easily. He peered inside—and hit pay dirt. The trunk was filled with photo albums, diaries, old letters, faded Christmas cards.

Respectfully he worked his way through the yellowing photographs (one of which showed Ginny as a child—plump, long-haired, looking awkwardly away from the camera as she stood before a two-storey frame house in the Bronx), the old report cards (mostly B-minuses and C-pluses, but with one A from high school, in social dance), and, ultimately, a collection of old birthday and Christmas cards, bound together by a frayed rubber band. He undid the band and flipped through the cards, noting the relatives' names inscribed within—Sal, Dominick, Carrie, Margaret—finally coming to one with a quiet snow scene on the front, like something out of Currier & Ives, the fake granular "snow" falling off the card as Michael opened it. Inside was an appropriate poem, and it was signed, *Merry Christmas, Ginny. Love, Nonno and Nonna*.

The envelope the card had arrived in had also been lovingly preserved; it was postmarked some fifteen years ago, and the return address read, *Angelo & Lillian Benedetti, Rural Route #1, Middlebury, Vermont 05753*. Excitedly, Michael unfolded his map and consulted the index, looking for the town of Middlebury. His finger ran along the grid lines until it came to the small dot in the middle of the state which represented the town.

His heart seemed to skip a beat as he fought back a sudden rush of terror.

The town of Middlebury lay less than a sixteenth of an inch—not more than half a mile—from the pencil line marking the point of no return for Michael and Ginny's astral bodies.

By three that afternoon, Michael was aboard a Greyhound bus bound for Barre, Vermont, the nearest major town to Middlebury; the bus rattled through the New England countryside, and despite his worry for Ginny, Michael began to feel calmer than he had in weeks. The gray, oppressive clouds of Manhattan slowly gave way to the clear, bright skies of New England; it was almost like traveling back in time, like the shadows of the past which he and Ginny could seemingly conjure at will, as glass-and-concrete office buildings were supplanted by gabled homes and wooden trestles, as New York gave way to Connecticut, Connecticut to Massachusetts, Massachusetts to Vermont. Michael sat beside a partially open window at the rear of the bus and watched the clean bright landscape hurtle past: tomato-red textile mills with crosshatched windows; churches topped by tall white steeples; lonely wood cabins dusted with snow; covered walkbridges straddling frozen streams; glazed and silent waterfalls emptying, like ice statues, into frozen ponds.

Michael had never been to New England before, save for one trip to visit relatives in Massachusetts when he was eleven, and now its beauty startled him. He watched the tall, thin birch trees whipping past, stripped by the wind, patient in the dictates of the season—knowing, perhaps, that in time their branches would come full, that the cycle had gone on for longer than any brief moment of chill such as this, that things had always come round before, and always would. The cycle of life continued here as it had for centuries of human generation, but it was more than the simple matter of deterioration and regeneration which Michael, standing on a bridge and looking down at black waters, had once envisioned: the land provided food, and the people provided for the land—building on it, raising their families on it, spending their lives with it.

Not everyone lived off the land, of course, but even so they were closer to it, a more integral part of their environment, than Michael had ever been to his own world. In New York, in most cities, nature actually intruded on the environment—a park here, a straggly line of trees over there. So much easier to forget that one lived on a planet of soil and sea and atmosphere; so much easier to forget you were a part of that, to forget that you were *alive* in the same way the ocean and the forest and the sky were alive. But here, Michael imagined, it must have been hard to forget that . . . hard to ignore the smell of pine trees, the scent of new-mown grass, the bitter chill of a New England wind, a wind like the one whipping at Michael now, cold and biting but *clean*, fresh, an honest reminder of the limits of one's endurance and an encouragement to transcend them . . .

. . . and it was then that Michael realized, with some astonishment, that he was shivering in that chill, biting wind; that he felt the cold as a real thing, harsh and unforgiving but wonderfully, beautifully *real*. All at once, sensations flooded him: he watched the landscape rush past and caught the crisp, clean smell of newly fallen snow; heard the laughter of children skidding across frozen streams on wobbly skates and remembered doing the same on the brook of his childhood in New Jersey, remembered the giddy loss of control as he slid dizzyingly over the ice and under a walkbridge.

He remembered it all, random sensations culled from thirty years of living: the scent of plants and shrubbery at night, sweet and heavy in the darkness; the smell of rain, the sound of it on a roof at night, a gentle drumming lulling him asleep; the feel of a woman's face against his, the way her hair brushed against his shut eyelids, the way his lips would gently nibble at hers, slowly working from one corner of her mouth to the other, then a hungry joining of tongues . . .

For an instant, he *remembered* . . . remembered what it was like to be alive, a feeling he now realized he had not had in many, many years . . . and then, too soon, it was over. The wind sliced through his astral form without cold, without chill, and the memories lost their vividness, turning flat, lacking in sensation. But he *had* remembered. For a moment, he had a vision of what his life once was, however briefly, and could be again . . . but not, he knew, until he had found Ginny.

Michael disembarked in Barre, catching another bus to Middlebury, where he went directly to the local post office. Finding a map of the rural and "star" routes, he quickly located Rural Route #1: a few miles north of town, perilously close to the border which only he could see, the point at which his astral body would start to lose its strength and fade away into—what? Heaven? Hell? Limbo? Once, any one of those might have seemed preferable to life; now, he wanted no truck with any of them, not for a long time to come. Suppressing his fear, he dashed out of the post office and struck up the dirt road outside town that would lead him to Rural Route #1.

It was nearly dusk when he finally spied the old wood-frame house standing in the shadow of a snowcapped hill; beside it was an abandoned barn and empty silo, the doors of the barn long ago boarded up, the barnyard still and deserted. Michael walked through the delapidated picket fence enclosing the front yard, every third or fourth stake either missing or askew, and down the snow-laden path to the house.

The house itself had probably been charming in its time; paint on the wooden siding had flaked away over the years, leaving now only scabrous red patches, here and there, but strangely enough the white trim on the doors and windows had weathered the years far better. Attic rooms peered down blindly from above; a red brick chimney stood, half-fallen, toward the front of the roof. A yellow lantern swung from the porch awning, and icicles hung like bars before the near-opaque windows.

Michael stood on the porch, suddenly frightened. If she was not here, he did not know where else he could look. If she was not here, he had lost her. He stared at the front door a long moment, paralyzed— then took a deep breath, stepped forward, and tingled

as his astral form passed through the door into the
house.

The foyer was dark and chilly; Michael followed it
to the living room, large and spacious and empty.
The fireplace had fallen in on itself, bricks and ash
lying scattered at its mouth; mounds of plaster dotted
the bare floors. Michael shivered even though he
could not really feel the chill. He moved back into
the hall, poked his head into a bedroom; it, too, was
deserted. He felt a rush of despair—why would Ginny
have come here? It was a tomb. He almost did not go
any further . . . and then he heard the voice.

"Oh, that looks wonderful, *Nonna*. Can I have
some?"

It was Ginny's voice. Michael's heart leaped; he
scrambled through the house, searching for the source,
finally bursting into the crumbling kitchen.

Ginny stood by the stove, her back to him, dipping
a broken ladle into a rusted saucepan. Michael ran to
her side. "Ginny!" he cried, nearly collapsing against
the kitchen counter. "Thank God! I knew you'd be
here."

But Ginny did not respond. She leaned over, sniffing something, sighed with pleasure and took a sip of
air from the empty ladle. "Mmmm," she said, "that's
wonderful, *Nonna*."

Michael blinked; he was not yet thinking clearly.
"Ginny, I'm sorry," he said, thinking she was ignoring him; "I should never have asked you to do it, but
it was important to me, and I wasn't really—"

She was not responding at all to his words; she
continued to sip from the empty ladle, her eyes fixed
on something just beyond. Michael took a step forward,

directly in Ginny's line of sight; she seemed to look right through him. "Can I help you with supper, *Nonna*?" she was saying, and Michael shuddered as he slowly came to understand what was happening. "I could go out and help *Nonno* with the firewood. No? I'll tell you what—I'll whip some cream for dessert, okay?"

Michael looked away as Ginny, a dreamy, satisfied smile on her face, skipped happily toward the rusted, doorless refrigerator, pulled open a door that was not there, took out something only she could see, then moved to the dirty counter and—her right hand tightly grasping something equally invisible—began a series of short, brisk whipping motions. She was whistling a Christmas carol as she worked.

Michael sank into one of the tumbledown kitchen chairs. No. No, please. He felt very weak, very tired, and knew that it was not just from the long ride here, nor from the shock of seeing Ginny this way; he was close to the edge, the point of no return only a few hundred yards away. But perhaps he could make that work for him. He looked up, watched Ginny stirring her nonexistent cream, then shut his eyes, allowing his mind to go blank. There were shadows here and he would catch them, as Ginny had. It was easier, somehow, to fall into that quasi-mystical state here; they were so close to the edge, the border, that their psychic defenses were down, as they had been when falling from the plane. It was easier to drop back into the past—and easier, Michael reminded himself, for Ginny to stay there . . .

When he opened his eyes, the kitchen was bright, clean, and homey, filled with the smell of pumpkin pie being baked in the large cast-iron oven. The refrigerator was whole and nearly new, and in the middle of the room, where only moments before had been nothing but cracked linoleum and the lonely chair on which Michael sat, there were now four high-backed chairs and a long wooden table covered by a red-and-white checkered tablecloth.

By the stove, a feisty-looking, white-haired woman in her seventies energetically diced celery while, not three feet away, Ginny stood happily whipping cream in a porcelain bowl. Michael stood, about to go to her, when suddenly a small, girlish voice called out from the corridor: "*Nonna! Nonna,* you in there?"

The elderly woman smiled as an animated, roly-poly little girl bounded into the kitchen to her grandmother's side. Michael recognized the girl from a yellowing photograph in a time now distant. It was Ginny.

"*Nonna,*" the girl said, very soberly, "Maggie won't play with me. All she wants to do is sit and watch the dumb television." Her chubby face was wrinkled in a frown, and Michael had to smile. Such a serious little girl. A lot like him, at that age.

Her grandmother squatted, bones creaking slightly, and brushed hair out of young Ginny's eyes. "*Ach,*" she said, waving a hand, "let her play with the television. We'll play in here. Here," she said, handing Ginny a bowl of diced onions, celery, and a container of sour cream. "We'll put the celery salad in your hands, Virginia. Mix in the sour cream and the vinegar—just a touch, now—and bring it back to me when you've finished. All right?" Young Ginny eagerly took the bowl, the container, and a large soup spoon, climbed onto a chair and began earnestly stirring the salad, bits of celery occasionally flying out of the bowl under her onslaught.

Michael looked over to where the adult Ginny did much the same thing. When little Ginny had entered the room, her adult counterpart had glanced quickly away, as if from an intruder; now she stole envious glances at the little girl, at whom her grandmother smiled and spoke and made small noises of approval. The adult Ginny whipped the cream harder, faster, as though by so doing the shadows in the room might be able to see her, but *Nonna* still made no recognition of her presence.

Nor had Ginny yet seen Michael. He took a step forward, almost reluctant to break the quiet, tender mood.

"Ginny?" he said, gently.

Ginny spun round, at first pleased that someone had addressed her, then stunned and embarrassed as she saw who it was.

"Michael?" she said, flushing briefly. Her eyes were wide, she seemed confused and disoriented; then her face abruptly darkened and she turned back to her task, whipping the cream harder still. "Go away," she said, as soberly as the eight-year-old across the room.

"Ginny, please, don't," Michael said, hurt by her tone. "I know how you feel—"

"Michael, go *away!*"

"I'm *sorry*, Ginny! I had no right to involve you in my crack-headed scheme, I never wanted to hurt you, but you can't stay here! Please. Come with me. We'll go back to New York, okay?"

Ginny turned, fire in her eyes. "Sure. There are at least three million other people there I haven't dumped on yet. That should keep us busy for a while!"

Michael reached out to touch her. "Ginny, it wasn't your—"

"Leave me alone!" Ginny screamed, recoiling violently at his touch; Michael was hurt deeply, tears sprang to his eyes. "I'm better off here, Michael, just leave me be!"

"Better off?" Michael said, incredulous. "Ginny, you don't belong here! No one can even see you."

"Yes, they can!"

"No, they can't! They're shadows, Ginny, ghosts, that's all!"

"That's all *we* are, isn't it?" she snapped, tossing her spoon into the sink with a clatter. "I should fit right in."

"We're not ghosts, goddammit!" Michael said, more vehemently than he had intended. "Don't you understand? This is our essence, our soul, whatever it is that makes us *us*, without all the damned heavy baggage the world dumps on top of us. If we can't figure out what it's like to be alive now, Ginny, we never will." He grabbed her by the shoulders, pleadingly. "You *are* alive, Ginny. You may not feel it—you may not want to feel it—but you are! You don't *belong* here."

Ginny flew into a rage, wresting away from him. "This is the only place I *ever* belonged!"

"No. *She* belongs here," Michael yelled back at her, pointing at the eight-year-old still happily stirring her salad at the table. "This is *her* Christmas,

Ginny. Not yours. Not any more. I swear to God, Ginny, you'll have other Christmases. You *will*."

"*Leave me alone!*" Ginny screamed. She clapped her hands to her ears and bolted the kitchen; Michael ran after. She zigzagged through the now-homey, now-brand-new hallways, flung open the front door, and stumbled down the front steps. Teddy, the old dying huskie, ambled right through her as she ran, weeping, into the front yard. Michael's heart raced as he saw that she was running north—toward the unseen edge of their world.

"Ginny, stop, please!" He picked up speed and quickly overtook her, grabbing her by the arms, preventing her from running any farther. She cursed, yelled, cried, slowly sinking to her knees; she looked up at Michael, tears streaming down her cheeks, voice ragged.

"Michael, don't you see," she said plaintively. "I hurt Dennis, I hurt Paula, I hurt Annie . . . and one of these days I'll hurt *you*. I don't want to do that, Michael. I've never wanted to hurt anyone less in my whole life."

"Ginny, you won't hurt me."

"I will. I *will*. I can't help it; I just *do*. For God's sake, can't you see you'll be better off without me?"

Michael squatted down beside her, touched her cheek, gently. "Ginny, I'd be dead without you. I love you."

Ginny shut her eyes, hearing the words as a mockery, a ploy. "Don't, Michael. You just want to get me away from here. Don't lie to me. Please."

"I'm not lying," Michael said, his voice catching. "I *love* you, Ginny. I've never said that to anyone before . . . never thought I ever would. I'm not just—"

But Ginny could not bring herself to believe. "Just like Paula!" she yelled, barely coherent now. "Just another lie! Just another stupid scheme! God damn you to *hell*, Michael! Get *away* from me! Just get the fuck *away!*"

He had never heard such hatred in her voice, and Michael suddenly knew that she was gone; lost. He was too late. He had always been too late. He stood up, numbly, blinking back tears, and looked down the road toward town. God, no. He couldn't go back. He couldn't face it all alone, knowing that he had hurt someone as much as this; he knew now what Ginny was going through. No, he couldn't go in that direction . . . and that left only—

He looked north. A small creek, its surface a sheet of glimmering ice, stood a few hundred yards away. Yes. That was about right. It would be as good a demarcation as any. All he had to do was think of it as a . . . a finish line. The end to a long, tiring race which he had lost without even knowing how. He turned back to Ginny.

"All right," he heard himself say, as if from a great distance. "I'll go away, Ginny." She looked up, something in his voice making her stop crying; Michael felt his stomach coil. He felt weak, just this close to it; it wouldn't take long. "See that creek over there?" he said, pointing. "I'm going to run to it. I'm going to run as fast as I can. And somewhere between here and there I'm going to fall, but I'll get up again, and run some more, and maybe I'll fall again, but I'll keep running till I can't *move* any longer, till I melt into the goddamn snow, till I fade away like I *should've* done on the plane. And that'll be it. No more pain. No more anything. Because if you're not coming back with me, there's no goddamn reason for me to crawl back into that frigging body and go through all the same crap, all the same pain! You understand, Ginny? No fucking reason at *all!*"

His voice built in intensity until, at the finish, it ended in a ragged yell. Ginny recoiled in surprise, not certain what he was talking about, but before she could say anything, Michael had turned on his heel and was running out the front yard.

Ginny stared after, a horrible feeling coming over her. "Michael—Michael—?"

Michael passed through the picket fence, his legs wobbling as he ran. It was starting.

Ginny's heart skipped as she saw him falter, the motion suddenly all too familiar. *My God, the plane.* She jumped to her feet, cried out: "Michael, no!"

Michael ran through a neighboring yard, his strength draining; he stumbled, pitched forward, fell.

Ginny started running after. "Oh my God, Michael, no!"

Michael scrambled to his feet and kept running, hot tears streaming down his cheeks, not hearing Ginny's cries. His legs felt like water, it was getting harder to breathe, but he continued running, the creek only a few dozen yards away now.

"*Michael!*" Ginny watched as Michael's body shimmered, turning first translucent, then transparent.

She screamed. "*Michael!* Oh, God, Michael, *please stop!*"

He was beyond hearing, past caring. He fell again, picked himself up. The frozen creek glistened like diamond ahead of him. The sea, he thought. The creek would carry him back to the sea. He stumbled again, lurched forward, regained his balance and kept running.

Ginny felt weak herself; her legs threatened to buckle, and she felt her own strength ebbing. Michael was still ahead of her; sunlight poured through his body as he ran for the creek. Points of dazzling light, reflected off the frozen stream, shone through his glassy figure, like stars shining through a cloud that looked, briefly, like the figure of a man.

"*MI-CHAEL!*"

The scream robbed her of her last bit of strength; she collapsed, sobbing, into the snow. She tried to get up, but her arms wouldn't support her.

Dimly, the scream filtered through Michael's pain and desperation; on impulse, he looked back and saw Ginny, her body also transparent, the figure of a woman etched on glass, just getting to her feet. She ran, stumbling, forward. His horror at seeing Ginny fading away overwhelmed his own pain; he stopped, turned, ran toward her.

"Ginny—go back—for God's sake—"

Ginny sprang forward and grabbed him, held him, began pulling him back, away from the dazzling creek. Leaning on each other for support, they stumbled back toward the farmhouse, with each step their transparent bodies becoming more opaque. The strength gradually returned to their legs; by the time they staggered through the picket fence, they were whole again.

They fell into a snowdrift, holding one another; Michael kissed her, and Ginny eagerly returned it, filled with wonder and astonishment, unable to believe that someone would really want to kiss her like this. Michael stroked her back as they embraced, astounded by her nearness, by the fact that she was not drawing away, like so many others had drawn away. They lay there in wondrous silence for a moment . . . then Michael raised a hand, stroked her face tenderly, and smiled. "I love you," he said, and tears came to his eyes.

Ginny bit her lip, didn't know whether she would smile or cry. "I didn't think anyone would ever say that to me," she said, softly.

Michael touched her face again. "I didn't think anyone would ever let me."

Ginny could hardly believe the words were coming from her mouth. "I love you, too, Michael."

They lay in the snow, then, and held each other, and when Ginny looked up she saw that her grandparents' house was once more old and deserted, the windows boarded up, the chimney half-fallen. She thought she heard the last traces of a little girl's laughter from within, fading like a phonograph winding down. And she smiled, thinking: Goodbye, *Nonno*. Goodbye, *Nonna*. And hoped the little girl inside would take good care of them.

14

Of all the trials and humiliations of childhood, for Dennis the worst by far had been Sunday afternoons. Even now, years later, he did not like to think about those long, numbing days which began promisingly enough with the arrival of the *Daily News* and its splendid comics section (reading the best strips—*On Stage, Brenda Starr*—first, then saving the real losers—*Dick Tracy, Dondi, Moon Mullins*—for the dead reaches of afternoon) and tumbling rapidly downhill after that. Because after the comics and the old movies and the cartoons on Channel 5, things went to hell in a handbasket: around noon he found that TV was dominated by interview shows and religious programs; half his friends were away (dragooned into visiting relatives in Far Rockaway or New Rochelle); and Dennis himself often found himself hauled off to Long Island to visit aunts, uncles, grandparents—you name it, he visited it. That had been torture, sitting in an overstuffed chair in a corner of a busy room, reading the Family Weekly section of the local newspaper while screaming cousins two or three times removed ran end-runs around the furniture.

Since then, he had made a point to contrive ways of occupying himself on Sundays, be it going to a movie or just sitting at his typewriter, working on another story for the *New Yorker* to reject; but this Sunday he could do neither. This Sunday Dennis sat at his desk, staring out at the alley below, crushed by the guilt and embarrassment and shame of Friday night's date with Paula.

He had run the evening over in his head a thousand times in the last forty-eight hours, each time finding a different point at which he might have reversed the terrible flow of events. Hindsight was wonderful. Why had he even told her he'd sent the flowers in the first place? Why didn't he deny it, but take the opportunity to ask her out anyway? The more he thought about it, the more he believed that that had been the single most important factor in the way the date had turned out: he had been so nervous, so uncomfortable about his lie, that he had allowed it to consume him.

Tired of thinking about it, unable to think about anything else, he got up and headed for the kitchen to make lunch. As he pulled the ground round from the fridge, however, he became aware of a sound from the small, functional living room: the hum and clatter of his electric typewriter. Puzzled, he put down the meat and re-entered the living room. The typewriter was silent, but as he approached he noticed that there was something written on the sheet of paper he had left in the machine.

He took the paper out and read:

WE'VE GOT TO HAVE A TALK, DENNIS.

Dennis crumpled the paper into a ball and chucked it into a wastebasket. Terrific. Now he was typing things without remembering that he had typed them. Maybe he was becoming a dual personality. Well, why not? Another personality sure as hell couldn't do any worse than this one. He turned, headed back into the kitchen.

Behind him he heard a click, a hum, and the clatter of the typewriter once more. So much for the *Sybil* theory. He dashed into the living room again, ready to confront whoever the hell was fooling around with his machine (had someone entered the apartment without his knowing it?)—and found the room totally empty. Another sheet of paper had been placed in the typewriter, and another message written.

I KNOW THIS MAY BE DIFFICULT TO BELIEVE, it said, BUT THINK OF ME AS YOUR . . . GUARDIAN ANGEL.

Dennis immediately went to the door to see if it was still locked; it was. Jesus. Either there was some bizarre conspiracy going on here, or that date Friday had so unhinged him that he was now seeing things. "No," he said, trying to remain calm, "I'm sorry. It's been a long, humiliating weekend, thank you, and I don't need hallucinations, too." He yanked the plug from the wall, started to walk away.

Before he took three steps, the machine was clatter-ing again. He spun around, angrily, to find not only the plug reconnected to the wall socket—but the typewriter actually *typing by itself*.

Dennis froze, disbelieving. He watched as the keys depressed by themselves, as the margin guide ad-justed itself, as the typewriter suddenly stopped in mid-sentence, backspaced, crossed out a word with a series of ///s, then continued blithely on.

Fear shot huge globs of adrenaline into Dennis' bloodstream; he wanted to scream, run, get the hell *out* of there. But fear also kept him bolted to the spot. Finally, the typewriter stopped, and Dennis, after a moment's hesitation, inched closer and peered cautiously at the new message. Something moved the platen up a few lines so, apparently, he could read it more easily; instead, he nearly fainted.

OKAY, the new message said. LET'S GET THINGS STRAIGHT. YOU'RE NOT HALLUCINATING; YOU'RE NOT GETTING OFF THAT EASILY. IF I'M NOT REAL, THEN WHO DO YOU THINK SENT THOSE FLOWERS TO PAULA? THE TOOTH FAIRY?

Dennis went numb. He sank into a chair, stared at the typewriter. Suddenly he remembered the phone book in his office, the restaurants circled in red. Jesus God, could it be? But no. No, he had to be going crazy; surely that was the preferable alternative. Better to be warped than haunted. Better to be—

The machine started typing again. This time Den-nis didn't even blink. He thought he might be going into shock.

NOT A *REAL* GUARDIAN ANGEL, the paper read, JUST THINK OF THAT AS A METAPHOR.

Dennis stared. Suddenly his life had turned into a

Luis Buñuel film. "Metaphor. Sure," he repeated, dully. "At least I'm being haunted by a literate ghost. What are you, anyway, a dead English major?"

I'M NOT A GHO

The machine began typing the sentence, then went back, ///ed out the words, and started over:

FORGET IT. THAT'S NOT THE ISSUE. LET'S TALK ABOUT YOUR DATE ON FRIDAY.

Dennis stood, suddenly defensive. "I'm not talking about a goddamn thing to a fucking Corona portable!" he snapped, suddenly aware of how absurd the entire situation was. "If you really are what you say you are, goddammit, do something . . . supernatural!"

There was a moment's silence as whatever was in the room seemed to consider its options . . . and then, a few feet from where Dennis stood, a cheap-looking old vase in which Dennis stored pencils and pens suddenly *floated* up off his desk . . . wobbled its way through the air to the center of the room . . . spun around as though being juggled, then rocketed into the kitchen where it shattered with a crash against the refrigerator door.

Dennis stared for a moment at the porcelain wreckage, then cleared his throat, still uncertain that he had actually seen what he had, but willing to accept it for the nonce. "I, uh, guess that'll do," he said meekly.

The Corona clattered into life again:

ABOUT PAULA. YOU'VE GOT TO CALL HER BACK, DENNIS.

Dennis' eyes widened. "Are you kidding?" he said. "Okay. So maybe you are real. I'll accept that for now, since the alternative isn't any better. But if you really sent Paula those flowers, you're the one who got me *into* this mess in the first place! Why? Why'd you do it?''

There was a short pause, and then, slowly:

I WAS ONLY TRYING TO HELP.

"Yeah?" Dennis said defiantly. "Well what makes you think I need your help? I've got a good job, good friends . . . what's wrong with that? Isn't that enough?"

Several moments, then:

IT IS IF YOU THINK IT IS. DO YOU?

Dennis started to say something, then stopped—considered the question seriously—and, reluctantly, looked down. He shook his head.

"No," he admitted. "I guess not."

CALL HER, DENNIS. YOU KNOW YOU WANT TO.

Dennis sighed. "I can't. I just can't." He began pacing nervously. "Look. Whoever—whatever you are. You probably mean well, but . . . it's too late. I'm out of step; I've always been out of step. I'm twenty-four years old and I'm still a goddamn virgin. I never learned what you said, how you acted . . .''

IT'S CALLED A SELF-FULFILLING PROPHECY, DENNIS, the machine said. Dennis did not reply.

I KNOW WHAT YOU'RE GOING THROUGH, his visitor went on. I'M NOT AN ANGEL OR A GHOST, DENNIS; I'M A GUY, JUST LIKE YOU, WHO FELT THE SAME THINGS YOU'RE FEELING NOW. I FELT HOMELY, CLUMSY, AWKWARD. AND ALONE.

I COULD NEVER WORK UP THE COURAGE TO DO THINGS OTHER GUYS DIDN'T THINK TWICE ABOUT—TAKING A GIRL'S HAND, KNOWING WHEN TO KISS HER, KNOWING HOW AND WHEN TO ASK HER TO MAKE LOVE. I FELT LIKE IF I TRIED, AND FAILED . . . THE WORLD WOULD COME TO AN END. LIKE IF I KISSED A WOMAN

AND SHE DIDN'T WANT ME TO, I WAS COMMITTING A CRIME
PUNISHABLE BY DEATH BY LETHAL INJECTION . . . OR AT THE
VERY LEAST, THE WOMAN WOULD HATE ME. EVENTUALLY, I
BECAME TOO AFRAID TO DO ANYTHING AT ALL.

Dennis looked away, the words coming uncomfortably close to home.

FINALLY, WHEN I COULDN'T MOVE AT ALL . . . WHEN I
COULDN'T STAND THE PARALYSIS ANY LONGER . . . I ENDED IT
THE ONLY WAY I COULD THINK OF. I TRIED TO KILL MYSELF.

Dennis started, a chill running up his spine.

I COULD SAY A LOT OF THINGS, DENNIS. I COULD SAY THAT
YOU'VE GOT TO BELIEVE IN YOURSELF OR NO ONE ELSE WILL,
BUT THAT'S A CLICHE AND YOU'VE PROBABLY HEARD IT SO
OFTEN YOU'RE SICK TO DEATH OF IT. I COULD SAY YES YOU'RE
SCARED AND YOU'RE LONELY, AND WHAT YOU DON'T REALIZE
IS THAT *EVERYONE'S* SCARED AND LONELY. BUT YOU MIGHT
NOT BELIEVE THAT EITHER.

The machine paused a moment, and then:

BUT IT'S AS SIMPLE AS THIS, DENNIS.

SOMEDAY YOU'RE GOING TO DIE. I MEAN, IT'S NOT AS IF
YOU'VE GOT A WHOLE LOT OF CHOICE IN THE MATTER, RIGHT?
BUT YOU DO HAVE A CHOICE AS TO *HOW* YOU CAN DIE. YOU
CAN DIE KNOWING THAT YOU ACCOMPLISHED WHATEVER IT
WAS YOU WANTED TO ACCOMPLISH IN LIFE—OR AT THE LEAST
THAT YOU TRIED, YOU MADE THE ATTEMPT. OR YOU CAN DIE
WITHOUT EVEN MAKING THE ATTEMPT . . . WITHOUT EVER HAV-
ING REALLY LIVED.

I KNOW WHAT YOU'RE THINKING, the visitor added. THE
VERY FACT THAT I'M HERE TO TELL YOU ALL THIS DEMON-
STRATES THAT THERE *IS* SOMETHING BEYOND THIS WORLD . . .
THAT MAYBE WE DO GET ANOTHER LIFE, ANOTHER CHANCE.
RIGHT? MAYBE THE NEXT LIFE WILL BE BETTER THAN THIS ONE?

IN THAT CASE, DENNIS, LET ME ASK YOU:

IF YOU DON'T HAVE THE COURAGE TO REACH OUT TO ANYONE IN THIS LIFE . . . WHAT MAKES YOU THINK YOU WILL IN THE NEXT?

Dennis stared at the words a long while, waiting for the presence to continue . . . but it did not. Somehow he knew, that the room was now empty, but for himself and that his life was again his own. The thought was a frightening one . . . but it was also, to his considerable surprise, an exciting one, as well.

Paula sat curled up on her sofa, disconsolately spooning yogurt from a container as she watched a Sherlock Holmes movie on WOR; she was wearing only a bathrobe, sitting with her knees up in front of her, as though bracing for an attack, with her eyes studiously blank as she watched the flickering black-and-white image on her TV.

Ginny entered, passing invisibly through the door into the apartment. She frowned as she caught her first glimpse of Paula, looking again like a wounded bird. For an instant Ginny wanted to turn and leave, unwilling to risk hurting her again; but she knew that Michael had been right, that no matter what the wisdom of their original plan, they had a responsibility now to try and set right what they had bollixed up.

Now all I have to do, Ginny thought with a sigh, is figure out how to communicate with someone who can't see me or hear me. Sure; that's all.

She sat down on the edge of the couch as Paula, restless now (could she somehow feel Ginny's presence? did she remember the time that Ginny had touched her?), got up and started flipping channels on the TV. She flipped past a news conference, a war movie, and a sitcom before settling briefly on an old, weepy Jeanette MacDonald/Nelson Eddy romance from the Thirties, and despite herself she leaned forward, her attention snared. Her gaze was momentarily wistful, envious—then, abruptly shaking off the feeling, she twisted the channel selector back to the war movie.

The sound of cannons going off startled Ginny, who had become absorbed in the romance. She looked at Paula, frowned. "Won't even let yourself think about it, will you?" she said, as though Paula could hear. An idea popped into Ginny's head and she smiled sneakily. "Well, we'll see about *that*."

As Paula began to return to her fetal position on the couch, Ginny reached over, twisted the channel selector, and switched back to MacDonald and Eddy. Paula blinked, frowned. Part of her sensed something strange, something she had felt before, but a larger part of her wanted nothing to do with it; she got up, switched back to the war movie, turned . . .

. . . and again Ginny flipped the dial. Nelson and Jeanette exchanged quiet whispers, then kissed long and tenderly. Paula became angry. She did not need to see this. She slapped the OFF button with more vehemence than Ginny had expected, then stalked off toward the bedroom, muttering something about buying a Sony the next time around. But somehow she knew that there was more to it than that. . . .

En route to the bedroom, Paula turned on the radio; loud rock music on WNBC filled the room, helping Paula to drown out her own nagging thoughts. Paula continued on to the bedroom; Ginny immediately sprang to her feet, spun the selector on the radio, and settled on a soft, plaintive love song.

Paula froze, turned. For a second the music transported her to a time when she still had hope, a time before the taunts and indignities of high school and adolescence; then, angrily, she stalked over to the radio and switched back to WNBC and a loud, metallic rock number. She glared at the dial as if daring it to do something; then, when it did not, she turned cautiously away.

Ginny promptly switched it back to the love song.

Paula's composure cracked. All the horrors of the last forty-eight hours fell in on her at once; she shrieked and lashed out, slamming into the radio with the flat of her hand, sending it crashing to the floor.

Ginny jumped back, startled and a bit alarmed, as Paula stood in the middle of the room, angry, upset, aware that there was something *here*, something trying to make her think of things she'd rather forget, something trying to mock her. "That's enough!" she yelled, eyes darting around the room, seeking some clue, some presence. "You hear me? I've had *enough!*"

Ginny shrank back, uncertain how to deal with this, as Paula went on: "For God's sake," she cried, "who's here? Why are you *doing* this to me?"

She stood, trembling with rage, tears starting to well up in her eyes. "I don't want to think about it anymore—you understand?" She bit her lip, took a short breath, tried to make sense of the jumble of pain and frustration inside her. "Everywhere you turn, that's all you hear, all you see—love songs on the radio, romantic novels in the supermarket! No one ever leaves the Love Boat sexually frustrated—oh, no! And no one ever has a romantic interlude in a movie without a little poignant background music! Why the hell can't they leave you *alone?* Why do they tell you there's music when there *isn't* any!''

By now the tears were rolling freely down her cheeks, tears she had held back for too long; she suddenly felt absurd and embarrassed, crying her eyes out, screaming at—what? Ghosts? Demons? God? She sank onto the couch, sobbing uncontrollably, shoulders quaking. Ginny went to her, sat down beside her, voice low.

"God, I wish I could touch you," she said softly. "Just once. Just so you'd know somebody gives a damn." She searched for the right words, hoping that somehow, perhaps, Paula might feel the words as she had felt her presence. "You deserve more than this, Paula," she said tentatively. "I know it's hard to believe . . . I never believed it, either . . . but it's true. You *deserve* to be *happy.* That was my trouble, too . . . I never thought I was good enough, or pretty enough, or nice enough to have someone love me. So nobody ever did. But it—it's not a *privilege*, Paula, it's a *right*. It's your *right* to be happy. It *is*.''

She raised her hand, aching to reach out, still holding back. "But if you keep on like this, you never will be. Instead, you may wind up"—Ginny's face clouded over—"lying in some hospital room somewhere . . . not dead, not alive, just . . . existing." She shook her head. "But don't you see," she finished, softly, "that's just what you're doing *now?*''

A moment's hesitation—and Ginny reached out and touched her, gently, on the shoulder. Paula felt something like a breeze, a feather brushing her skin; she blinked, looked around, and realized that she had stopped crying. She took a breath, feeling less afraid, but didn't know why.

With wonder and delight, Ginny took her hand away. For the second time in as many days, she had touched someone and had not hurt them. First Michael, and now Paula. She stared at her hand and tears came to her eyes. She laughed, softly, to herself.

The phone rang, and both Paula and Ginny nearly jumped out of their seats. Paula got up, sniffed back the last of the tears, hovered above the phone a moment, then slowly picked it up.

"Hello?"

By the look of astonishment on Paula's face, Ginny could tell who was calling.

"No. No, that's all right," Paula was saying. The trace of a smile tugged at her lips. "Well, I never have known anyone who could spill anything over the phone, so I'll take the risk." She wiped at her eyes with the sleeve of her robe. She listened for several moments, then nodded. "I know," she said. "So was I. You could've said 'Boo' to me and you would've had to pry me off the ceiling with a spatula." She sat down, cradling the phone between her chin and shoulder, and Ginny thought she saw the tension slowly ebbing from her. Paula smiled: "Yeah, I know. Amazing how funny two frightened people can be when they're on opposite ends of a phone wire." She laughed at something Dennis said, settling in for a long talk. Ginny decided to give her some privacy; she got up and headed for the door.

She looked back only once; Paula sat, the conversation coming more easily now, punctuated by occasional laughter. Ginny felt an immense sense of pride; she smiled, turned, and left the apartment. They had done all they could—now it was up to Dennis and Paula.

Ginny took the bus from Paula's apartment to La Crêpe, where Michael was waiting, fairly bubbling with excitement. "Dolly Levi, I presume?" he said, grinning, and kissed her lightly on the lips. She smiled back: "We did okay, didn't we?"

"We at least got them talking. That's all we can do." He led her into the restuarant. "But enough shop talk. I've reserved the best table in the house for us."

"The kitchen again?"

"I said it was a good *table*; I didn't say where it *was*."

The next few hours passed like a dream for Ginny; it hardly seemed to matter that the table they sat at was a counter in a noisy kitchen, and that instead of a candelabrum they had track lighting. They sat, nibbling on puffed Roquefort sticks and staring into each other's eyes, and Ginny almost thought that she could actually taste the food, the way she used to. Once, a cook spied a half-empty plate and tried to carry it away, but Michael merely grabbed him in a hammerlock while Ginny took the plate back; the cook, thinking himself paralyzed, watched as the plate floated out of his hands and back onto the counter.

The kitchen staff gave that particular corner a wide berth for the rest of the evening.

After dinner, Michael became very mysterious—leading Ginny halfway across town, his arm around her, evading her when she asked where they were heading. In truth, Ginny didn't really care; it was enough that they were walking, that they were together, that she could feel Michael's body against hers. But the farther along Third Avenue they walked, the more it seemed familiar to her, though how or why she could not quite put a finger on; finally, on the corner of 48th and Third, Michael abruptly stopped and gestured grandly. "Well," he announced, "here we are."

Ginny was confused. "Michael, what are you talking a—"

She stopped as she looked up at the street sign . . . and suddenly knew exactly where she was. She spun round, looking down 48th Street, where halfway down the block an old, ornate building stood—a reconverted theater, elegantly refurbished, a blue crescent moon emblazoned above its marquee. Tears sprang to her eyes.

"Oh, Michael," she said. It was nearly a whisper. "The Moonrise! I used to work here when I was in high school."

"I know. You mentioned it that night in the park— before we started screaming at each other."

"But it's Sunday night. It's closed."

"Not to us," he said, taking her hand. They passed effortlessly through the wall of the building; the tingle they both felt was not simply an effect of their passage.

Inside the darkened ballroom, Michael made his way among the spectator seats as Ginny squinted, eyes adjusting to the darkness. The last time she had been here, she had been a waitress, an observer; but now . . .

Michael took a large white gift box from beneath one of the seats and handed it to Ginny. "I brought this in this afternoon. Had to unlock the entrance from the inside to get it in," he said. "I, uh, hope the size is right. I popped over to your apartment and took a look in your wardrobe closet, just to be sure."

Ginny laughed. "Michael, what on earth—"

"Take it into the ladies' room and see."

Ginny shrugged, padded across the dance floor to the ladies' room, as Michael set about unpacking another box he had deposited here earlier. He cleared off one of the spectator tables, extracted a pair of wineglasses and a bottle of champagne from the box, and began pouring, enjoying this hugely. He felt uncannily like William Powell.

A few minutes later, Ginny emerged from the ladies' room—dressed in the powder-blue evening gown she had worn briefly on a night of shame and loneliness. But this was a different night, and Ginny looked, and felt, almost like a different person— radiant, transformed. "Oh Michael," she said, feeling like something out of a fairy tale. "It's beautiful."

Michael took her hands, kissed her on the cheek. "So are you."

"But Michael . . ." She hesitated. "How did you know? About the dress?"

"Know what?" Michael said, seemingly innocent. "I just wanted to get you a nice dress, so I went to Macy's and looked around. That one just seemed to appeal to me."

Ginny was dubious, but willing to be convinced.

"You didn't see any of that . . . psychic residue stuff, did you?"

"Should I?"

Ginny smiled; it really didn't matter. "No. I guess not. Thank you, Michael."

"Now wait here a sec." He moved to the rear of the room, flipped a lever—and the ballroom burst into light, lamps with gels of amber, blue, rose, and violet illuminating the multicolored dance floor.

Ginny, entranced, went to the table Michael had set up. Michael handed her a glass of champagne; they lifted them in a toast. "To absent friends," Michael said.

Ginny nodded; they both knew what had to happen before long. "To absent friends," she agreed. They touched glasses and drank, peering at each other over the rims.

When they had finished, Michael went to the bandstand, dragged out a rather bulky, old-fashioned reel-to-reel tape recorder, and began threading a tape into the machine. "I went through half their tape library," he said, "before I found this." He switched on the machine, went to Ginny's side, bowed slightly.

"May I have this dance?"

Ginny giggled. "Gee, I don't know. My dance card is awfully full. But you look like a nice enough fella." They put aside their wineglasses as the tape began to play—a lush, waltz-like melody filling the room, slow, sad, but quietly transcendant . . . a Sixties pop ballad called "Saturday Night at the World":

It's a Saturday's night at the world
I am thinking about a girl
And how useless to search it becomes
When you seek all the answers in one . . .

Michael took her hand, led her nervously onto the dance floor. "It's been a long time since I've done this," he said, feeling clumsy as his feet moved awkwardly in a simple two-step.

"You're doing fine," Ginny said. "Just loosen up. Don't shuffle . . . turn on the balls of your feet; that's right, just brush the floor . . ."

Michael took her advice and found himself moving more gracefully than he had thought himself capable of. "Hey," he said, "you ever think of doing this professionally?" She laughed; they became more daring, the two-step turning naturally into a long, sweeping arc across the dance floor as the music soared, carrying them with it:

But her voice seemed to answer
the echoing silence
From yesterday's asking, and waiting,
and listening,
For something resembling a song
to be sung back to me . . .

Alone under the bright lights, they danced.

Later, they made love, not the fumbling, desperate attempt of a few weeks before, but a slow, tender passion filled with wonder bordering on awe. Afterward, they lay in their bed at the Waldorf, holding each other, feeling warm and safe and happy—emotions which only a few weeks ago they had been so certain they would never know that they chose to end their lives rather than live without them. And here they were, not quite alive, not really dead, and they finally knew what it was like.

After hours of simply holding one another, caressing each other's bodies, getting to know the shape and feel and texture of one another, Michael finally looked at her in the way she knew he would, eventually, and smiled sadly. "You know what we've got to do, don't you?" he said.

She nodded, full of uncertainty and fear, but nodding nonetheless. "Practice what we preached," she said with a smile. He grinned, nodded. Her face darkened momentarily. "Michael . . . how do we know what'll happen? Suppose . . . suppose it doesn't work?"

He longed to have an answer for her, but he could only shake his head. "I don't know, Gin. All we can do is try. After what we told Paula and Dennis, we'd be some kind of hypocrites not to try, wouldn't we?"

"I just don't want to lose you."

"You won't lose me. I won't let you."

She kissed him on the lips. "I love you," she said.

"And I love you," he said, his embrace tightening.

"Don't let go," she said.

Toward dawn, they got up, dressed, and, hand-in-hand, left the Waldorf for the last time—at least in this existence. The air was cold and moist; sunlight crested the far buildings. They walked slowly all the way down First Avenue to 30th Street, their stomachs coiling as the familiar buildings came in sight. They entered via the Emergency Room, passed through Admitting, and tried to fight back the fear which gripped them as they drew closer to their destination.

Finally, they stopped—in front of Ginny's private room. Ginny looked at Michael, embraced him. "Michael, I'm scared," she said, shutting her eyes, not wanting to let go.

His heart was pounding wildly. "So am I, Ginny. But it's gonna be okay. We're going to go in there, and in a little while we'll wake up, and pretty soon we'll be visiting each other's rooms. It'll be okay."

They kissed again, held each other for several minutes as nurses and orderlies bustled back and forth around them, and then, finally, they separated. "See you in a little while," Michael said, moving off.

Ginny smiled, held back tears. "In a while," she repeated. Forcing herself to move, she turned and entered the room. Michael looked after for a moment, then continued on down the hall to his own room, and entered.

Michael went to the foot of his bed, looked at the body lying so deathly still before him, and, slowly, climbed in beside it. Ginny, in her room, took a deep breath and did the same. They shut their eyes, lay back, and merged with their corporeal bodies, sharing the same space, both wanting more than anything in the world to open their eyes and feel the sun on their faces, the wind in their hands. They allowed the hum of the body monitors to lull them asleep; drifting, their last conscious thoughts were of each other, and then they fell into a long, peaceful darkness.

*   *   *

The first thing Michael felt when he woke was the
sun on his face. He didn't know why, but he felt that
that was important somehow. He opened his eyes, saw
bright white light, winced. He smelled the sharp
scent of antiseptic and he knew he was in a hospital.
He tried to get up . . . and discovered that he could
not move his legs. After a moment of panic, he
realized that his legs were bound in casts, and that he
had feeling in his toes. Thank God. His left arm was
bandaged and his right felt stiff. Suddenly he remembered the bridge, the water, the dizzying fall. He
emitted a low, rueful moan.

All at once there seemed to be nurses all around
him, looking startled, amazed, checking his pulse,
asking him questions.

"Mr. Barrett! Are you all right? Can you speak?"

"My God, he's awake. Call Dr. MacKenzie. Hurry!"

"Everything's going to be fine, Mr. Barrett. Welcome back . . ."

They looked so pleased, so happy, Michael felt he
should feel happy, too . . . but all he felt was a
gnawing sense of emptiness, as though he had lost
something, something very important, and he could
not recall what it was nor where he had misplaced it.
He lay there, trying to summon up the memory, but
nothing came, nothing at all; the last thing he could
recall was the bridge, the water, the fall, the blackness.
And that was all. That was all.

15

Ginny was sitting up in bed within twenty-four hours, uncomfortable and embarrassed by all the attention she was getting; all this TLC for someone who had stupidly tried to overdose on sleeping pills. Remembering that night, it was almost like watching a movie, seeing someone else crying uncontrollably, pulling out the bottle of pills, nearly choking on a handful; it seemed like another person, somehow, her and yet not-her. She felt as though she had aged years in the month she had been unconscious: strange new feelings bubbled within her, old fears relegated to a far corner of her mind. She felt as though there were a reason for this, some pivotal thing or event she couldn't quite place . . . but again she drew a blank, as she had these past twenty-four hours, trying to recall. The last thing she remembered was drifting off to sleep, in bed, at home—then, waking up here. Between those two points, something had changed for her, but she could not for the life of her think what.

Margaret was sitting at her bedside, looking haggard, drawn, but immensely relieved. And terribly guilty. "Oh, honey," she kept saying, genuinely happy to see her sister, "I'm so sorry. If I hadn't gone off to the Bahamas . . . if I'd stayed home—"

"Maggie, I'm not going to dump all that on you," Ginny said, her tone very calm and controlled. "I didn't try to . . . to kill myself just because you didn't spend Christmas with me. There were a lot of other reasons."

Margaret looked confused. "You never told me," she said.

"You never listened," Ginny said flatly. Margaret blinked, apparently taken aback by the firmness, the confidence in Ginny's voice; so, for that matter, was Ginny. She sounded different, even to herself, but she liked the sound.

"Well, from now on . . ." Margaret began, but Ginny just smiled, interrupting:

"From now on," she said, "I talk to people who want to listen to me. I . . . I hope that includes you. If not . . ." She let the sentence hang, but there was certainly no indecision in her tone. Margaret could not believe she was hearing this.

"There was this nice doctor in here a few hours ago," Ginny went on. "A psychologist. I'm going to start some therapy when I get out, Maggie—try and get a few things straightened out. I think it'll do me good.''

Now Margaret was alarmed; things were happening too quickly for her to assimilate. And there was something else, something she didn't even want to admit to herself. ''Do you . . . do you think that's wise, Gin? Maybe you need some more time to think about—''

Ginny looked at her, smiled; she put a hand on hers. ''Maggie, my getting well won't make you anything less. I'll still be your sister, you know? Except maybe I won't be your *little* sister anymore. You . . . think you can live with that?''

Tears welled up in Margaret's eyes and she embraced Ginny. They hugged each other for several moments, eyes moist, until Margaret pulled back slightly and managed a small smile. ''I think I can live with it, yeah,'' she said.

Ginny smiled, feeling genuine affection for her sister for the first time in God knew how many years, and tried to shift to a lighter subject. ''So tell me. How's Tony? When's he gonna come by and say hello?''

Margaret looked faintly stricken, said quickly, ''Oh, I haven't *told* you, Gin—I met this wonderful man, his name is Ben, he's—''

''Maggie,'' Ginny said, undeterred, ''what happened to *Tony*?''

Margaret hesitated, looked down. ''He . . . left me,'' she finally admitted, voice low. ''But you're not interested in—''

''Would you like to talk about it?'' Ginny said, not

prodding, just asking. Margaret paused, looking at her sister with new eyes and some uncertainty; then, as though working up her courage, she nodded, slowly.

"Yeah," she said softly, with the trace of a smile. "Maybe I would, at that."

Shelley and Josh were standing beside Michael's bed, Shelley's eyes shining with relief and affection even as she held tightly on to Michael's hand—as though to prevent him from ever slipping so perilously away again. Josh was hefting a stack of newsmagazines onto the tray/table beside the bed. "*Time, Newsweek, Newsday* . . . we even saved you selected issues of *Us*. Only the most scandalous cover stories, though. You've got some catching up to do."

Michael considered that. "Still trouble in the Mideast?"

"Of course," Shelley said.

"Continued deadlocks in Congress?"

"Last time I looked."

"Nuclear tensions at an all-time high?"

"Uh huh."

"Then I'm all caught up," Michael grinned, pushing aside the magazines. Shelley and Josh laughed, just as the door to the room swung open and Bob and Susan entered—Bob carrying a portable but still quite hefty video recorder, Susan with about half a dozen cassettes in her arms. "Fuck this informed-citizen shit," Bob declared, swinging the VCR onto a table beneath the hospital's TV set. "*We've* got the real goods here."

Michael's eyes widened. "Bob . . . is that a—"

Susan held up two of the cassettes, grinned. "Three weeks' worth of your favorite programs," she announced, "plus the latest movies to hit HBO. They say you've gotta be in here a few more days before they can let you recuperate at home, so you might as well catch up on cultural trends, hm?"

Bob presented Michael with the remote control, as though handing him a royal scepter. Michael was immensely touched. "Guys," he said, quietly, "I don't know what to say."

Shelley squeezed his hand, looked at him soberly, her tone quiet. "Just say," she said, her voice nearly catching, "that you won't leave us again."

Michael's eyes felt moist; for a moment, all he could do was nod, and when he found his voice, it was, to his surprise, confident and assured. "Not if I can help it," he said. "I promise." And indeed, he found that, looking back, he could barely remember why he had wanted to kill himself—how he ever could have forgotten how much love he had in his life. It seemed like the actions of another person . . . some other Michael Barrett . . . an earlier, sadder Michael Barrett. For the first time he could see himself as a succession of Michaels, and he began to realize that he owed no allegiance to any of them— that if he were to suddenly become happy one of these days, it would not be a betrayal of the lonely, unhappy adolescent he had been . . . but, rather, a vindication.

"I almost forgot," Shelley said, producing a large gift-wrapped package from her tote bag. "I brought you something." She handed it to him, and puzzledly

Michael began unwrapping it. It was an odd shape, partly padded with tissue paper, and as he tore off the last scrap of tissue, Michael found himself holding—

His horn. His French horn, all polished and shining as though brand-new. He looked up at his friends, who seemed to be enjoying his stupefaction. "The hospital probably wouldn't take kindly to impromptu recitals," Susan said, "but you can play it when you get home. We just thought you'd like to have it here."

"Yes," Michael said quietly, turning the horn over in his hands as he might a precious stone, as dear to him as these people surrounding him. "I do." A pause, and then: "Thank you."

He was still holding the horn hours later, after his friends had left. Once or twice he raised it to his lips as though to play, then thought better of it; but the desire to play was there, and it amazed and delighted him.

"Well, you really don't have to announce my entrance with a fanfare, but if you insist—"

An attractive young nurse entered the room, smiling and carrying a blood-pressure gauge; Michael laughed as he set aside the horn. "Cathy, if I blew this thing every time you came in to poke or prod me with something, I'd never stop playing."

She wrapped the pressure cuff around his upper arm. "Probably not a good idea after recovering from a pneumothorax anyway." She held the stethoscope to his middle arm and began pumping the inflation bulb. She was a very pretty young woman, with short dark hair and dark eyes, and as she checked his BP, her soft fingers touching his skin, Michael

felt himself getting . . . excited . . . for the first time
since awakening. Immediately he fell into a daydream,
imagining the nurse's hands touching something other
than his arm.

—You know, Cathy, you really do have magic
fing
· No.

He looked up as she finished taking his BP and
began shaking down a thermometer. "Uh . . . Cathy?"

"Um?"

"I'm not usually this . . . forward, but since I'm
going to be leaving here in a couple days, I was, uh,
wondering if maybe I could call you after I'm back
on my feet. Maybe we could have lunch sometime,
see a movie . . . ?"

She blinked, considering. "Well, you know, we're
not supposed to get involved with patients. Hospital
policy and all that." A moment, and then she grinned.
"So I'll just have to wait till after you've checked
out, then, won't I, before I can give you my number?"

Michael beamed, amazed that she was interested,
and even more amazed that he had asked.

Later, he held the horn fondly to his lips, not
making a sound, just liking the kiss of brass, the feel
of the instrument in his hand. For a moment, he
seemed to hear something—a fragment of music; a
gentle, waltz-like melody, like something out of a
ballroom dance—but it quickly faded, and he did not
dwell on it. Not when there were enough things
ahead of him to dwell on; more than enough.

Margaret Benedetti pushed a puzzled Ginny down
the corridor in the mandatory departure wheelchair.

"What do you mean, you have a car waiting?" Ginny was saying. "You don't drive. You mean a taxi?"

"Nope."

"Did Ben come with you?"

"Uh-uh."

"Then what—"

"You keep on asking so many questions," Margaret warned, smiling, "and you're gonna be the first patient in Bellevue history to leave here at fifty miles an hour through the front door. Be patient, Gin."

Ginny smiled back, shook her head. "For a nice Italian girl from the Bronx, Maggie, you've got a heckuva lot of chutzpah."

"A heck of a lot of what?" Margaret laughed. "I've never heard you use that word. Where'd you pick it up?"

Ginny blinked, momentarily confused, then shrugged. "I don't know. I just did, I guess."

They turned a corner and headed down a final corridor toward the exit. Behind them, Bob and Susan wheeled Michael—in neck brace and leg casts—out of his room and down the same corridor. "Your teaching certificate?" Susan was saying. "What brought this on?"

Michael shrugged as they pushed him down the hallway. "I was just thinking, that's all. I've got the B.A. in music—all I need is another ten, twenty units of comprehensive, then about thirty units of specialized concentration—"

"Yeah, but why?" Bob said.

Michael frowned. "I can't stay at Multigraphics

all my life, can I? I mean, I'm going to be thirty years old, people—time to grow up a little, wouldn't you say?''

Bob and Susan exchanged pleased but puzzled glances and pushed him toward the exit.

Out by the curb, Ginny got out of her wheelchair and Margaret gently pointed her toward an idling Volkswagen. Ginny looked up—to find Annie McGuire holding open the door, smiling hugely, eyes bright. "Welcome home, Ginny," she said, and her voice trembled a bit when she spoke.

Ginny was stunned at first, then felt tears spring to her eyes; in moments she was running toward her, the two women embracing, laughing, crying together.

"Annie . . . oh God, Annie, I'm so sorry—"

"So am I, Gin," Annie said. "I should never have tried to push you into something you didn't want."

"But I did want it, don't you see?" Ginny said, shaking her head. "I wanted it so much I was terrified I might get it. You understand?"

Annie studied her, startled at the new confidence in her voice, the new contentment in her eyes. She was glad to see it there. "You seem so different," she said, squeezing her hand. "What happened, Gin?"

Once, the idea of being *different* would have made Ginny bristle, and, in a knee-jerk reaction, become even more frozen and inflexible. But now she just smiled. For an instant she seemed to see a flickering trace of something—the distant, faraway image of a man's face—but it was just a moment, and then it was gone.

She looked at Annie, shrugged. "I don't know, Annie," she said, truthfully. "I wish I did."

Margaret helped Ginny into the car as Annie got behind the wheel. The door on the passenger side snicked shut; Ginny buckled her seat belt.

A few dozen yards away, Bob and Susan wheeled Michael down the sloping sidewalk toward the curb.

Annie keyed the ignition; the car revved up.

Michael glanced to his right and saw a yellow Volkswagen pulling away from the curb into traffic. He blinked, feeling a bittersweet sense of loss, of pain and—something else.

Ginny suddenly turned around in her seat, searching desperately out the window for—what? A red Buick cut into the next lane, obscuring Ginny's view of the hospital; in moments the feeling of urgency was gone, and slowly she turned round in her seat, feeling as though she had lost something and gained something, a sound of pages turning and doors closing.

Michael saw the Buick change lanes again, and by the time it did the Volkswagen was heading north on First Avenue. The bittersweet feeling lingered, and now he felt something else, too, something he could not account for. Gratitude. He watched the Volkswagen disappear into traffic, and he thought: Thank you. And had no idea whom he was thanking, or for what.

"Mike? Ready to roll?"

He shook himself awake. "Oh. Sure. Anchors aweigh." An intern helped Bob lift Michael into the car. Michael sat there, thoughtfully, as Bob started the ignition and swung the station wagon into traffic. Up ahead, the Volkswagen started to make a right turn as Bob prepared to make a left. Michael tried to crane his neck around to the side, but the neck brace prevented him; he caught only a fleeting glimpse of yellow in the distance before it turned the corner, and was gone.

15 + 15

Ginny left her studio in Northampton a little after five o'clock, but what with the rush of holiday traffic on Route 9, she didn't get home to Amherst until nearly six. She bustled into the modest suburban house, weighted down with the last of her Christmas shopping, to find the rooms already filled with the smell of pumpkin pie, turkey, and cinnamon. She dropped the gifts under the Christmas tree in the living room, then, with a certain amount of relief, put away her work ledgers and apppointment book in the china hutch in the dining room. As much as she enjoyed her work, she was glad for the vacation, even for only a week. (The one appointment she had let stand, however, was with a bright, plump, rather shy young woman who had come to her in a panic, desperate to learn enough dance steps to make it through a New Year's Eve party on Friday. The girl, her voice trembling and her eyes wide, reminded Ginny of herself as a teenager; she couldn't find it in herself to refuse.)

The twins burst into the dining room just then, yelling and chasing one another, as usual; when they saw Ginny, they immediately skidded to a halt and assumed expressions of beatific innocence. "Hi, Mom," Chris said, shuffling by. "Hi, Mom," echoed Lillie, following suit. It was like a Tom & Jerry cartoon: the minute they had inched past their mother and gained the relative sanctuary of the stairs, they bolted up the steps, resuming their chase. Ginny smiled, shook her head, and entered the kitchen.

Dave stood hunched over the oven, ardently basting the turkey she had begun that morning and left to his ministrations. It was golden brown, crisp, and smelled absolutely wonderful. "Mmm," she said, coming up behind him. "Smells great."

He turned, put his arms around her waist, kissed her. "Get everything squared away at the studio?"

"Pretty much. Just one client next week, the Simmons girl. Kids give you any trouble?"

"Nope. I just let drop that their presents were hidden somewhere in the house and they spent most of the day tearing around looking for them. I figured even if they found one, it'd probably be worth it, keeping them occupied."

Ginny laughed. "I'll have to remember that one." They kissed again; Ginny looked up at her husband's smiling face and traced the line of his mouth with her finger. "Maggie called me at work. She'll be up around nine. With her, uh, latest."

"That reminds me. Annie and Bruce are coming over a bit early—should be here in another twenty minutes."

"Whoops. Better get ready, then." She pecked him on the lips and padded up the stairs to their bedroom.

After showering, she sat at her dressing table, absently combing her hair as she stared out the window at the snow flurries falling gently on Kellogg Street below. She heard the first of the Christmas carolers making their rounds of the neighborhood, kids who worked at the food co-op around the corner, their slightly off-key rendition of "Silent Night" drifting up to her second-floor window. Pulling on a bathrobe, Ginny opened the window and leaned out, catching a snowflake in her hand; it melted quickly. She'd didn't know why, but the feel of snow on her skin always raised her spirits, somehow. Ever since that other Christmas Eve, fifteen years ago, when she thought she would never want to see another Christmas again. Odd, how distant that seemed, so impossibly remote; yet some things still bound her to that time, and she would not have had it any other way. Because despite all the pain, all the mistakes of her early life, the pain had shaped her, given her a viewpoint, made her better able to cope with the disappointments and frustrations she would encounter later. That, and—something else.

Sometimes, when her life seemed to be faltering—like the time Chris had been in the hospital for surgery following the car accident two years back, and she and Dave had sat numbly in the waiting room, unable to speak, unable even to hold one another—she would cry, and close her eyes, and seem to see, floating there in the dark, the face of a friend. That was the only way she could describe it: the plain, somewhat horsey, but immensely warm and reassuring face of a man she almost knew, a man whose mere presence, such as it was, helped her through the pain and anchored her, somehow, to the good things she still had. It was a face she would seem to see once in a while in a crowd, a face she would find in her mind after a long night's sleep. She had long ago stopped trying to puzzle it out: perhaps it was the face of someone she had known in childhood, someone she had liked and forgotten, repressed along with so many of those bad years. Whoever it was, she was glad he was there, and glad that he stayed.

The carolers were at her house now, bursting into a chorus of "Hark, the Herald Angels Sing"; she waved to them and they shouted greetings, plumes of breath trailing after them as they moved on to the next house. Bruce and Annie's car suddenly swung around a corner and pulled toward the curb; Ginny broke into a wide grin, excited at the thought of seeing her friend again after so many months. She shut the window, taking one last look at the swirling snow, one last touch to the moist fingertip where moments ago a snowflake had melted, then began to dress, happy at the arrival of another Christmas Eve.

*   *   *

Michael dismissed his 1:00 Music Appreciation class early this afternoon, partly his usual custom on holidays, partly to buy himself time to pick up one last gift for Laura. As his students filed out of Orvis Auditorium, calling out season's greetings to him as they left, Michael smiled and packed his briefcase—wincing slightly at the stack of papers to be graded over Christmas break. He made his way through the cluster of low, palm-shaded buildings in which most of the music theory and performance courses were held and, within minutes, was tooling out of the parking lot in his Datsun, down University Avenue toward the Lunallilo Freeway.

From the freeway he saw the pastel towers of Waikiki in the distance, and beyond them the Pacific, deep sapphire against a pale blue sky—the waters so clear, so rich, so much a fulfillment of the dreams he'd held for so long, that even now Michael was occasionally filled with wonder and gratitude that he lived here; that every day he could walk to the beach, watch the sailboats dotting the horizon, follow the surfers riding the crest of waves begun perhaps three thousand miles away, on the western edge of the continent he had left behind years before.

He felt a pang of loneliness as he thought of Shelley, and Bob, and Susan, and all the others he had left behind as well . . . but it wasn't as though he never spoke with them, as his mammoth monthly phone bills would attest, and if there was one thing you could rely on living in Hawaii, it was the annual visit from friends in cold climates. Shelley and Josh had been here three times in the last four years;

Morrie and Val, twice, and Bob and Susan were
preparing for their first trip to the islands in May.
And of course there were the yearly trips back to
visit Laura's family in Rhode Island, with the inevitable side trips to New York. No, he had not lost his
friends by moving here, not really . . . and he had
gained so much else.

He picked up the gold pendant for Laura in the
jeweler's shop on Ala Moana; it was a simple, elegant teardrop with an even simpler inscription on
the back, a word which for Michael expressed everything he felt about his life these past few years, but
most particularly Laura, and their marriage: *Mahalo*,
Hawaiian for *Thank you*.

On a whim, he decided against returning to the
freeway, opting instead for the beach road circling
Diamond Head; he could pick up the highway again a
little past Kahala, and from there, home to Wailupe.
He continued on Ala Moana, driving through the
heart of Waikiki—packed, as it usually was in winter,
with tourists—toward Kapiolani Park.

Still thinking of New York, his thoughts drifted—as
they invariably did this time of year—to another
Christmas, many years ago, when he had tried to
take his own life. It was strange, but even knowing
all the things he would never have known had that
misguided attempt succeeded—his life with Laura, the
satisfaction he derived from teaching, the pleasures
of living in the islands—he still only had pleasant
memories of that Christmas. It was irrational; he had
spent, after all, the better part of a month in a coma;
but whenever he felt depressed, whenever the frustrations began to build and his faith in himself began to

ebb, he had only to think of that Christmas to feel
calmer, serene, at peace. It was almost as though all
his strength emanated from that one point in time, as
though all his reserves of confidence he drew from
those three weeks of oblivion. He did not understand
why, but by now had learned better than to question
it. He simply accepted it, and for that, too, *Mahalo*.

As he rounded the very tip of Diamond Head, the
two-toned waters of Maunalua Bay—the deeper the
water, the deeper the blue; coral reefs marked by a
brilliant aquamarine—commanded his attention, and
on impulse he stopped at the Amelia Earhart memorial on the eastern edge of Diamond Head Beach
Park. He stood at the lookout, staring into the distance,
the faint rolling contours of Molokai, Lanai, Maui,
and, way in the distance, the Big Island visible on
the horizon. He shielded his eyes from the glare of
the sun, and, for a moment, seemed to see something
flickering in the brightness—a smile, a laugh, a face
not unlike the one which came to him sometimes in
the morning, fading after a long night's sleep, vanish-
ing before he could catch it in the light of day. After
a moment, Michael returned to the Datsun and swung
back onto the road, a fragment of music inexplicably
running through his head—a sweeping, waltz-like
melody—as the palm trees swayed and bent along the
road, sheltering him, like old lovers, all the way
home.

And sometimes, in their dreams, they would meet
in a winter wheatfield beneath bright Pennsylvania
skies, and tell each other of their lives, their lovers,
the dreams fulfilled and the dreams still waiting.

They would laugh in the good times, cry for each other in the bad, hold one another like the old, dear friends they were, and then, as morning approached, they would return to their sleeping bodies, so many miles apart, knowing that there would be other nights and other meetings. And they would wake, a voice dimming in their minds, a face retreating into memory, and go about their lives 'for that day—refreshed, somehow, renewed—drawing their strength from a place beyond dreams.

Dedicated, with love and hope,
to the cherished memory of
Asha PenAmber
a kindred spirit